THE SKY'S THE LIMIT

"What does Terra have the most of? More than anything else, what does she most need a—a relief of?"

There was a brief silence, then Leif piped up, "People."

"Right," I said. "Archy, what was the population of Terra, last count?"

"Nine-point-three billion at the 2000 census, Star."

"Are Terrans starving?"

"No," Archy said carefully. "The air is pretty foul and the quality of life literally stinks. People aren't actually starving, but they are getting thinner. And there's the ozone depletion, too."

"You would not describe life on Terra as pleasant, then."

"No."

"Thanks, Arch. Okay, boys and girls, here's the deal." I looked around the room and took a deep breath. "Multiple-family dwellings, mass produced for lowest cost, sold on site or delivered upon request at extra charge."

Simon said, "What, you want to go into the prebuilt home construction business?"

I said softly, "Try the prebuilt *world* construction business."

Praise for *A Handful of Stars* . . .

"A great story . . . exciting, fun, spell-binding . . . For the SF fan, this is a must-read."

—Voice of Youth Advocates

. . . and *Second Star*

"This story is action packed and the settings visualized with almost cinematic vividness . . . Recommended."

—Roland Green, *Booklist*

"Reminiscent of Heinlein. [*Second Star*] is an impressive first outing that sho⸻

—*Locus*

Ace Books by Dana Stabenow

SECOND STAR
A HANDFUL OF STARS
RED PLANET RUN

A HANDFUL OF STARS

DANA STABENOW

ACE BOOKS, NEW YORK

This book is an Ace original edition,
and has never been previously published.

A HANDFUL OF STARS

An Ace Book / published by arrangement with
the author

PRINTING HISTORY
Ace edition / December 1991

ISBN: 0-441-31615-8

ACE®
Ace Books are published by The Berkley Publishing Group,
200 Madison Avenue, New York, New York 10016.
ACE and the "A" design
are trademarks belonging to Charter Communications, Inc.

PRINTED IN THE UNITED STATES OF AMERICA

10 9 8 7 6 5 4 3 2

For
Joanna Carlson,
a civilized human being

—1—

Nonlinear Computers

> ... a nonlinear computer weighing only 160 pounds, having a billion binary decision elements, that can be mass produced by unskilled labor.
> —**Scott Crossfield's description of an astronaut**

The captain spat out a hank of my hair and swore. "Star, either you tie up that mess or I take a knife to it here and now."

"I'm sorry, Crip," I said meekly. He was right. The cockpit was a small one and crowded enough with crew and controls and backseat drivers as it was. "Does anyone have a piece of string?"

"With all the zerogee traveling you do I don't know why you don't just shave it off." He rubbed a hand over his own smooth scalp and resettled his headset. "Where the hell's my checklist?"

"Move to parking orbit checklist, Captain," the navigator said. She handed his copy to him and a roll of gray tape to me. I gathered my hair into a hasty braid and wound a piece of the gray tape around the end of it.

1

"Why don't you strap down in your cabin, Star?" Crip said, peering through one of two tiny forward ports. "Ellfive Traffic Control, *Hokuwa'a*, radio check, one, two, three, four, five, four, three, two, one."

"*Hokuwa'a*, Terranova Traffic Control, it's Terranova now, Crip, how many times do I have to tell you? Your radio check is five by. Stand by for the mayor of Terranova."

Crip glanced back at me and rolled his eyes. "Standing by. On the intercom, Denise."

"Aye, Captain, on the intercom."

We waited. There was a click and a low buzz. Someone muttered a curse down the channel. The static cleared, and sounding like fingernails scraping a blackboard, Mayor Panati's voice bounced off the bulkhead all the way downship from bridge to crew quarters to galley to freight to pressure plate and back again. Crip lunged for the volume control and Panati's voice dropped to a more endurable level. I settled back and resigned myself to the standard hearts and flowers farewell. After a few unintelligible whispers, Panati's voice said, "Is Star Svensdotter in the audience?"

"I am, Your Honor."

"Good. Now then, where'd I—oh, thanks." He cleared his throat. He was still squeaky, like someone rubbing a balloon. "Members of the First Terranovan Mining Expedition, this is Mayor Charles Panati of the independent nation of Terranova speaking." He paused. "Think about those words for a moment. Mining expedition. Independent nation. Sound good, don't they? Well, keep in mind that there would be no mining expedition and only an American Alliance colony known as Ellfive were it not for the courage and determination of one woman. I'm sure you know of whom I speak. I'd bet big money she's riding in the jumpseat behind Crip right now because she's convinced he can't get the *Hokuwa'a* out of orbit without her."

Denise gave Crip a swift, sidelong glance. I glared at the back of his head and dared him silently to laugh.

"Well, maybe she's right," Panati went on. "Star Svensdotter led Ellfive to freedom in the One-Day Revolution, and on to independent nationhood as Terranova."

Sort of, and kind of from behind.

"Star Svensdotter opened a dialogue with the first extraterrestrial visitors to our solar system."

If you can call a one-way, one-time tête-à-tête a dialogue.

"Star Svensdotter oversaw the construction of the first self-supporting, self-governing space colony in human history, which made all of the foregoing possible."

I did do that.

"And now Star Svensdotter is leading a mining expedition to the Asteroid Belt in search of those elemental materials so desperately needed here at Terranova for the completion of construction of Island Two. Terranova will never be able to repay Star Svensdotter all that we owe her. Of course we are grateful, but gratitude alone doesn't balance the books. Star, so you know that wherever you go and whatever you do, you will always have a home on Terranova, the Habitat Assembly has deeded to you title in perpetuity to the house and accompanying plot of land in the Rock Candy Mountain foothills, heretofore occupied by the director of construction of Lagrange Five Space Habitat, Island One. It will be maintained by the Terranova Assembly against the happy day of your return. And the heartfelt thanks of every Terranovan goes with it."

I was dumb. Without looking Crip reached a hand around behind him and smacked my leg, hard. I jerked and stammered something into my headset, God knows what. It must have been all right because Panati sounded satisfied.

"You are very welcome. Now then. To Star and to her crew at the beginning of this momentous voyage, we bid farewell and bon voyage. But it has been said before me, and better said at that." Panati cleared his throat yet again and his voice deepened. " 'A health to the man on trail this night. May his grub hold out. May his dogs keep their legs; may his matches never miss fire.' "

The last echoes of Jack London's Klondike toast echoed throughout the ship. I had a lump in my throat the size of a cantaloupe.

"Cleared for separation, *Hokuwa'a*," Terranova Traffic Control said in a low voice, "and safe journey, Crip."

"Roger that, Terranova," Crip said gruffly, "and thanks, Bolly. Navigator, you have comm."

"Aye, Captain, I have comm."

Crip fiddled with the controls in front of him for a few seconds. He cleared his throat and swiveled around to look at me. "You look like you've been stuffed, woman. Why don't you go on down to your cabin like I said? There's nothing for you to do now but sit back and enjoy the ride."

I was determined to match him nonchalance for nonchalance. "Was that a tactful way of telling me to get the hell off your bridge? In your dreams, Crip."

Crip gave a slight smile, one a little rusty around the edges, but a smile nevertheless. It was good to see. I checked my straps and worked on getting my gut under control. I coped with travel between Terra and Ellfive by willing myself to sleep through the entire twelve-hour flight. We were leaving for the Asteroid Belt today. It was a journey that would take six-plus weeks and I had long since faced up to the grim fact that I'd have to be awake at least some of the time.

"Captain," Denise said, "we have a go for egress from Terranova Traffic Control."

"We have a go, aye," Crip said. "Make ready to fire forward verniers."

"Making ready to fire forward verniers, aye."

"Increase to forty percent thrust."

"Increasing to forty." Her hands moved, flicking switches, pushing buttons. One by one, red lights changed to amber, amber to green. "Green board, Captain."

"Fire verniers, starboard one, portside one, on my mark. Mark."

"Firing verniers."

We heard the vernier thrusters, distant pops like firecrackers around the corner and down the block. I leaned forward and craned my neck to watch through the cockpit's portside viewport. The long, silvery cylinder of Ellfive began to recede.

"Switch monitor to aft camera."

"Switching monitor now."

The picture on the main screen centered above the cockpit instrumentation panel changed. The Warehouse Ring was a designated stationary orbit surrounding Ellfive's equator ten klicks out. We could see the LIMSH tender dock and the netlike mass catcher and the windowed soccer ball that was Maria Mitchell Observatory. The spaces between were taken up by assorted spacecraft in parking orbit, from SeaLandSpace freighters to Piper solarsleds to Patrol shuttles. We were headed for transient parking. Seated behind and a little above, I watched Crip's hands work the controls. Lean and sinewy, sprinkled with gray hairs, they were almost careless in their competence. Almost.

He reached overhead and pushed a toggle switch. "Fire aft verniers, fifty-two percent thrust, port and starboard, on my mark." The Express-class ship had eighty-eight separate directional thrusters spaced around the hull. Crip was using two. He was also looking out the viewport. With all the state-of-the-art electronic gear and computer instrumentation and digital readouts at his fingertips, he was eyeballing our way in. Pilots. "Mark."

"Firing verniers now, Captain."

Crip waited, his hands relaxed on the yoke. I leaned forward to glance over his shoulder at the telltale. The little toy ship on the screen slid effortlessly into the little toy parking space, no pitching, no yawing, no rolling, just one smooth slide right into the money.

"Fire reverse thrusters."

"Firing."

"Dead slow, and . . . stop. Position."

Denise consulted her control panel. "Maria Mitchell Observatory a thousand kilometers off the port bow. We have achieved orbit in Transient Parking Space One. Bull's eye, Captain. TTC says nice work."

He yawned. Like I said. Pilots.

The monitor switched to Mitchell. "Magnify image now." And there was Tori Agoot and Ariadne Papadopoulos and the rest of Mitchell's crew crowded into Mitchell's largest viewport, along with approximately half the population of Terranova, including Petra Strongheart, Rex Toranaga, and Ariadne-Two, Ariadne Kennedy, who used to ride shotgun for Crip but had chosen to sit this trip out. I wondered if she regretted her decision yet. It wasn't a question of if, only of when.

They were all waving furiously. Tori was yelling something. He probably wanted me to run just one more navigational sim, get me lost just one more time in the Greater Magellanic Cloud. And Sam, who was along for the ride, would probably see to it that I did. Whoopee.

They couldn't see us, of course, but I found myself lifting a hand in farewell anyway. "Want me to punch 'em up?" Crip asked.

"No," I said. "We said our good-byes last night."

"Launch checklist, Captain," Denise said. She handed Crip yet another clipboard.

"Security, report."

"Security reports all secure." As usual, Caleb sounded composed, unexcited, if anything a little bored.

"Everyone strapped in?"

"Everyone I could find. Is Star up there?"

"Yeah, she won't leave."

"You want me to arrest her and throw her in the brig?"

"I don't know." Crip looked over his shoulder at me. "Do we have a brig?"

Crip had actually made a joke. I'd thought he'd forgotten how. Denise, a serious-minded professional who objected on principle to levity during business hours, tapped her fingers meaningfully on the control panel.

"Cargo bay, report," Crip said obediently.

"Cargo bay reports everything liable to kick up a fuss is strapped in, tied down, tethered, lashed and leashed better'n my mamaw's mule on a Sunday-go-to-church morning! Let's light this candle!"

Crip looked around at me. "Claire sounds pretty confident for someone who learned how to pack an Express-class spaceship just last month."

"Doesn't she, though?"

"I hope she knows what she's doing."

I did, too, especially when I thought about some of the cargo. Please, oh, please, I prayed, let me not have forgotten anything. At least not anything important.

I didn't get an answer. I didn't expect one. When you're leading a mining expedition to the Asteroid Belt through 450 million kilometers of merciless vacuum, the only God there is, is you.

"Red light firing panel," Crip said. "Stand by."

"Red lights across the board, Captain," Denise said. "Standing by."

"All hands, all hands, stand by for primary ignition. You've got five minutes"—Crip checked the readout—"correction, you've got four minutes fifty-seven seconds to double-check your areas. It's going to be a bump and a half, people, so look sharp."

There wasn't exactly a thunderous rumble of activity downship. It was more of a rustling, like mice in the grain bin. I thought of my 250 handpicked mice, all skinny tails and pink noses and inquisitive whiskers. Half of them were on board the *Hokuwa'a* with me, the rest would follow on the *Voortrekker* in a week. Were they as smart as I thought they were when I hired them? As able?

"All stations, sound off," Denise said.

"Archy gives us the go, Crip," Simon said.

"Engineering standing by, ready for ignition, Captain," Whitney Burkette said crisply. He was the only other crew member besides Denise who called Crip Captain.

"Cargo, aye, go, go, go!"

"Security?"

"Security, aye," Caleb drawled. "Kick it."

"Medical secure for thrust, Crip," Charlie reported. "Mind the babies."

That reminded me. I slid inquiring hands over my bulging stomach and was soundly kicked for my pains.

"Make ready for drop," Crip said.

Denise's hands fluttered over the controls. More lights turned green. "Ready to drop, sir."

We were moving nose forward, out of Warehouse Orbit now, making ready to boost. I knew enough of the process to follow it mentally. By now the propellant charge would be shifting into the ejection shute.

"Fire CAK."

"Firing."

"Drop charge."

The bullet-shaped nuclear charge, pushed by small blasts of compressed air, would be sliding down the shute and out the *Hokuwa'a*'s tail.

Denise watched a monitor, her small, sharp face lit by the readout on her screen. "Charge clear of hull, sir."

"Move charge out to thirty meters."

"Thirty meters, aye, sir."

"Switching to aft camera."

We looked up at the monitor. Maria Mitchell Observatory disappeared, to be replaced by a close-up of the propellant charge. It was a tiny thing, for all of its power, tiny and silver and glittering brightly in Sol's rays. The *Hokuwa'a*'s pressure plate dwarfed it. I could feel every muscle in my body begin to tense.

"Launch a remcam."

Denise set a dial, pushed a button. I heard a thud. The scene on the viewer changed again, this time taking in a section of the *Hokuwa'a*'s pressure plate with the silvery projectile floating off its stern. The Orion propulsion system was simple and pretty unsubtle; still, fission was fission. And I was not what you could call relaxed.

"Triangulation."

Denise entered figures on a keypad. "Triangulation confirms, propellant charge at thirty meters." By now I was stiffer than the seat in which I sat.

"Acknowledged. Did you know, Star," Crip said, running absentminded fingers over the control panel, "that the tide on August 3, 1492, that Columbus sailed on to the New World was the very same tide that exiled the first boatload of Jews from the Spanish Inquisition?"

"No." But I knew that back in the last half of the last century, Von Braun's Saturn series completed thirty-two launches without a single major failure.

"I figure we're just like Columbus."

"Really?" Of course, only fifteen of those Saturn rockets were manned.

"Except we know where we're going."

And I refused even to think about the *Challenger* or the *Challenger II* or the *Zumwalt* or the *Tereshkova*. I swallowed and said, "You heard 'em, Crip. Kick it!"

Crip smacked the flat of his hand down on the large red button on the lower right-hand corner of his board. The kick came moments later, the boot thudding into the back of my chair. It pressed me into the jumpseat even as it thrust me up from high earth orbit, out of the plane of the ecliptic, away from Terranova. Me, and 113 crew members, and 10 nuns, and a cartographer from the Royal Geographical Society, and a hold stuffed with coffee beans, microchips, Tampax, and the other necessaries of life. And at the end of our journey? Who knew?

Crip was wrong. I didn't feel like Columbus. I felt like Marco Polo. I wondered how he'd staffed and provisioned his caravans.

— 2 —

Space Apes

Even a space ape must urinate.

—Desmond Morris

Don't let anybody kid you, space travel is not romantic or thrilling. The smell is such that you wish somebody would bring back the common cold. The same seven weeks that pass in the blink of an eye when you're growing starstones in Terranova's Frisbee can seem like seven years breathing Terran air on board a spaceship between planets. Eating was the nearest thing to recreational activity that we had on board. The food, and I employ the term loosely, was vacuum-packed, freeze-dried, and reconstituted. It was stored in lumoil packets and nuked in the microwave one minute before eating and then sucked out through a straw. It was uniformly bland in taste and texture and had the sole virtue of being compact. "The savor of the mornings was a great delight," Crip remarked morosely one morning (ship's time) at breakfast.

"Who said that?"

9

"Christopher Columbus. On his first trip over. Only took him thirty-three days. And the sun shone the whole way."

"Only took Apollo 11 4 days, 6 hours, 45 minutes, and 39.9 seconds to get to Luna," Caleb said, equally morose. With mutually glum expressions they surveyed what passed for bacon, eggs, and toast on the *Hokuwa'a*, and sighed heavily in unison.

We were crowded, and not just with crew. The *Hokuwa'a* had treadmills bolted to every available square meter of deck, bulkhead, struts, spars, and I-beams, in the galley and down the companionways. Those treadmills represented Charlie's victory in the bitterest battle we fought over outfitting the First Terranovan Expedition. We had yet, she informed me, to find a way to circumvent the old Ten-Ten Rule, which says that spacers lose ten percent of their bone mass for every ten months spent in zerogee. Her standing orders called for a mandatory two hours a day on a treadmill or the equivalent exercise by all personnel in twenty-four-hour zerogee. If you have 125 people to a ship and 24 hours in a day you need 250 treadmill hours per day. That works out to ten point something treadmills, if you are willing to have them going day and night. On a ship the size of an Express I wasn't. In vain did I point out that we would be in transit for less than two months and without gee for less than six. "You want a bunch of people with spaghetti where their muscles used to be when we get to the Belt?" Charlie demanded. Mother Mathilda concurred, gently but firmly. I could have ignored my sister, but there is something about the pronouncements of a nun. I okayed the treadmills.

Mother Mathilda was the head of our contingent of the Sisters of St. Anne, ten of them, from a nursing and teaching order. I figured one of the first things we'd do upon arrival in the Belt was set up a primary school for the Belters' kids. It would be good public relations; with Terra-Luna Mines and Standard Oil and Solar bidding against us we were going to need all the leverage we could get to meet our tonnage quota. Helen Ricadonna had set a ten-year completion date for Island Two; I wasn't going to be the one to tell her we'd fallen short. I wanted those miners to want to sell to us, if possible without us getting into a bidding war with the other buyers. It wouldn't hurt to bribe the sellers with their kids' education, and it certainly wouldn't hurt the kids.

In spite of every effort on my part we'd wound up with supercargo, too. "I still don't know why we had to bring him," Simon said. He was unhappy enough about the addition of the Sisters of St. Anne to the roster, and Simon Turgenev in zerogee was already unhappy just on general principles. "We've got astrographers, pro and am, up the wazoo. What the hell do we need with another?"

"A representative of the Royal Geographical Society lends the expedition a certain, shall we say, cachet," Whitney Burkette said austerely. "The prestige of the Society is not inconsiderable, don't you know."

"I don't know that prestige counts for all that much with somebody who's head-down ass-up grubbing for uranium in the Belt," Simon said. A biotech pulled her way down the companionway. Simon ducked her feet and grabbed for another handhold. In our silver-blue jumpsuits we looked like globs of mercury rolling up and down a test tube.

"My dear fellow," Whitney Burkette said, raising his voice to be heard over the thumping of the treadmill bolted to the bulkhead right next to us, "from the Schomburgk brothers in French Guiana in the 1830s, to the conquering of Everest in the 1950s, to the circumpolar navigation of Luna in the 1990s, the Royal Geographical Society has funded expeditions that have provided sound, solid, sensible research into the makeup of our world. They wish to extend that research farther into the solar system." Whitney Burkette permitted himself a wintry smile. "History is about chaps, don't you know. Geography is about maps." And with that little epigram he sailed off majestically downship.

"It's not enough already the binary brat decides he's coming with us," Simon moaned in his basso profundo voice, "now we've got mapmakers and nuns crawling out of the hatches." Simon's brown hair stood up in cowlicks all over his head. His wide, thin-lipped mouth drooped down at the corners of his shovel-shaped jaw. His cavernous brown eyes were mournful. He needed a shave. He always did.

"I heard that," Archy said over the communit strapped to my wrist. "Just for that it's check and mate in four moves, bub."

"Hah!"

"Watch me. Bishop to king's knight five."

"What! Why, you little—"

I looked at Simon. "Just swear to me you plugged the Asimov inhibitors into him before anything else when you transferred him on board. Just swear it. Please?"

Simon built computers. Sort of. He took other computers apart and mixed up their parts and put them back together again. Then he wrote software to make them run better, like about one thousand percent faster and with ten times the memory and fifty times the precision, which made their original manufacturers gnash their teeth and tear their hair and give him lots of money to show them how he did it and to do it again. The upshot of all his tinkering was that Simon was a millionaire before he was thirty and bored with it, so when I came along and dangled the prospect of designing a computer capable of running a space habitat in front of him he grabbed at it. To this day he tells anyone who asks and a few who don't that I drafted him, which is slander and calumny and I make sure I look hurt whenever I hear him say it. The truth is that I rode in like the White Knight and rescued him from the sheer tedium of sitting around counting all that money and he should be grateful. I also introduced him to his loving wife, although I'm never quite sure exactly how grateful he should be to me for that.

Archy was Simon's magnum opus. Archy was the most advanced computer in the solar system. Simon built him, provided him with a data resource base equal to none, and gave him the semblance of a personality. Our contact with the Librarians had nudged him over the edge into sentience and Simon had yet to forgive them for it. For that matter, neither had I. Archy was almost as mouthy as Charlie, and for some reason he unnerved people. Human people, that is. The Librarians had offered him an all-expenses paid tour of the Milky Way; he had declined with thanks, and little Elizabeth, Simon and Charlie's daughter, had gone instead. Simon had yet to forgive Archy for that, either. But when Archy said he was ready to come with us to the Belt, he'd cut our lead time in half. Loading computers takes time, even for Simon, and even into a ship the size of an Express.

Panati, the interim mayor of Ellfive, or Terranova, as I supposed I must accustom myself to calling it, had generously offered the Orion ship *Theodore Taylor* to carry us to Ceres orbit. I extended my gracious thanks to the mayor and told him and the interim Habitat Assembly that I wanted at least four ships, one of them an armed scout. I also demanded one of Boeing's new experimental 1X1 shuttles with the tandem-rig robot arm and a complete set of waldo remotes, specifically designed for servicing solarsats and commsats.

Well. You'd have thought I'd demanded the sacrifice of someone's firstborn child. First the mayor and then the Habitat Assembly screamed like a Frisbee entrepreneur making only a fifty percent profit. Colony Control, in the reluctant process of disbanding following the One-Day Revolution, made it a high-pitched trio.

After some squalling myself, I allowed the expedition to be pared down to the *Taylor* and the *Freeman Dyson*, nuclear-powered sister ships in the Orion class. I slunk out of the assembly's chambers so obviously a beaten woman that several of the assembly members tried to console me. It was difficult not to burst out laughing right in their faces. Aging, a trifle shabby, and almost obsolete, nevertheless two ships of the same provenance meant burning the same kind of fuel and stocking the same kind of spare parts, which in turn meant more cargo space to jam pack with tomato seeds and toilet seats and hand grenades.

What little room left in cargo was in flight given over to classes. When we weren't eating or on the treadmill or whining about the crew complement, we were in training.

There were 125 people on board the *Hokuwa'a*. We were physicists, chemists, computer techs, drillers, metallurgists, explosives experts, exogeologists, hydrobotanists, hydroponics techs, communications technicians, engineers, mechanics, riggers, pilots, teachers, tinkers, tailors, soldiers, sailors, doctors, lawyers, and one Indian chief—me. Even excluding the Sisters of St. Anne we were slightly more than half female and would have been more so if I'd had more time for crew selection. Women mass less than men, they eat less food than men, they breathe less air than men, and they are more radiation resistant than men. It was like the old joke—they might not be easier to live with but they sure were cheap, or at least cheaper than men to support in vacuum. A few days out Charlie made some crack about having to defend Simon's honor. "Not that Simon has all that much honor to defend," I retorted, "but at last report Belters are four-to-one male. I don't think finding friends will prove that much of a strain on anyone. Now, come on, Roger's going to teach us how to grow beans."

"And this day started out so well."

Roger Lindbergh was teaching a course in basic hydroponics techniques, hand in hand with Zoya Bugolubovo. At the end of the first class Simon looked from Zoya to me and asked, "I was afraid to ask before we set sail; how'd you get Roger to sign on?"

"No, Simon," Charlie said, "the question is, how did Star get Zoya to sign on."

"There's no mystery about it," I said. "She's the foremost hydrobotanist of our time. Feeding the Belt Expedition presented a challenge."

Simon regarded me with a sapient eye. "What'd you do, hire somebody to sleep with Vitaly Viskov and somebody else to take pictures to show Zoya?"

"I most certainly did not."

"Don't sound so indignant. Actually," he told Caleb, who was looking amused, "she probably didn't have to do anything. Viskov'd been pissing and moaning about the trigger-happy imperialist military forces of the American Alliance ever since the One-Day Revolution. He got caught between the Patrol and Jerry Pauling's bunch in the Frisbee and I hear he almost took a round." He reflected. "Would have been easier for Star if he had."

Charlie nodded. "As it was, all she had to do was sympathize with his outraged feelings, make sure a shuttle was at his disposal, and call General Feodov to make sure Viskov was welcome at Tsiolkovsky Base. Voilà." She grinned. "Star told Roger that Zoya was coming with us and Roger forgot all about leaving the chief agronomist's position at Ellfive—excuse me, Terranova—and taking the Richard Bradfield Chair in Agronomy at Texas A and M and becoming Farmer Emeritus and a legend in his own time."

I ignored them. I was practiced at it. When Roger and Zoya were through with us, we all sat down together to learn fiberoptics for intraship communications and suprasonics for extraship communications from Maile Kuakini. Bolly Blanca had put the big Hawaiian's name forward for consideration to run communications for the expedition and after an interview I hired her on. She was the exception to my woman-cheap/man-expensive rule, though: she massed almost as much as Caleb did. She had small, merry brown eyes that saw the joke in everything, even when there wasn't one, and had a cheerful smile for every occasion. She always agreed wholeheartedly with the opinions expressed by the last person she talked to. She was the least likely candidate for ulcers I had ever met.

Next was a series of lessons in how to read and maintain an Express ship's inertial-measurement unit, or space compass, which Sam Holbrook tied into astronomy lessons from charts projected onto the galley bulkhead. Then everyone sat at the feet of Don Albach, our most experienced pressure suit maintenance technician, who taught an intensive forty-hour course in fifty-hour p-suit reconditioning.

Down in engineering powertechs instructed in the manufacture of electricity and water from oxygen and hydrogen through the use of fuel cells, in case Murphy struck and something went wrong with the E-generators. Waste management operators gave lessons in how to flush the toilets, a procedure that, on an Orion Express, practically required an advanced degree from CalTech. They also taught us how to change the molecular sieves that purified cabin atmosphere and how to vacuum the filter screens on the air-conditioning system.

Charlie gave classes in tooth extraction and emergency appendectomies and tracheotomies and zerogee CPR. Caleb organized the crew into oncall security squads with assigned squad leaders and taught a refresher course in basic weapons and zerogee tactics. I signed up for it and thought Charlie was going to have a stroke. "What happened to my sister the pacifist?" she wanted to know.

"She's buried back on Ellfive next to Paddy," I replied, and Charlie had the grace to look ashamed. When the drill (field-stripping sonic rifles, I was never again not going to know which end did the shooting) was complete, she came up to me and said soberly, "Nothing worthwhile comes without cost, Star."

"Now you sound like me," I said, racking my rifle. "Sometimes the price is too goddam high."

"Paddy would have thought it was worth it."

Charlie was right. Knowing it didn't make me feel any better. She tugged at my arm. "Where we going?" I said.

"Time for your monthly checkup."

A pelvic examination at one full gravity is not fun. A pelvic examination at zerogee is even less so. Grumbling loudly, I followed her down to her cramped clinic.

I'm blond and blue-eyed and come in extra large. Charlie

is brunette and petite and chic and every other one of those French adjectives designed to describe those women who make the rest of us feel like milk cows. She has hair as long and as straight as mine; hers is a deep, inky black. Her tilted eyes are big and brown and her skin is the color of fireweed honey. She has a wide, full-lipped mouth that teeters always on the edge of a joyous grin. She's a year older and thirty-five centimeters shorter than me. What she lacks in height, she more than makes up for in mouth.

When Helen Ricadonna yanked me off an oil platform in the Navarin Basin to supervise the construction of Ellfive, my first official act was to recruit Charlie. Four hundred thousand kilometers from home is no place to be without one friend in whom you can place absolute trust, even if she did steal your building blocks for the first ten years of your life and your boyfriends for the next ten. When Helen Ricadonna recruited me to ramrod the Belt Expedition, my first official act was to sign on Charlie. One-point-eight AUs from home is no place to be without at least one friend in whom you can place absolute trust, either.

When the examination was over she sat at her keyboard, playing something circa Franz Joseph II. Her eyes were on a monitor mounted on the wall of the clinic where lines of brightly colored symbols maintained a rolling readout of encoded test results, gobbledygook to the uninitiated. The keyboard was switched to straight piano, no percussion, no brass, no strings.

Charlie used music to solve particularly hairy medical problems and each specialty had its own composer. Shanghai Wang worked the cardiovascular system because only the hottest jazz could get the heart moving the way Charlie thought it ought to. She used Brahms lullabies for pediatrics and Beethoven for orthopedics. Glenn Miller worked from the neck up, on Charlie's theory that a clarinet and a saxophone an octave apart were the best stimulants for the little gray cells, her own and the patient's. Today it was Mozart.

"Everything okay?" I asked.

She grunted.

"Charlie?"

"Huh? Oh, yeah, you're as healthy as the proverbial ox." She stopped playing and surveyed me critically. "You're starting to look like one, too. Better spend some more time on your treadmill." She wrote the monitor data to a chartdisk and filed it.

"Thanks a whole bunch. And the twins?"

"They're fine. Did I tell you they've decided they are going to be a boy and a girl?"

"You mentioned it. Charlie, did you ever find out what the hell happened with my implant? This is the twenty-first century. People don't get pregnant by accident in the twenty-first century. Especially not with twins." One twin kicked out in contradiction and for an instant a tiny foot was outlined against the silver-blue of my jumpsuit.

Charlie shrugged. "Most of the time contraceptive implants work. Sometimes they don't. Yours didn't."

"It did the whole time I was with Grays."

She grinned the kind of wicked grin that only another woman can fully appreciate. "Well, it didn't with Caleb, did it?"

I looked pointedly at her own bulging belly and said, "It didn't with Simon, either."

"At least I keep it to one at a time," she said cheerfully.

"You're really enjoying this, aren't you, you bitch?"

"You bet I am. You know why? It's because you're always so—so—" She groped for a moment and then brightened. "Invincible, that's what you are."

I was hurt. "That's a terrible thing to say. I am not."

"It's what you seem to be," she said. "Ask anyone who has ever worked an hour for you, friend or foe. You lay track for the Iditarod TGV from Anchorage to Nome over seventy-two hundred of the roughest kilometers in Alaska and you finish it five months ahead of schedule and half a billion under budget. You go out into the Bering Sea in the middle of the worst weather and tides in any ocean, not to mention armed Russians who think the entire northern Pacific Ocean belongs to them anyway, and you bring in the St. Paul discovery well and a super-giant oil field. Then your old college roomie calls up and says, 'Want to build a space habitat?' Tell me the truth," Charlie said, leaning forward, "you probably said something like 'Might as well. Haven't got anything better to do.' Right?"

She shook her head, I was pretty sure not in admiration of her little sister's many talents. "You climb a wall no one else can climb, cleave a dragon in record time, swim a moat in a coat of heavy iron mail. Lancelot had nothing on you. No," she said, holding up one hand to stave off my rebuttal. "Don't bother. You've always got a mission, Star, and you always go at it in a straight line. When something or someone gets in your way you go over them or you go through them or you go around them." She sat back, her lips curving. "Okay. Let's see you get around this. Or I should say, these. You named 'em yet?"

"Sean and Patricia." After Patricia Sioban O'Malley, Fenian, poteen brewer, ballad singer, Crip's dead love, my dead friend. Ellfive patriot and martyr, although she would have hooted to hear herself so described.

"Paddy for short?"

"Yeah."

"Who's the Sean for?"

"Caleb's father."

"What was he like?"

"From what Caleb's mother told me, a great, roistering bear of a man with a laugh the size of Africa herself."

"Good names."

"We think so."

"Speaking of twins—I'm thinking of writing a paper."

"Oh, God, not another? You've practically got your own byline in the *American Journal of Medicine* as it is. What's this one about?"

"The effects of unfiltered cosmic radiation on human conception. Did you know the odds are up more than twenty percent that a woman conceiving upstairs will deliver twins? IQs are up, too, maybe not significantly when you consider the smarts of the average spacer, but they are up."

I looked down at my belly and intoned, "A super race. And now, live from Ellfive, in-tro-DU-cing, homo"—I searched for the proper adjective—"homo *superlitavus!*"

"Yeah, right," Charlie said, shifting gears from deep thinker back to big sister, "not if you're any indication."

"I'm hurt."

"But it's worth looking into."

"Umm."

We sat in silence for a while. Talking about children who came in extra smart naturally led my thoughts to Elizabeth, so I wasn't surprised when Charlie said, "I wonder if Elizabeth knows."

Charlie rarely and Simon never spoke of their firstborn, by now studying the lore of the universe somewhere on the other side of the galaxy. For them the loss was still too new, too acute for even the most casual reference. For me, too. Elizabeth had been my friend, my coconspirator from the day she looked up at me from her crib and signed "hello" with clumsy baby fingers. With some difficulty I said, "I don't know, Charlie. I'd like to think so. The Librarians could be watching us and we'd never know it. We didn't last time."

"No." She said the word softly, sadly.

Only half a dozen of us rated cabins; between me, Caleb, and Caleb's orchids, mine was a tight fit. I rolled over in our bunk and stuck my nose in a bunch of phalenopsis and sneezed. The twins high-kicked in protest and I groaned. Caleb woke up enough to rub my belly with one huge, comforting hand. "Ha," he said sleepily. "Trapped you."

Caleb was the size of Sasquatch and the color of coffee with cream. His hair was a cap of short black curls. His mouth was wide and his grin wider, over a chin that was very square and very firm. Someone had been just dumb enough or just lucky enough to get just close enough to hit him in the face, one time. It had bent his nose and left a scar that twisted his right eyebrow up and gave him the look of a benevolent Lucifer. His eyes were lake green and limpid and he was looking at me out of them. "Better?"

I snuggled back against him. "Better."

He rubbed my belly. "Not long now."

"No."

His hand moved farther south. "And then another six weeks. Too long."

"Too long," I agreed.

He was quiet, his hands warm and strong on me. "Now that you've got two in the oven, how do you feel about abandoning your first child?"

"Excuse me?"

"Ellfive. Sorry, Terranova. All thirty-two kilometers of your handmade space habitat, including two farming toroids, zerogee manufacturing module, astronomical observatory, and solar power station. You just gave her away. How do you feel about that?"

I lifted his hand to my cheek. "I didn't give her away. She grew up and moved out. I am now a dictator without a constituency."

"And as all good dictators know, once you have had free run of an autocracy, a democracy can feel pretty cramped."

"Mmm."

"And so awa-ay we go."

"Mmm. Caleb!" I twisted around to meet his eyes. "I just realized. I didn't even ask you if you wanted to come."

He kissed me. He took a nice long time over it, and it was filled with the promise of things to come. When he lifted his head his eyes met mine and for once their usual lazy amusement was gone. When he spoke, it was like he was taking a vow. "Whither thou goest, Star. Whither thou goest."

I had to struggle not to cry and I am not a weepy woman. "I love you, Caleb," I said, when I could speak.

The lazy amusement was back in a flash. "Naturally. What's not to love?"

Over the next ten days Whitney Burkette taught a comprehensive course in ship propulsion, from construction and maintenance to detonation. The man had a walrus mustache and a walrus's appetite for women; I knew that from pre-Caleb experience. In addition, he was a pompous ass, but when he was done teaching that class there wasn't one of us who couldn't dropkick an Express. Theoretically, anyway. And his real specialty was zerogee construction.

Claire Bankhead taught exogeology. One of her ore samples got loose and floated down a companionway to be inhaled by Maile, who was sleeping with her mouth open, which gave Charlie something to do. The rest of us slept and ate in shifts, studied hydroponics and astrogation and p-suit maintenance and zerogee first aid, read, marched on treadmills, and got more pregnant.

And, hourly, the Asteroid Belt got closer.

The proper term for the individual objects orbiting through our destination was "minor planet." Asteroid means "starlike." Asteroids aren't. Astronomers call them "the vermin of the sky," which is understandable when you realize that to accurately predict asteroidal orbits it is necessary to calculate the gravitational attraction of each of the major planets on each asteroid, and then the perturbing effects each asteroid has on the other. In the solar system there are ten planets, a hundred moons, and a minimum of fifty thousand asteroids.

Who wouldn't refer to an object that caused that much tedious work as vermin?

The Asteroid Belt is sort of the shape of a doughnut, as wide as the distance from Sol to Terra, and fills up the space between Mars and Jupiter. The only rule of size, shape, orbit, inclination, or composition in individual asteroids is that there isn't one. 1566Icarus has an orbital period of thirteen months. 1Ceres takes four and a half years to travel the same distance around Sol, and 944Hidalgo, fourteen. Yes, years. Ceres is less than a thousand kilometers in diameter, Icarus, little more than one. The bulk of the Asteroid Belt is only somewhat inclined to the plane of the ecliptic in which the planets revolve, but Feodosia has an orbital inclination of over fifty-three degrees.

With the help of Maria Mitchell Observatory, the Belt had become more familiar territory, and more provocative, and by 2005 independent prospectors and energy company–financed expeditions as well as geologists sponsored by every Terran government that could afford it were sniffing around the Trojans. Before long news of oxygen, hydrogen, and uranium strikes were commonplace on the trivee.

None of these mining finds would have been possible without safe, swift, and economical space travel, which development of would not have been possible without The-War-of-the-Worlds hysteria created by the Beetlejuice Message in 1992, which caused in part the USSR's invasion of (or voluntary confederation with, depending on whose history book you were reading) the Warsaw Pact countries and the European Community.

Then, in 1996, the United Eurasian Republic went to Mars.

Well. The United States promptly formed the American Alliance with Canada and Japan and negotiated the historic SALT VII agreements, banning nuclear power in all but transportation and generation fields and providing for watertight verification. Frank Sartre won his first Nobel for negotiating the treaty. The ink was barely dry before the American Alliance handed a blank check to the newly created Department of Space and told them to solve the fallout problem in the Orion's exhaust and get it operational as of yesterday.

To the surprise and pleasure of those of us who since the Beetlejuice Message had been working our butts off on the heretofore underfunded habitat project, suddenly all things were possible. LEO Base, HEO Base, Copernicus Base, and

Ellfive were completed ahead of schedule and under budget, at which time Frank won his second Nobel, this time sharing it with Helen Ricadonna.

No bucks, no Buck Rogers, I think I heard someone say.

And then the Librarians' ship arrived to pick up Archy and took Elizabeth away instead and any argument about whether or not we were alone in the universe was put to rest once and for all.

Our spaceships weren't quite as snazzy as the Librarians'. Our entire vehicle was only 125 meters long and looked like the bishop piece from a chess game, with an aft pusher plate that was 57 meters across. We rode up front, with the freight modules between us and the fuel storage, and the freight modules and fuel storage and the pressure plate between us and ignition, about a hundred meters. It never felt like nearly enough of a safety margin. After TMI and Chernobyl and Seabrook, there wasn't enough room in the universe to put between me and fission. I've been to Hiroshima. Eighty thousand dead on impact, a hundred forty thousand by the end of 1945, and they were still counting inherited genetic defects handed down by survivors well into the twenty-first century. Solar flaring is my personal bogey, but next up is traveling in an Orion ship. Once they work the kinks out of a fusion drive, or think of a way to speed up solar propulsion, I'm jumping the fission ship.

What's all this got to do with a mining expedition to the Asteroid Belt?

Everything.

The Orion starship was powered by the controlled velocity distribution of nuclear explosions DOS called "pulse units" and the Space Patrol called "charge propellant systems" (and Simon called nuclear farts) but which were nothing more or less than nuclear bombs modified into nuclear fuel after SALT VII. Nuclear bombs were made with plutonium, bred from uranium, which was in short and diminishing supply on Terra and Luna. Which was why we were going to the Belt. The Librarians plugged into stars when they ran low on fuel. This is a trick we have yet to learn.

The original Orion starship, conceived in the late fifties and constrained by late fifties and early sixties technology, had been expected to take anywhere from three to six months travel time from Terra to Mars. Technology had improved somewhat between 1963 and 2008, and we expected to be a little over a month and a half in transit, 47 days Ellfive to Ceres, at 5.7 million kilometers per day, or a little over 238,000 KPH. The Librarians probably parked faster than that.

Hurtling beltward in our little tin can, we fine-tuned the plans we would put into effect after our arrival. Our stated purpose was to find and ship raw materials back to Terra geosync so Ellfive could complete Island Two on schedule. What the job boiled down to was, we were going to be throwing rocks at Terra and missing. That wouldn't take a lot of finesse or, once the operation got going, much more than a standby monitoring process. With this kind of crew, ambitious and too bright by half, tedium was bound to set in pretty fast. In vacuum 1.8 AUs from Terra is not a good place to be suffering from boredom. You get bored, you get careless. You get careless in vacuum, you get dead real fast.

"So?" Charlie said.

"So we think of something to keep ourselves occupied. Where we'll be, we'll have two important things, the only two really essential items." I ticked them off on my fingers. "One, unlimited raw materials. Two, unlimited solar power to fashion those materials however we wish. Start thinking up projects." I grinned, and it was a dirty, low-down, sneaky kind of a grin. "Preferably profitable ones."

"Gimme a fer instance," Simon said. Nothing got Simon's attention like the word "profit."

I shrugged and spread my hands. "Use your imagination. For example. As time passes in the Belt, some depletion of essential minerals will become inevitable and we will need new ways of processing low-grade ore. Certain bacteria and fungi, either naturally occurring or artificially created, are known to have an appetite for rocks and metals and generate their own energy through metabolism. Standard Oil and Solar's been using polyporus versicolor on Terra for years to turn lignite into a water-soluble liquid. The liquid is then treated with an artificial fungi, which turns it into methane for fuel, which is then sold at a very handsome profit. I don't see why we can't at least investigate the possibilities of similar refining processes during our stay at Ceres."

"Well, as long as we're there," Charlie said.

"And using electrophoresis in zerogee to purify biological materials such as enzymes and hormones makes—"

"Insulin and interferon," she said. "They're already doing that in the Frisbee."

"It's a free marketplace," I said. "And at last count there are between five and eight thousand miners in the Belt, with more arriving on every ship. We've got a market. All we have to do is define it, fill the demand, and count our take."

"And you want us to find something to sell them that they literally can't live without?" Charlie said.

"How will we distribute this theoretical take?" Simon said. "Between the ship's crew, allowing for expenses and Terranova's cut, I mean?"

I hid a grin. "We'll work out an equitable split on crew shares when the time comes."

We were running out of training programs and planning seminars and Caleb was beginning to wonder aloud what orchids sautéd in oleo might taste like when Crip called for the crew to strap themselves in their couches and brace for braking. The vibrations from a mighty, shipwide cheer almost sent the *Hokuwa'a* half a degree off course, but we were already performing our lazy somersault on verniers. When the pressure plate was facing into the wind, so to speak, Crip dropped a series of propellant charges and ignited them one at a time. Our speed dropped by half, and we sighted our first asteroid. Another cheer threatened to cause us to intercept it, and I was glad I'd insisted on the portholes.

Due to a few erratically moving rocks in unexpected places we were a day late braking for the orbit that would take us into Ceres. Crip, Sam, and Simon had a blasphemous time recomputing the trajectory, and at that Denise had to ride the joystick on three different occasions to avoid collisions. Communication with the *Voortrekker,* a week behind us out of Terranova, went blurred and erratic as soon as we put the first rock behind us. "We'll have to set some commsats out of the plane of rotation, first thing," Maile said.

"Agreed," I said. "Have you heard anything yet from Piazzi City?"

She and I and Caleb were crowded onto the flight deck, trying to raise Ceres on what we knew was the Belt's standby frequency. "Nothing. Nothing at all. You'd think we'd have gotten something from one of the outlying claims, at least, but we haven't heard a word."

"We did come in kind of skewed," Crip said. "They may be blocked, or still out of range. They don't have a very powerful transmitter."

For three days we drifted in space. There was no traffic, no chatter over the net. It was as if we were on the very first wagon train ever to travel the Oregon Trail. When I said as much to Caleb he replied, unsmiling, "Yes, and I'm seeing hostile Indians behind every rock."

When we finally matched orbit with Ceres, Crip cut the maneuvering thrusters and turned to me. "Now what?"

The cockpit was crowded. The twins kicked out protestingly. At eight and a half months, they were anxious to get out into the real world, although not half as anxious as I was to get them there. "Still no communication with Ceres?" I said.

"No," Maile said. "I've picked up a few garbled sentences here and there, but I can't tell if it's something someone just said or it's been floating around for years. I get better response from Terranova even though it takes twenty minutes."

I gnawed my lip. "I don't like this," I said. "I don't like this at all. Caleb?"

He nodded. "I'll put my people on standby." He left.

"Put Ceres on the viewer, Archy," I said.

The viewer above the instrument panel showed us a large, pitted rock, seemingly lifeless and stationary. It stood alone at the center of a black stage against a distant backdrop of shimmering, unfocused stars. "Archy, call up the Piazzi City coordinates. Okay? Launch a remcam."

There was a sharp snap and the pop of jets from the hull somewhere aft. We waited. Shortly, Ceres faded from the viewer. It was replaced by a low-level sweep of some bumps that may or may not have been the roofs of Lunabuilts, submerged into the surface of the asteroid.

"Look, over there. Lights."

"Archy, left and down." Archy's remote zoomed in. The lights were mounted on poles, over hangars, personnel locks, what looked like freight bays. All were deserted. What space-buggies and solarsleds we saw were grounded. There wasn't a sign of life to be found anywhere.

Maile said, with a cheerful smile, "Why do I keep expecting someone to jump out and yell 'Boo!' "

I resisted the impulse to gag her and activated my communit. "Caleb," I said in a low voice, "go from standby to alert."

"Still no sign?"

"No. I don't like the feel of it. Stay sharp. Maile, run the bands again."

"Okay, Star, but we know they stand by on Channel 9."

"Do it anyway."

The red figures on the digital readout climbed rapidly, searching for traffic. When the speaker erupted into life we all jumped.

"*Hokuwa'a, Hokuwa'a*!" an excited voice said. "Can you read me?"

"This is the *Hokuwa'a*," Maile said. "Who's this?"

"Name's Strasser; have you got the serum?"

Maile looked at me. I shook my head. "What serum?" she said.

There was a long pause. The voice came back tense and angry. "Those bastards on Ceres told us you had a cure for it! That's why they locked us out and told us to wait for you!"

"A cure for what?"

The voice said despairingly, "We don't know! That's the problem!"

I tapped Maile on the shoulder and nodded at Charlie. She pulled herself within range. "Sir," Charlie said, "this is Dr. Carlotta Quijance, medical officer of the *Hokuwa'a*. Do I understand you to say you have some kind of disease?"

The voice came back, almost laughing, but the kind of laughter that sent a shiver down my spine. "Disease! We've got a goddamned epidemic on our hands, and those bastards on Ceres have locked us out of their medlab!"

board ship, they'll infect the crew."

"But you're pregnant!"

"You noticed!" Charlie closed and sealed her bag. "I won't get out of my suit, Simon, but I have to be on the scene. I'm the only doctor here."

"But we don't even know what it is!"

Charlie turned and headed for the hatch, talking all the way. The rest of us pulled ourselves down the corridor behind her. "Star."

"Yes."

"You're sure you can run the Yalow?"

"You checked me out on it yourself, Charlie. You know I can."

Charlie nodded curtly, looking far from satisfied. "The Sisters will do the blood sampling. They'll feed you the data to begin the RIAs. I plugged the plague card into Blackwell so she's ready to run symptom matches." We entered the galley, crowded with Sisters of St. Anne already in their pressure suits. Charlie began stuffing herself into hers. Seven and a half months along and she looked like she was wearing a beltpak. I envied her. "Archy?"

"Maile has a downlink dedicated to you and connected to Blackwell in the dispensary," Archy said. "I'll be standing by the link at all times."

"Very good." Pausing, her helmet beneath her arm, my sister looked at me. "As chief medical officer of the Terranovan Belt Expedition, I formally direct that the *Hokuwa'a* be placed under quarantine until further notice. Nobody in unless I okay it and Archy has a positive match on their voiceprint identifying them as a member of our crew. Secure all hatches, with the main hatch set for ascep and bleed double bleed. Nobody gets on board, crew member or not, who hasn't been through the bug spray. By the book, Star."

I nodded. I allowed myself one, and one only, bitter, self-condemnatory reprimand for the scoutship tucked safely away in the *Voortrekker*'s hold. If the scoutship had been loaded on board the *Hokuwa'a* Charlie would have had a ready-made mobile lab and I wouldn't be sending her as good as naked into unknown territory and a dangerous and volatile situation. Strasser had sounded on the edge of hysteria. "Understood and acknowledged. Archy?"

"Logged and dated, Star. All hatches sealed."

I looked around. "Whitney, get your people to double-check all hatches, and set up a schedule for a twenty-four-hour guard by each one."

Whitney Burkette straightened with a nearly audible snap, almost saluted, and hustled aft. He bumped into Simon in the companionway door, Simon half in and half out of his pressure suit. Charlie, when she saw him, looked as if she would liked to have stamped her foot, but in a p-suit on board a spaceship you don't dare.

Simon held up one gloved hand. "Don't argue. I'm coming."

"Simon, I'm working!"

He gave an abstracted nod, fiddling with a control on his helmet. "You have spent the last six months training me in medtech. I'm qualified to help. I'm coming."

"You're staying," I said. My back hurt. His head snapped up. "You're second in command, Simon. I need you more than Charlie does. She's got the Sisters with her. They're all experienced physician's assistants. You're staying." He opened his mouth to protest. "That's an order, Simon."

There was a brief, sizzling silence. For a moment I thought I was going to have to add mutiny to the growing list of Things That Must Be Dealt With In The Next Five Minutes. Simon moved first. He stepped forward to kiss Charlie good-bye. Her set, unsmiling face disappeared beneath her helmet. Simon locked it down for her. Three by three they crowded into the lock. It hissed and cycled and delivered them into the arms of the jitney pilot waiting outside the hatch. Behind me I could feel Simon, tense with unvented spleen. I tugged myself back to the bridge with him close behind me. Crip sat at the controls, relaxed, alert, and wary. "Caleb. Report."

Caleb's voice was deep and calm. "Nothing yet, Star. Every hatch into Piazzi City we've seen so far has been locked and sealed and a couple of them even look like they've been welded shut. We're homing in on Strasser's transmission beam now. He says they're in a geodome west of the city."

There was a long silence, productive chiefly of sweat.

"Holy shit," Denise blurted.

"What *now*?" I said.

"Traffic off the port bow and it's big."

"Take a look."

The picture on the monitor changed. "Sweet Jesus H. Christ on a crutch," Crip breathed.

The *Voortrekker* hove into view. My back hurt worse than ever.

"I don't believe it," Crip said blankly. "Austin, you bitch, what'd you do now?" And we all stared at the monitor with our mouths open, the medical emergency temporarily forgotten, as we looked at what Perry Austin, that bitch, had done now.

"I really don't believe this."

"Archy, back off a little on the image."

The *Voortrekker*'s pressure plate was dwarfed by the asteroid looming up in front of it. The ship trailed along behind at the end of a tripod of slender plasteel cables that looked entirely too flimsy for their load, like a grizzly bear on a dog's leash.

"I really and truly do not believe this," Crip said one more time, his voice echoing hollowly down the transmitter.

"You don't have to," said someone acerbically over the ship-to-ship frequency. "We matched orbit with it halfway here."

"Matched orbit? How the hell—"

"An Apollo asteroid," Sam Holbrook said. He crammed himself the rest of the way into the cockpit, his eyes fixed on the *Voortrekker* with an expression halfway between incredulity and delight.

"A what?"

"An Apollo asteroid," Sam repeated impatiently. "The astronomers figure there's about two thousand of them with solar orbits that bring them relatively close to Terra. Like 1566Icarus. At perihelion it passes within the orbit of Mercury."

I said, "Perry, I don't suppose that is Icarus?"

Her voice came back at me. "Where do you think we've been, Star? Icarus is inclined twenty-one degrees out of our flight path. No, this is just a stray."

"How'd you get here so fast? You must be a week ahead of schedule."

"Five and half days is all. We hitched a ride," Perry said, and even at that distance I could tell she felt more than a little smug. Well, she'd earned it, and her paycheck for the duration of the expedition if that asteroid was worth saving. "Crip. Tell

Claire to run a snake, and to switch in the geiger."

Denise took a sight. Crip maneuvered the *Hokuwa'a* with the vernier thrusters so Claire could take pictures of Perry's rock's best profile.

"How am I supposed to make maps of the Belt if people keep shifting the asteroids around?"

I looked over my shoulder and saw Bob Shackleton, our supercargo disguised as an RGS cartographer.

"Welcome to life in the Asteroid Belt, Bob," Crip said. "I think Perry's just demonstrated that the days of fixed orbits are long gone, at least for the duration of our expedition."

"It's not going to be just us moving them, is it," Bob said, and it wasn't a question.

"We probably perturbed some on our way here, just by virtue of our superior mass."

"How'd I get myself talked into this job?" the cartographer muttered, but he sounded less alarmed than resigned to his fate.

Ten minutes later Claire shoved her way into the very crowded cockpit with what looked like a long, narrow picture of the Manhattan skyline.

"So, Claire?" Perry said impatiently over the channel. "How's it look?"

"Black as a Yankee's heart and dirty as his underwear," Claire replied exultantly. "That boulder y'all got tied to your tail is twenty percent pitchblende or my momma's no lady."

"That's the way we read the albedoscope," Perry said in a satisfied tone. "It was just too good to pass up."

"No argument here," I said. "How big is it?"

"Maybe a hundred meters in diameter. It's flat on one side and kind of pointed on another and sort of scooped out on a third, so don't go figuring volume just yet."

"I hate to interrupt this entrepreneurial business conference," Charlie's voice broke in, "but we've got this teensy little medical emergency going on at the moment. You think you can hold off breaking out the picks and shovels until we stop people dying?"

Caleb's voice made us jump when he said suddenly, "Stand by. We've found them." There was another silence, during which the ache in my lower back continued to nag at me. Caleb's voice said, "Switching to viewer."

"Archy?"

"Got it, boss. Viewer on."

Everyone on the bridge looked at the screen.

Caleb was in a cramped geodesic dome, the ceiling so low he had to stoop over. His chest camera played over the interior. I saw an AtPak presumably churning out oh-two and nitrogen. There was a screened latrine and a stove with a box of food packets set next to it. It looked like the standard Miner's and Prospector's Geodome Kit Series K from Eddie Bauer Outfitters, a guaranteed ninety days of food, fuel, water, and shelter for the independent miner, geologist, astrographer, astronomer, and scholar-gypsy clutching the inviolable shade. It looked a little like an igloo, including the tunnel entrance. It was built for a maximum of four occupancy, but there were ten—eleven including Caleb, twelve if you counted his p-suit—crowded into a tiny space that looked less than four meters square. They were sitting with their backs to the wall and their knees drawn up because there wasn't enough room for all of them to stretch out.

Caleb's camera played over their faces, one by one. They all had a strange kind of skin rash made of large, dark uneven spots that looked like flat, sloppy moles. Two of them had limbs that seemed distended, the others looked emaciated to the point of starvation. None of them seemed able to summon up enough energy to move. No one except Strasser, one of the two swollen ones, was able to speak at all.

Archy turned up the gain and we heard his thin, tired voice. "It's some kind of sexually transmitted virus, we've figured out that much. Maggie's was the first place to get hit and then her customers, but only the ones who got laid. It's got a two-week incubation period. Then you break out. Thirty days later, you die."

Caleb, still with his helmet sealed, said, "And you've had no medical attention? What about the hospital in Piazzi City?"

"What hospital?"

"There's no hospital in Piazzi City?"

I heard what could have been a laugh.

"Does that mean no hospital?" Caleb said patiently.

"SOS and T-LM, they run the place. As soon as the plague broke out they sealed the city. We came here all the way from our claim on Eldorado and they wouldn't let us in. They won't let anybody in. They've got the only real doctor in the Belt. We've just been dying—" His voice broke.

"Caleb," I said. I had to stop and fight back a wave of fury before I could continue. "Caleb, those people need shelter. Get it for them."

"Break seal?"

"Break seal, break heads, open up Piazzi like a tin can, I don't care. Get them shelter."

There was grim pleasure in his reply. "Happy to oblige, Star."

"You getting all this, Charlie?"

"Yes, Star."

"Trip Caleb's locator beacon and follow him down." I turned from the viewer and found Maile behind Simon. "Maile, get on the Ceres standby frequency, as many watts as it'll take for them to hear the message in the fillings of their teeth. Tell them who we are. Tell them we're coming in, the hard way if we have to, but we are coming in. Tell them we're armed and we'll burn down anyone who tries to stop us. Caleb, *are* we armed?"

"We are."

"Good. Tell them, Maile, that I expect every doctor, P.A., nurse practitioner, and medtech they've got standing by to offer their services. Tell them that if I find out later that anyone shirked the duty, I will be very annoyed." I rubbed my back. "Tell the miners what we're doing and to head this way. Anybody who's sick and who doesn't have transportation, call in and we'll find it for them. Crip, you hear?"

"I hear. I take it I'm supposed to—ah—acquire said transportation on Ceres?"

I managed a smile that was little more than bared teeth. Crip swarmed out of the bridge. I said to Maile, "Put both messages on tape and run a loop, broadcasting every fifteen minutes. Go." Maile vanished up the companionway to the radio shack.

"*Hokuwa'a, Voortrekker,* what's going on?"

I nodded to Denise, and she accessed the transmitter. "*Voortrekker,* they've got some kind of plague down on Ceres."

Perry was silent for a moment. "Son of a bitch," she said finally. "What flavor?"

"We don't know yet. We've got security and medical people on the way now."

"Security?"

"Piazzi City's locked the Belters out."

There was another pause. "You're kidding, right?"

"I'm not kidding. I suggest you secure all hatches and go to standard debug every time you cycle."

"Ah—"

"What?" I snapped. "Those instructions too difficult for you to follow?"

"No," Perry said. "They're late, is all."

"What!"

"I got a couple passengers with your name on them. They're in transit right now."

I looked at Denise. She pointed to the monitor. A dinghy with three p-suited figures straddling it grew larger as it moved toward the *Hokuwa'a*.

"Helen and Frank," I said grimly. "It just has to be." I forgot my backache and pulled my best time ever bridge to galley. The lock was cycling as I entered the room. Three figures in pressure suits tumbled out, one the size of a midget. They needed more help than they should have in getting their suits off and that made me even madder. "Just what I need, zeegee rookies bumbling around the ship—"

One of the two larger figures finally got her helmet detached and off and turned to help the midget. My jaw dropped and whatever curses I had been going to rain down all over the new arrivals backed up in my throat.

It would have been hard for Gauguin to choose which, my mother or my sister, to use as his model. At seventy-three well-lived years of age Mother's black hair was only winged with gray, her brown skin was clear and unlined, her almond-eyed gaze was steadfast in its customary calm, and her tiny frame was as lithe and graceful as ever. The last time I had seen her, downstairs on a public relations tour a year ago last December, she had looked drawn and much thinner. Today she looked healthy, almost glowing.

"Mother!" I said. "Mother?"

"Hello, dear," she said warmly, as if I were eleven again and she had just returned home from a quick trip to the store. Instead of which she had just made a voyage of nearly two astronomical units via TAVliner, shuttle, and Express, and this was the woman who refused to get on a Cessna 180 for the twelve-minute ride between Seldovia and Homer. She kicked herself forward and enveloped me in a somewhat breathless embrace.

"Mother!" I repeated stupidly. "What have you done to your hair?"

Mother pirouetted, floating upward in the zero gravity. "Do you like it, dear?"

"Well," I said. "It's short."

"Thank you, dear. And so much easier to care for in zero gravity."

"Natasha!" Simon said from the companionway entrance.

"Simon, dear!"

"Never mind that, Mother," I said, "what're you doing here?"

Mother bestowed her special smile on the tech who took her helmet and he reeled away with a dazed expression on his face. He couldn't have been more than twenty-five. "I'm late for work as it is, dear," she said to me. "It took me longer than I'd hoped to settle my affairs on Terra."

"Late for work?"

"Yes, dear. On Mars."

"Work?" I said. "On Mars?" I said. "The American Alliance hasn't even got a colony on Mars yet, Mother."

"I know that, Esther dear, but the only way I could get Professor Eakins to underwrite my trip was to promise I could get into Gagarin City by virtue of my Russian ancestry. My job is to report back to him on the social dynamics of a closed frontier. It's a once-in-a-lifetime opportunity for a Darwinian social anthropologist."

"Mother," I said. I think I even chuckled. "While it is true that Piotor Romanov became your great-grandfather when he walked across the frozen ice of the Bering Strait to marry Luba Shugak, your great-grandmother, we haven't spoken Russian in our family for three generations. We're not exactly kissing cousins to the Martians."

Mother waved this away as a point unworthy of serious consideration. "I expect they'll be glad to see anyone by the time I arrive. And in the meantime," she added serenely, "I can do fieldwork in the Belt. I'm sure studying its culture will be most beneficial to my major work on Mars."

"What culture?" I said before I could stop myself. "No, no," I added hastily when she opened her mouth, "no anthrosociological lectures today. And who is this?" I said brightly, nodding at the young boy who had emerged from the smallest pressure suit. "Your assistant? I suppose he's going to work on Mars, too? Little young, isn't he, Mother? Even for you?"

"No, dear." With one gentle hand she pulled him forward, a thin boy, too thin, all arms and legs and thick, straight hair. It was so fair it was almost white and he was continually pushing it out of his eyes. Those eyes were so blue that meeting them was like staring into the heart of a starstone. There was a hint of determination around the jawline that could easily slide into stubbornness. He looked oddly familiar. Behind me Simon gave a muffled exclamation and Claire was eyeing me curiously.

Mother placed her hands on the boy's shoulders and said gently, "This is Leif, Esther dear. Your son."

I looked again into those blue eyes and this time it was like looking into a mirror. The ache in my lower back increased. "Simon?" I said in a muffled voice.

"What?"

"You—" I looked beyond Mother and the boy. "What the hell!" Everyone swiveled around to follow my gaze and what little noise there was inside the galley died away to a dead silence.

The third figure had shed her pressure suit with more facility than the other two, to reveal the unmistakable black-and-silver uniform of the Space Patrol. She was patting it down when the silence in the galley registered and she looked up to find herself the cynosure of all eyes. Not noticeably discomposed, she looked us over with an impartial stare and her gaze came to rest on me. She stiffened into a freefall brace and saluted. "Patrol Lieutenant Ursula Lodge, reporting for duty, Ms. Svensdotter." She reached into a zippered thigh pocket and pulled out a disk. "My orders."

The ache in my back stiffened into a cramp that coiled around my belly and caused me to double up, gasping. "Simon. You have command. Take over. *Now*."

"What? Why? What's the matter?"

"I'm in labor, you idiot, that's what's the matter!"

"What?"

"What!"

My water broke, and I mean it really broke, flooding my jumpsuit and splashing all the way down to my shoes. Lucky for everyone in the room it adhered instantly to the cloth of my jumpsuit. I winced, first from the sound of Caleb's voice

roaring at me over my communit, and second from the strength
of my first contraction. "Please don't shout. I don't think this
is going to take very long."

"But they're almost three weeks early!" Charlie sounded as
upset as Caleb.

"Archy!"

"Jeez, boss, is this it?"

"Archy, keep Caleb and Charlie off my channel, they can
talk to Mother but not to me." I should have done that before,
but dammit I couldn't think of everything, especially when
I was about to drop two kids on their heads. But this was
zerogee, another voice said in the back of my mind, and I
groaned. No gee meant I would be doing all the work.

My memory of the following nine hours, fifty minutes and
twenty-two seconds is confined to flashes, sharply edited
miniscenes, like previews at the beginning of a showtape.

Large drops of sweat rolling off the tip of Leif's nose and
floating away in the zero gravity as I hauled on his hands.

Archy counting minutes down between contractions as if he
were launching a Saturn V rocket.

Simon alternately yelling "Push!" and "Breathe!" at me and
"Don't touch anybody!" at Charlie over his communit.

A little demon dressed up in Mother clothes insisting that I
"Bear down, dear."

Somebody yelling. Somebody yelling a lot.

And pain. A great deal of pain.

I don't like pain.

Never have.

Pain hurts.

I distinctly remember wanting to speak to Caleb. I remember
having a great deal to say to him, none of it complimentary.

It wasn't supposed to be like that; for one thing, Crip had
promised me at least half a gee by the time I went into labor
if he had to swing the *Hokuwa'a* around on the end of a string
to get it, and for another, on the strength of her and Mother's
past performance, Charlie had predicted a quick, speedy, and
practically painless delivery.

You can't trust anybody anymore. I concentrated on my
heehees and to hell with whatever was going on down on
Ceres.

Eventually two other voices started yelling, too. I slid unresisting beneath a big warm wave of painless peace.

I surfaced to the low hum of machinery and the soft murmur of my mother's voice. For a moment I thought I was back in the chartroom bunk of my father's crabber, headed for Kachemak Bay and home. My eyes drifted dreamily around the room, and came to rest on the digital readout next to the patient monitor. It was thirty-six hours later than it had been—when? I had a vague recollection of—what? a scarred, pitted bowling ball on an ebony lane, with stars for pins? with smallpox? and sirens howling? That couldn't be right, but I wasn't worried. I was cruising. I was copacetic. I was not in pain.

"That's right, dear," Mother was saying into her headset. "Hudson's Disease, or acquired immune deficiency syndrome." She listened. "Some new fast-acting strain, Blackwell says, so the symptoms differed somewhat from the classic text. Archy and that nice young medtech of yours are formulating a vaccine to Blackwell's specifications. When the ship's crew has been inoculated, we'll ship a load down to Ceres. Yes, dear. Twins, just as you said. No, dear, no trouble. Esther was in labor a little over ten hours. She went into hard labor almost immediately, for some reason, and I'm afraid she had rather a difficult time of it. Yes, dear. Yes, dear. Certainly. Carlotta, dear, I do know how to take care of new mothers. I was one twice myself." She looked toward the dispensary hatch and said comfortably, "And now here's Caleb, in case I have any trouble with her."

"Natasha? I'm Caleb. Nice to meet you in person."

"I know, dear," Mother said, embracing him, "I feel the same way. Viewscreens are wonderful inventions but they aren't quite the same as being there, are they? Although the wedding was very nice."

My head twisted around and I woke up from my dreamy state. "Caleb!"

"Star!"

"How are things at Piazzi City? And the *Voortrekker*?"

"The hell with that! How are you? How are Paddy and Sean?"

I remembered then. I was a mother. Gulp. "I don't know. I haven't seen them yet myself."

"Here you are, dears," Mother said, pulling herself in from the next room with a double cradle in tow. "Star, you're holding Sean. Caleb, this is Paddy."

They were identically tiny and identically red. Neither one had any hair to speak of and their eyes were shut tight like newborn kittens. My soft little package lodged neatly between the elbow and wrist of one arm. Caleb could hold his in one palm. I looked down into their faces, asleep with a kind of frowning concentration. Unnoticed by either of us, Mother slipped tactfully out of the room.

Caleb looked at me with a dazed expression. "Wow."

I felt a little light-headed myself. "We did good, Caleb."

"We did good, Star." He pulled himself over to the bunk and kissed me.

"Star?"

We disentangled ourselves. "Yes, Leif?"

He pulled himself all the way into the room, kicking his foot into a strap on the wall next to the bed. "Can I see them?"

I looked into his anxious blue eyes and smiled. "You practically delivered them, Leif. You can see them whenever you want to."

Caleb reached up to give his shoulder a friendly shake, which yanked the boy out of his strap and sent him cartwheeling across the ceiling. "Thanks, kid. I owe you one."

"I take it you've met," I said.

"We have," Caleb said.

"Did Mother tell you—"

"Uh-huh," Caleb said, and grinned. "Surprise."

"No kidding," I said with feeling. I looked at him curiously. "You don't mind?"

Caleb shrugged. "What's one more kid more or less?" and I remembered his dozen half brothers and sisters. He added, "It's not every family that arrives with its own built-in baby-sitter."

Leif, recovering his balance against the opposite wall, grinned and it looked pretty much like a fait accompli. I gave in gracefully, keeping my reservations to myself for now. "This is true." I settled Sean at my breast and he didn't need to be told how; he latched on like an octopus and I could feel the milk in my breasts let down in a rush. I ran my fingertips over his forehead and down his tiny little nose. He was so perfect. I couldn't believe I was responsible for something this perfect. "Oh, Caleb," I said huskily.

I heard soft smacking sounds. I looked over at Paddy and she was making yum-yum motions with her mouth. A baby bottle floated in the door from the next room. Leif snagged it out of the air and sent it on its way to Caleb and Paddy.

And then I remembered. "Caleb."

"What?"

"There's a Patrolman on board."

He nudged the nipple of the bottle into Paddy's mouth and readjusted her in his arms. He watched her feed for a moment, took a deep breath, and looked up at me. "We got a dozen Patrolmen on board, Star."

"What!" I guess I kind of yelled it out. Sean lost his place and let out a protesting wail. Okay, this mother stuff came first, I knew it, I'd known it when I'd decided to go through with rather than terminate my surprise pregnancy. "Okay," I told Sean, "no yelling during feeding time." He latched back on and the noise stopped like someone had thrown a switch. I looked back up at Caleb and in a lower voice demanded, "What do you mean, a dozen Patrolmen on board? The Patrol doesn't maintain a presence in the Belt. What're they doing here?"

"They came on the *Voortrekker* with Perry. Perry says the Alliance wished 'em on her at the last minute and there was nothing she or Helen or Frank could do. It's another reason she hitched on to the asteroid; talk about crowded, she couldn't get here fast enough."

I leaned my head back against the bulkhead. Something was nagging at me, some elusive little thought . . . "Oh, God. Oh, God, Caleb."

"What?"

"She said her name was Lodge."

He nodded, a rueful expression in his green eyes. "Ursula Lodge."

"Any relation?" I asked without hope.

"Let's find out." He raised his voice. "Archy? You on?"

"Of course I'm on, I'm always on. Boss?"

"Hey, Arch."

"Boss, don't you *ever* do that to me again!"

"What? Don't do what to you, Archy?"

"All that bleeding! All that yelling! All that almost dying!"

"Archy, I didn't almost die, I—"

"Yeah, right, boss, you can tell that to the marines! I'm not ever going through that again, you hear? I'll move down to Ceres, I'll go to Mars with Natasha, I'll even go back to Terranova if I have to! No more baby-having! Is that clear?"

"It's pretty clear, Archy," Caleb said solemnly.

"Don't you even talk to me, you ten-toed New South African slug, I'm not speaking to you, this was all your fault in the first place!"

"Hear, hear," I murmured.

"Whaddya want, anyway?"

"Could you find Lieutenant Lodge and have her report to us here, please?"

"And that's another thing! The Space Patrol, yet! They already pulled my plug once! What do you—"

"Archy," Caleb said firmly, "just have her report to us here. Now. Please."

There was the distinct sound of a huff in Archy's voice. "As you wish, supervisor."

"Thank you," Caleb told him, and said to me, "This is what comes of letting computers grow up."

I knew he was trying to get me to relax but with every passing second I could hear the Patrolman get closer. When the knock came I almost jumped out of my restraints.

"Come," Caleb called. "Leif, wait outside, please."

Lodge's silver-and-black dress uniform looked parade-ready, the ceremonial dagger on her hip was gleaming and the bars on her collar shone. Compared to our rumpled selves and especially to me she looked smart and professional. She had brown eyes and brown hair cut short that made her look like a sculpture by Praxiteles. Her figure was compact and muscular, her jaw square and heroic.

Caleb looked her over and appeared unimpressed. "I admit my memory is not what it was, Lieutenant Lodge, but I do seem to recall making a request that all Patrolmen on the Belt Expedition adopt the uniform of the crew."

I lifted Sean to my shoulder and patted his back. Paddy was sound asleep in Caleb's arms. This domestic scene might have lulled a less wary or less intelligent person into relaxing. Lodge was neither unwary nor stupid and her shoulders tensed. Caleb didn't say much, but it was how he didn't say much that made him such an effective security chief. When Caleb interrogated, he leaned forward with an expression that told his victim there was nothing more important in the entire solar system than he was at that very moment, that Caleb would be nothing less than enraptured by any confidence his victim might care to share with him. Under the influence of that compelling green gaze, his victim became anxious to unload everything he knew, to confess every sin, real or imagined, to lay his burden down in the sure knowledge that Caleb would pick it up and in so doing grant absolution and a full pardon. When Caleb had a subordinate on the carpet, that same bright green gaze turned bored and impersonal and it soon became painfully obvious that no excuse however ingenuous or even true was ever going to compensate for any dereliction of duty, no matter how small or insignificant. Usually even the most self-possessed subordinate had been reduced to terminal stammers before Caleb had even opened his mouth. I settled back and watched him go to work.

Lodge's face reddened slightly. She did not shift her stance. She had yet to meet my eyes straight on. When she spoke her voice was unexpectedly soft, low, and gentle, an excellent thing in a woman, not to mention all the better for soothing the ire of an angry superior officer. At least I hoped Caleb was her superior officer. "I feel more comfortable in the uniform of my own service, sir."

Caleb didn't say a word. He looked at her, unwinking, unsmiling, completely disinterested in her comfort or lack thereof.

I'll say this for her, the woman had backbone. She stuck out that cold stare for a full sixty seconds without wilting, which had to be some kind of record. Then she crumbled. "Permission to be excused, sir."

Caleb shifted Paddy to his other arm and looked at the blinking red chronometer on his communit. "You have ten minutes, Lieutenant."

She was back in eight, breathing heavily. This time she was clad in a standard-issue crew jumpsuit, which silver blue color actually did things for her dark complexion. There was a tiny barred silver-and-black shield beneath the nametag below her left shoulder.

Caleb lifted his eyes from his communit and said pleasantly, "Lieutenant Lodge, I believe you have yet to be formally introduced to our boss, Star Svensdotter." No words of censure, no hint of reproof. Sometimes Caleb scared even me.

"No, sir," Lodge said woodenly. "Ms. Svensdotter."

I nodded. "Lieutenant Lodge."

She made as if to hold out her hand, then thought better of it. I recognized the ring she wore, though. A West Pointer, God help us. Those brown eyes, thick-lashed and intent, looked me over and weighed me up with a measuring, assessing, altogether speculative look. I stood it with what I felt was composure for as long as I felt necessary. "Sorry," I said finally. "No horns."

She smiled. Like her low, soft voice it was another surprise, lighting up her square face with humor and intelligence. "No tail or pitchfork, either, I see."

"No."

"You can't blame me for looking for them."

"No," I said. "I imagine what your family has been saying to the trivee lately is nothing compared to what they've been saying among themselves."

"What are you doing here, Lodge?" Caleb said.

"The American Alliance convinced the Terranova Habitat Assembly that a detachment of Patrolmen would enhance the security of the Terranova Belt Expedition." She recited it by rote. "As well as establish a Patrol presence in an area of expanding Terran interest."

"Uh-huh," I said.

Her brown eyes looked at me a moment longer, and then shifted to Caleb. "Permission to speak freely, sir."

"Granted."

She turned back to me. "I understand your reasons for being suspicious of me, ma'am, but this isn't Terranova and I am not my uncle."

"Grayson Cabot Lodge was your uncle?" She nodded and I swore beneath my breath.

"The One-Day Revolution is an historical fact," she went on. "Terranova is today a free society. I have neither the ambition nor the inclination to attempt to change that."

"Or to help anyone else do so?" I couldn't help asking.

"Or to help anyone else do so," she affirmed. "I volunteered for this expedition and I agreed to work under your authority because I wanted to be a part of exploring the Belt, not to pursue some quixotic mission of familial revenge."

I concentrated on removing a tiny speck of lint from Sean's blanket. "Lieutenant, either your naivete is so complete as to be almost incredible or it's one hell of an act. Must I remind you that during the so-called One-Day Revolution, I was directly responsible for the death of your uncle, Grayson Cabot Lodge, commodore in your service?"

"Ahem," Caleb said.

"It was my responsibility, Caleb, I was in charge. I was also responsible for Terranova's declaration of independence, Lieutenant. That, if you remember, put a considerable dent in the prospective profits of one Standard Oil and Solar, a corporation of which your grandfather happens to be majority stockholder and CEO. I gave the order to hijack five Patrol Goshawk fighters for the Terranovan fleet, and—"

"Excuse me, Star, but you were unconscious at the time," Caleb interjected.

"Yes," she said. "I was next in line to command that squadron at my next promotion."

Wonderful. "In short, Lieutenant, if the Patrol starts shooting, there's reasonable cause for me to be uncertain of which way they'll be aiming." I settled Sean in his crib and fastened the safety straps as I spoke. I turned to face Lodge squarely. "Tell me I'm paranoid about your reasons for coming along on this trip. And make me believe it."

Her square jaw worked for a moment. "Ms. Svensdotter. My name could be Smith or Jones or Clinkerdagger, and if I screwed up an assignment you'd ship me out. If it comes to that, do it for the right reason."

"And your name isn't a sufficient reason?"

"Not in my opinion, no. Ma'am."

We stared at each other for a long time. Caleb's head swiveled back and forth between us like a spectator at a tennis match. I blew out some air and looked at Caleb with a slight shrug. Caleb nodded to himself as if he had known it all along, and said, "Lieutenant."

She went back into her brace. "Sir."

"It's no use saying you won't be working under a cloud, because you will. You'll be watched and followed and second-guessed and leaned over. It's not fair, I know, but that's the way it's going to be, past history being what it is. You'll have to prove yourself, you and the rest of your squad. You come under my authority out here, according to your orders, and I won't make it easy for you."

"I understand, sir. All I want is the chance." There was real relief in her voice. Relief that she would be given a chance at the job, or at me? I wished I knew.

"You've got it. Dismissed." She left. Caleb said, "I believe her, Star."

"Sometimes I've believed as many as six impossible things before breakfast."

He laughed a little and shook his head. "I'll put her to work as soon as I can. Keeping her busy will keep her out of mischief."

"I can live with it, as long as she's working for you and not the other way around. Now get Mother in here."

"Mother," I said in what I felt was a calm, rational tone, "if I'd ever been pregnant before I'm sure I'd have remembered it."

"Esther dear, don't push your chin out like that," Mother said. "It makes you look positively australopithecus."

"Mother," I said, some of my calm deserting me, "do I have to beat it out of you? Where'd he come from? Aside from that egg I donated to CalTech's egg bank for that publicity stunt Helen thought up eleven years ago. I have managed to get that far."

She settled herself more securely in the webbing affixed to the walls of the dispensary and folded her hands. She had small hands, neatly made, that were always either folded or taking notes. She looked down on me benignly. Mother never got excited. Getting excited wasted energy better spent in irritating her children. "Well, dear, as I am sure you recall, I strongly encouraged you to participate."

"That isn't quite correct, Mother. You demanded I do it or you'd disown me."

"If you say so, dear."

"I do say so. Mother, that egg bank maintains strict anonymity for the donor parents. It was the only way I would agree to enter the program. What'd you do, rob it? And if so, how dare you?"

"Esther dear, what was I supposed to do? There were my only two children, a quarter of a million miles away, and not likely to return home anytime soon, if ever. My only grandchild went gallivanting off around the galaxy without even consulting me." This with an expressive sweep of one hand that indicated Betelgeuse and other points north. "And there was I, alone on Terra, my husband gone, no other family to comfort me in my old age—"

"All right, Mother, you can cue down the violins."

"Yes, dear. So I called Helen—"

"Helen knew?"

Mother looked mildly surprised. "Of course, dear. How else do you think I managed to get hold of the right egg? After that—"

"Helen knew about Leif?" When I saw Helen next—

"I just said that, dear. Didn't I just say that?"

"You just said that, Natasha," Archy confirmed.

"I thought so." Mother carried on as if there had been no interruption at all. "It was simply a matter of finding a donor father and a host mother. When Leif was born, I took over. When you came downstairs last December and found me looking so strained it was because Leif had been ill, not I."

I thought of the thin, pale child and said, "Ill? With what?"

"He's fine now, dear, just the measles combined with the Arctic flu—do you know they still don't have a vaccine for the Arctic flu? I've never heard of such laggardness. I mean to speak to Carlotta about it."

"Never mind the Arctic flu, just when were you going to tell me about Leif, Mother?"

Her brow wrinkled thoughtfully. "I intended to tell you as soon as he was born, taking all the responsibility for his upbringing, of course. But then all that bother started with those Luddite creatures, and after that the Alliance Congress, and then the Space Patrol . . . well. Hardly a suitable environment in which to raise a child. I hardly ever saw you except when you came home on those awful publicity tours, and even then we were never able to spend more than a few hours alone together. There was never time to sit down for a nice cozy chat." She sat back, folded her hands, and prepared to dismiss the matter.

"Mother—" I said, and sighed. "I don't know what to say to you. Have you considered what you are doing to the child? Maybe you shouldn't have told him. Who says he has to want me for a mom?"

She granted me one of her rare smiles. "Ask him, dear."

Leif looked at me out of direct blue eyes and said simply, "Who wouldn't want you for a mother? You're Star Svensdotter. It's on the trivee all the time, how you worked to get Copernicus Base going on Luna, how you practically built Ellfive bare-handed. How you kept it free of the Space Patrol so Terrans could move into the sky. I've heard about you all my life, and not just from Emaa." He shrugged and repeated, "Who wouldn't want to be your kid?"

My face was burning. Caleb was grinning. I managed to say in a steady voice, "So you really feel okay about that?"

"Why wouldn't I?"

I cast about helplessly for something to say. "Because you weren't my idea. Because although I may be your parent biologically—"

"Oh, that." Leif's voice was almost scornful. "We did all that in school."

"Did what?" I said. "Who's we?"

"The Petri kids."

"Petri kids?"

"That's what they call us." He saw my blank expression and looked impatient. "You know. 'Born in a Petri dish, behind a Bunsen burner, in the lab on a Sunday afternoon'?"

I didn't recognize the words or the tune but I nodded anyway because I didn't know what else to do.

"We—the Petri kids—figured out that what we do for ourselves is more important than who we came from." He saw my face change and added, "It's not like we don't have people who love us." He smiled at Mother. "Emaa's been better than any two parents could have been." He met my eyes and said steadily, "Probably better than you would have been, too. You've been busy."

"How old are you?" I said.

"Ten."

I looked at Mother. "You didn't let the grass grow under your feet, did you?"

"No, dear, I didn't," Mother agreed placidly.

It had been a busy week. It wasn't until the next day that it occurred to me to ask who Leif's father was. The answer knocked me up against a bulkhead. "Grays?" I repeated in a stunned voice. "Grays? You gave that poor kid Grayson Cabot Lodge for a father?"

Mother said, as if she were reasoning with someone younger than Leif, "Well, Esther dear, he was the only man you were involved with in the entire fourteen years after you went to space."

"You never liked him, Mother," I said. "You wouldn't let me bring him to the potlatch when I brought him home that time. You wouldn't even let him stay in your house."

"What has that got to do with anything, dear? The geneticist said Grays's DNA was very clean."

"But he almost killed me!"

"Yes, dear, but he didn't."

"I married the man who killed Grays, Mother! Don't you think Leif might have a problem with that?"

"No, dear," Mother said simply.

The more indignant I got, the more reasonable Mother became. "Did he know?"

"Certainly, dear."

I rubbed my forehead. Of course he had known. *You won't kill me, Star,* I heard Grays's voice say distantly. *Never me.* Grays was dead and buried and now he was reaching out to me from beyond the grave. Damn him. Wearily I told Caleb, "Have I ever told you that the only member of my family I ever got along with is dead?"

"That would be your father," Caleb suggested.

"That would be my father," I agreed. "It's why I took his name. A more rational, reasonable man you'll never meet. You could talk to him. He—"

"Esther dear, I couldn't have your child fathered by a complete stranger, now, could I?"

"I don't know, Mother," I said. "I suppose not. I feel a little dizzy. I think I'll lay down for a while."

"Of course, dear," Mother said solicitously. "I do hope you felt all right during the journey. Zerogee is no fun when you're pregnant."

"How would you know?" They left, and I told Archy I was off line for the next eight hours.

The next day I told her she and Leif couldn't stay on with the expedition and that was that. I had help. Caleb suggested that after seventy-three years on Terra perhaps Mother might be unable to adjust to subgee life. Simon told her that the addition of two extra people, one of them a child not bred to space, was simply not feasible for the continued good health of the expedition. "Mother," Charlie said, tackling the problem from a different angle, "what about research materials? What about your paper on the society of the Alaskan Eskimo after ANCSA? What about the background statistics you need to prove your theory that assimilation is essential for survival of race as well as culture?"

"Carlotta dear, you have been telling me for years about Simon's computer. If he's good enough to run Ellfive single-handedly, and to receive an open invitation to browse through a Library somewhere on the other side of the universe, he can surely find some little corner to store the small amount of relevant sociological data I may require en route to Mars. Can't you, dear?" This last was directed toward the ceiling pickup.

"Certainly, Natasha. My data base is at your service, and I can access the library at the University of Alaska on your word." Archy's tone was grave and respectful, which made me wonder what was wrong with him.

"Yes, Simon dear, and I want one of those wrist thingies—"

"Communits, Natasha. Communits."

"—communits, then, dear, so I may communicate freely with Archy, and we can set up a program as soon as possible."

"I like your mom, Star," Archy said. "She reminds me of the Librarian."

"Thank you, dear," Mother said. She was quite unruffled at being compared by the only sentient computer in the system to a photonic being that traveled faster than light around the Milky Way doing research for the Encyclopedia Galactica.

"Mother," I said, squaring my shoulders and meeting her eyes womanfully, "you do not have a skill that will contribute to the success of this expedition."

Mother looked at me.

"We don't need you on this trip," I said, getting specific. "Exogeologists, hydroponics techs, astronomers, yes. A Darwinian social anthropologist, no."

Mother's gaze never faltered. I hoped that shine I saw in her eyes wasn't tears. "Well," I said. "That's that, then. I'll tell Maile to start looking for a vessel inbound for O'Neill. I'm sure Terranova will be happy to have you. Now there's an evolving society for you to study. You've even got a place to live, the Habitat Assembly deeded my house over to me. It's beautiful, you'll love it. It's even got its own cat." That wasn't precisely true, as Hotpants had been adopted out to Petra Strongheart, but I was getting desperate.

Mother said nothing.

"And don't try to argue with me about it, Mother, because my mind's made up."

— 4 —

Should-Be-Ables, Inc.

A human being should be able to change a diaper,
plan an invasion, butcher a hog, conn a ship, design
a building, write a sonnet, balance accounts, build a
wall, set a bone, comfort the dying, take orders, give
orders, cooperate, act alone, solve equations, analyze a
new problem, pitch manure, program a computer, cook a
tasty meal, fight efficiently, die gallantly. Specialization
is for insects.

—Lazarus Long
Time Enough for Love

Charlie was busier than a cat with two tails and no room to
swing either for the next month. She had that mutant strain of
Hudson's Disease just about whipped into line when a bunch
of miners who hadn't been getting their exercise came down
with hypercalcemia. While they were flat on their backs, an
epidemic of influenza swept through Piazzi City, another mutation. The cramped, crowded living quarters on Ceres and in the
claims encouraged proliferation of the most minor sniffle, so
what one got they all did, and then of course everyone spread
the infection to Piazzi City, which gave it back to the miners,
who brought it back to Ceres and so on ad infinitum. On Terra
or Terranova it would have been an overnight task for any
moderately sized hospital to isolate and identify the bug; in
the Belt, Charlie and Blackwell had to improvise. She lost ten
patients before she managed to come up with a vaccine, and

she was short-tempered and surly until she did. Immediately thereafter she gave birth, on schedule and with a minimum of fuss, which relieved Archy. As she pointed out in a fair-minded way, she did have more experience at it. Simon wanted to call him Norbert, after Norbert Wiener, but Charlie put her foot down and they called him Alexei after Simon's father. Alex was little and loud and born looking like he needed a shave. Simon immediately shot a message off to Terra informing his father of the happy event. As he explained, the old man would no doubt wish to alter his will immediately.

Charlie assigned weightless workout sessions for her hyper-calcemic patients aboard the *Hokuwa'a* on a rotational basis and the grunting and thumping could be heard all over the ship, nonstop around the clock. The difference between cozy and crowded on a spaceship among 127 permanent residents and God knew how many transients was too close to call. When she got them organized, she turned her attention to me and before I could say "Dr. Benjamin Spock" I found myself in the dispensary with my feet up in the stirrups.

"Uh, Charlie?"

"Yes?"

"How much longer?" She looked at me over my knees and grinned, and I added, "Caleb wants to know."

She laughed. "Sure he does. Well, the equipment looks in pretty good shape. Give it another two weeks and we'll see. Okay, I'm through." She pulled herself over to the clinic terminal and wrote a few notes to my chartdisk. "How do you feel, Star? Good, bad, indifferent? Mentally, emotionally, whatever?"

"I feel well enough for my first visit to Ceres," I said, looking up from where Sean was already rooting purposefully at my breast. "Is it safe?"

"I give you the booster for Hudson's?"

"Yes."

"And you're up-to-date on your flu shots?"

"Yes."

"The twins, too?"

"Certainly."

She sighed. "All right, if you feel up to wrestling your way into a pressure suit, far be it from me to stop you."

She tugged her way over to her console while I fought my way into my jumpsuit. I really hate zerogee. I keyed my communit and said, "Caleb? Charlie says I can go down to Ceres."

"I'm way ahead of you," Caleb said from the doorway, Paddy in her baby bag strapped to his chest. "Alert hizzonner that we're coming, Archy."

"I'll go with you, dears," Mother said from right behind him. "I want to look at the social structure of the place before our presence contaminates it."

Strasser, Charlie's first Belter patient, was in the dispensary for his booster shot and he asked if he could hitch a ride. "Sure," I said. "You're looking better."

"I'm feeling a whole hell of a lot better," he replied emphatically. "The doc is some kind of miracle worker." He pulled himself down the passageway behind me. "What's going on downstairs these days? The last I heard, Brazil had finally joined the American Alliance."

I gaped at him. "Just how long have you been in the Belt, Mr. Strasser?"

"Ten years and five months," he said proudly. "I was an engineer's mate on the *Sagdeyev* in 1996. I jumped ship to do some prospecting of my own."

"And got lucky?"

He grinned and didn't answer.

"And started selling your ore to Standard Oil and Solar."

He stiffened and his eyes became wary. "Terra-Luna Mines, actually, but it doesn't make much difference here."

"Really? Why not?"

He looked from me to Caleb and back again. "Why ask me? You're a relief train for them, aren't you? They're expecting you. You should know the setup."

"Let's get one thing straight, Mr. Strasser," I said briskly. "This expedition is not affiliated with either SOS or T-LM in any way whatever. We're a private enterprise, funded by the independent nation of Terranova. The most anybody expects out of us is a profit. Which we intend to give them."

"The independent nation of what?"

"Terranova, the habitat circling Terra at Lagrange Point Five."

"Ellfive," he said. "I thought Ellfive was an American Alliance colony."

"It was."

"It's independent now?"

"Since a year ago January. At any rate, Mr. Strasser, I repeat, Terranova is not going into business with SOS and T-LM. We're going into competition with them." I had to grin at his expression. "Now let's go tell them so."

Wriggling into a pressure suit wasn't as difficult as usual, mostly because Caleb had modified ours to accommodate one baby each suspended from a chest harness. Caleb and I both needed pressure suits custom made in our size; I was three centimeters taller, so mine had to be longer, but he outweighed me by twenty-three kays so his had to be bigger around. The twins snuggled into their harness and fell asleep almost at once. I had one of Whitney Burkette's engineers working on a design for an expandable pressure suit for growing girls and boys; I thought as long as expedition expenses were being carried by Terranova we might as well experiment on the twins and come up with a working model for eventual sale to Belters, not to mention my own crew. One prompt by-product of pioneering is always baby pioneers.

Outside the lock, I saw for the first time the solarsled Daedalus had fashioned for the expedition. It looked just like the Wright Flyer I'd had as a child, until I tried floating down the slough on it. The biggest difference was the shiny sail four times its size that unfolded from the stern.

"Hey, wait up! Can I hitch a ride with you guys?"

Bob Shackleton was making a game effort to pull his way across to the sled. He missed a handhold, grabbed wildly for purchase, and knocked himself loose of the *Hokuwa'a*'s hull. The reaction from the force of the blow caused him to begin to drift, and he began a frantic and futile wiggle, his pressure-suited arms and legs looking like fat white worms against the blackness of vacuum. "Hey! Somebody help! Heee-eelp!"

Strasser made a disgusted sound over the commlink. "All abooo-aaard!" Caleb said. We straddled the bench that ran the axis of the thing and strapped ourselves down. Caleb fiddled with the controls and we detached so gently from the *Hokuwa'a*'s hull that it was a surprise when I realized Shackleton was growing in size. Caleb lay the sled next to the drifting figure in one smooth maneuver. "You been spending some time in the cockpit with Crip?" I asked him.

"Got the boathook?" I passed it forward. "Shackleton? Quit thrashing around like that. Grab the hook."

Shackleton made a pass at the hook and missed. The wide swipe his arm made at the hook caused him to begin to revolve and he drifted out of our reach.

"Oh, for crissake," Strasser growled. "Gimme that damn thing. I'll reel in that yo-yo; you mind the store. Get behind him." He unbuckled, stood up in the stirrups, and took the boathook from Caleb. Caleb trimmed our solar sail and in a few moments we caught up again with Shackleton. Strasser made one pass with the boathook and snagged the emergency latch on the back of the cartographer's p-suit. "Relax now, dammit! We got you." He walked his hands up the boathook and, handling the other man the way a child would manipulate a doll, plucked him off the hook and jammed him down on the solarsled's bench. "Stick your feet in there. Not there, there! Jesus!"

"Whew." The cartographer sounded exhausted. "Thanks."

Strasser growled something unprintable.

"Your first EVA?" I inquired politely, restowing the boat-hook.

"First one outside of training. I thought I was a goner."

Strasser growled something else, equally unprintable, and Caleb said diplomatically, "Now we're all aboard. And off we go, into the wild black yonder." He punched in the coordinates for Piazzi City and when I looked around five minutes later I was amazed to see the *Hokuwa'a* a thousand meters astern.

"This sucker actually moves," I said over the communit. "How?"

"Beats the hell out of me," Caleb said cheerfully. "Heckel said something about the solar cells creating an artificial solar wind that pushes the sail that pushes the sled that gets us where we want to go, but I've only got his word for it, and it all sounds pretty unlikely if you ask me."

"Great. What happens if we break down?"

"We yell for help. Loudly."

Sean hiccuped and burped against my breast and I craned the back of my neck up against my helmet to look down at him. Everybody cleaned out their own pressure suits, and I devoutly hoped the twins were not going to make it more of a chore than usual.

Even from 1.8 AUs out the reflection of the sun's rays was blinding and I was glad when the bulk of Ceres came between us and Sol. I knew intellectually that the rock wasn't

a thousand klicks in diameter but at this distance it seemed
nearly the size of Luna, only a lot less welcoming. The surface
looked bare and skeletal. Escaping vapors from thousands of
lock ventings and leaks of pressurized construction gases hung
over the surface in a kind of shroud.

"It gets worse," Caleb said over our helmet communits.

"I don't see how it can," I replied dismally.

We docked in an unpressurized hangar hacked out of the
side of a cliff. The interior of the hangar was festooned with
other transports moored to every available surface in, to my
disapproving eye, very sloppy fashion with no discernible
organization. Nor was there any attempt made to standardize
moorings; ships were haphazardly attached to various cables,
tied down to eyebolts driven into the rock, with runners slipped
beneath U-bolts. I saw one weighed down with a rock. More
arrived every minute. All their drivers demonstrated a fine
disregard for courtesy of the road. I counted two midairs in
the few moments we stood watching, both of which involved
no great speed and therefore resulted in little more than a string
of curses over Channel 9, 1Ceres's standby.

I touched my helmet to Caleb's and said, "I knew we should
have brought somebody from Boeing with us. Tell me that isn't
an old Sammamish Scooter over there. I haven't seen one of
those since I worked on Luna."

"I wouldn't know, it looks more like a garbage disposal
to me."

Whatever it was, the one thing it had in common with all of
the various transports was an advanced case of acute disrepair.
I shook my head and then remembered Caleb couldn't see
me. I touched helmets with him again and said, "Where's the
lock?"

"They don't make it any too easy to find, do they? This
way."

Hiding behind an outcropping, it looked like any personnel
airlock I'd ever seen, except that it was unattended on either
side, letting dual lockseals do guard duty instead. There didn't
seem to be any vacant lockers available for pressure suits.

I popped by helmet and looked at my chronometer. "Less
than an hour, lock to lock. Not bad." I looked around. "Where
is everybody?"

"You were expecting maybe a brass band?"

"May we get out of our p-suits, dear?" Mother inquired.

He spread his hands. "Where we gonna leave them, Natasha? Come on. Through here."

I latched my helmet and gauntlets to my belt and stumped grimly forward toward the lights and noise.

Piazzi City occupied a large cavern below Ceres's surface. It had started out small, maybe the size of the hangarlock on Terranova, and it had been burrowed out until it was about the original size of Copernicus Base proper. The interior surface was filled in with a pressure-sealed silicate fixative, a dull, grimy gray in color. No sunlight whatever had been introduced into the interior and the result was pretty gloomy. What light there was, was provided by a haphazard array of halogen lamps hooked together with a tangle of cables—"You'd think they'd have taped them over at least," I muttered, tripping for the third time. It's not a good idea to fall down in a p-suit, even in minimal gravity. Electric generation did not seem to be any too steady or reliable as the lamps on the walls and the street poles flickered, becoming brighter or dimmer with no warning and for no obvious reason. A few lines of streetlights disappeared down several unfinished, hacked-out tunnels running off the main room.

The place was packed like a salmon stream in June and it smelled worse than the inside of the *Hokuwa'a*. Everyone seemed to be talking at once, loudly. I counted three shell games from where I stood, each deep in its own intent group.

"Feels like we're touring an ant farm from the inside, doesn't it," Caleb said, wiping his forehead and showing me his wet palm.

"It's too warm in here," I said. "Guaranteed low employee productivity."

"It's dry, too," Caleb said. "They're going to have some problems with dehydration if they don't watch it."

Mother sniffed the air appreciatively, her brown eyes bright with interest, her tail practically wagging with enthusiasm.

We came into the public square without challenge. People came and went around us, many of them from the Planetismal Trading Company, a building dug out of one wall, the outside of which was plastered with hand-lettered signs featuring the word SALE writ large in red letters. A typical one read "Deluxe Eldorado Prospector's Outfit, Supplies for One T-Year, Gourmet QuikFreeze Meals, Portable CampPak Available in Large Sizes. No Money Down, Credit Extended on

Your Good Name, We Will Not Be Undersold!"

Not likely, as the Planetismal Trading Company was the only general merchandising store I had seen so far. To its right stood a boardinghouse offering beds with guaranteed clean sheets in six-hour shifts for fifty Alliance dollars or equivalent confirmed-assay ore per shift, a five-minute hot shower for twenty-five Alliance dollars or equivalent confirmed-assay ore, and the services of a pressure-suit mechanic for one thousand Alliance dollars or equivalent in confirmed-assay ore per half hour, advertised as a bargain-basement rate, cheapest in the Belt.

"A thousand bucks per half hour?" I exclaimed.

Caleb shrugged. "Supply and demand."

I struggled to match his laconic drawl. "Well, if we strike out moiling for gold, we can go into the service industry, I guess."

"And probably make more money at it, at that."

Two other buildings, looking as if they had come from the same Lego set as the store, squatted side by side to the left. One bore the gold pan and pick of Terra-Luna Mines, the other the black-and-silver starburst of Standard Oil and Solar. The rest of the structures appeared to be saloons, out of which erupted much noise and the occasional body. Mother, already dictating to Mead over her communit, promptly disappeared into the nearest one. Strasser had vanished at the airlock and Caleb and I were alone.

"Doesn't look much like either Sodom or Gomorrah to me."

"Yeah," Caleb said, "it looks more like Tombstone. But then *Time* can't be right all the time, I guess." He looked around, dangling his pressure suit helmet from one hand. "There." It was a tiny one-room shack made of preformed silicon flats, set a little back from the square, with "City Hall" painted over the door in barely legible script. "Want to go on in?"

"No." Through the door of the office we could clearly see the bulk of someone sitting behind a desk, but I was already irritated enough at not being met at the airlock. Not that I expected the brass band, but common courtesy at the very least called for the provision of a guide. The slight was real; I could feel eyes on my back watching to see how I would take it.

Caleb looked at me warily. "Are you going to get mad?"

"Mad? Me?"

He looked even more wary. "I didn't like the idea of coming over here without a security detachment in the first place," he said in an undertone. "You behave, Star, or we'll both be sorry I didn't."

"Trust me," I said, and he groaned. "What's that?"

He followed my gaze and grinned. "Something you'll like. Take a look."

In the center of the square stood a four-sided post, a meter to a side and two meters tall. Someone had made a pitiful attempt to grow a few pitiful blades of grass around its base and the result was what you might expect—pitiful. But so far as I could see, they were the only growing things in sight. Roger would have a stroke.

We shouldered through the crowd for a closer look. The pillar turned out to be a combination newspaper, lost-and-found, community bulletin board, solarsled dealership, employment agency, and personals column. Faxsheets of the latest news beneath the UAPI byline were tacked up, the more recent ones over the old news, all much thumbed. Most of the notices were straightforward and businesslike, some were unintentionally hilarious, others poignant.

Will pay, trade, kill for book/filmtapes.
4C format ONLY, please!!!
See Bob in T-LM Assay on 1Ceres, around
corner to your right.

Silicon assaying and processing,
will do some fabrication,
experienced silicon technician,
reasonable rates.
Maggie on 1Ceres.

White lightning, Kentucky moonshine,
the genuine article.
Brewed of the finest natural ingredients
available in the Belt.
Reserve your liter now.
Dope, crack, snort also available
and certified chemically pure
by accredited lab techs.
Robber Joe's Fun House on 4Vesta.

Claim jumped, then wife. Dragging up on
next freighter going anywhere. Best offer
for complete outfit, including 2002 Dodge 512
rock buggy and trailer, homemade solar conversion.
It runs. Seller experienced longshoreman,
short-order cook, janitor, can drive anything,
looking for job starting yesterday. Will
stand by on Channel 9 from 0700 to 0800 each
morning 1Ceres time, or leave msg. with Maggie
for Harry on 19Fortuna.

BOOKS, TAPES—buy, trade, sell, loan,
any subject, any condition, any model tapes,
any price. Leave msg. with Maggie on 1Ceres
for Bill Shakespeare on 3839Caliban.

"Who's this Maggie person?" I asked.
"Runs a whorehouse outside the city. So I'm told."
"That's not all she does."
"She does seem kind of ubiquitous, doesn't she? Look at
this one."

URGENT! Calico cat in heat, looking for mate.
Will reimburse for fuel getting here and split
sale price on kittens seventy-thirty. Latest
going rate for weaned kitten $5,000 Alliance—
this means fifteen hundred per kitten for you!
Standing by on Channel 9 twenty-four hours
a day, call Arai on 2Pallas direct
or leave msg. with Maggie.

"We should have brought Hotpants along for the ride."
"I guess."
"What?"
"I don't know. I've got a feeling about this Maggie—"
"Here's her name again."

Buggy/Scooter/Sled tune-ups, aseptic abortions
and other first aid by qualified medtech,
fresh herbs, munitions, Tarot readings, XXX showtapes.
Mom-and-Pop's on 6789Cribbage.
Call ahead on Channel 3 or talk to Maggie.

Those arriving without prior appointment
will be shot on sight as trespassers.

"First chance we get, we introduce ourselves to Mom and
Pop."

"Deal."

Sunday Services, 7 pm weekly in lobby of
the Terra-Luna Mines building on 1Ceres.
Brother Moses of the
Divine Brethren of the Promised Land, Ltd.,
conducting. Wedding, baptisms, funerals
by appointment only. Versed in all
denominations, services recognized by
official churches everywhere, Catholic,
Lutheran, Jewish, Moslem, Buddhist.
Rate schedule available upon request.
Contact the Brethren on 55Pandora, Channel 9.

"Mother Mathilda's got competition."

Caleb nudged me. "That's him."

"Him?" I said. "Him who?"

"Brother Moses."

"He's here? Where?"

Brother Moses was indeed present in person, conducting what
we later learned were regular Wednesday afternoon sweeps for
converts. He was a tall, cadaverous figure in a jumpsuit so white
it hurt the eyes. He had hair to match that was longer than mine,
a glad hand and a gladder smile. He stood in one corner of the
town square pitching his deep voice to reach the very fringes
of the crowd. "I can promise you eternal salvation if ye but
trust in Him who created us all! I can promise you that! Praise
the Lord!"

There were a couple of "Amen"s and "Praise his name"s
from the crowd. Brother Moses' voice dropped. "But you all
know what waits around the corner for the backsliders and
soulless sinners among you! Yes! I'm speaking of eternal
damnation here! Thank you, Jesus! Yes, thank you, Jesus,
for giving us the choice, and for giving us the vision and the
backbone to choose the path of godliness and righteousness
and the way of our Lord!"

Brother Moses raised his arms, laid on hands, and transformed a heckler into a true believer there and then. The poor saved soul, looking as if he were overdosing on redemption, staggered to his feet and emptied his pockets of handfuls of what looked to me like rocks into a very large collection basket carried between two white-clad members of the Brethren. The crowd sucked in a collective gasp of breath and Brother Moses beamed.

I looked over at Caleb. "All I ask is that you keep him off the *Hokuwa'a* and away from me."

"Consider it done."

"A dollar a kay," a voice said.

"Huh?" We turned. Two men were standing nose to nose with their heads low and their fists clenched. One had no chin and the other only one eye.

"The going rate for freight to 2Pallas is seventy-five cents!" One Eye protested.

"Two dollars," No Chin replied.

One Eye hesitated.

"Okay, a buck seventy-five," No Chin said, "but that's my last offer. I got expenses, maintenance on my scooter, and my time's as valuable as yours any day." Their fists unclenched and the deal was closed.

"I *knew* we should have brought somebody from Boeing with us."

Caleb looked thoughtful. "Now there's a man who's more interested in finding someone who's already staked a claim than he is in finding a claim himself."

"Those are the ones who make the bucks in the end."

"Cigars! Hand-rolled Havana cigars! One to a customer! Cigars!"

I jerked around. "People *smoke* out here?"

The cigar salesman—short, stocky, and energetic—spoke around one of his unlit products clamped in one corner of his mouth. "Sure, lady, whaddya think, we're uncivilized or something?"

"What're you charging?" Caleb inquired.

The salesman surveyed Caleb with small, sharp eyes, his head cocked to one side like a bird's. "Well now, son, normally it's the item's weight in ore assayed to forty percent pure of total weight, or ten dollars in Alliance scrip, but for you—"

"How do you tell how much it weighs?" Caleb asked.

The salesman plucked a digital scale, seemingly from the air, and held it up.

"How do you know what kind of ore you're getting, or how pure it is?"

Again from the air appeared a traveling assay kit, complete with chemicals, solvent, mortar and pestle, and test tubes.

Caleb shook his head admiringly. "How's business?"

The salesman looked cautious. "Fair," he said, looking around him with a furtive air. "Fair." He espied a potential customer and was gone.

"Means he's already paid his way out and probably back, too," Caleb told me.

I was still in shock. "They *smoke* out here, Caleb! In an enclosed space habitat they actually light up a cigar! We could be incinerated at any moment!"

He patted my shoulder absentmindedly. "Um-hmmm. Listen, I wanted you to see this. No, up higher. Yeah. There."

I followed his forefinger back to the pillar and one of the more official-looking notices. It was dated less than a month previously. It was fancied up with scalloped silver edges and the SOS starburst at the top and declared Piazzi City reopened for trading, assaying, and general hoorahing twenty-four hours a Ceres day, seven days a Ceres week, in language so benevolent and magnanimous it reeked of bonhomie and good fellowship. And patronage. And not one word of apology to the miners for locking them out and denying them medical aid.

While we were reading, someone cleared his throat. We turned to see a short, pudgy man with black hair, narrow, tilted brown eyes, and a petulant mouth. "Kevin Takemotu." He shoved out a square, rather dirty hand. "I'm the mayor. Suppose you're Svensdotter."

I smiled at him. "How did you guess? Perhaps because we've been standing out here waiting for you for half an hour and more?"

His color deepened and he dropped his hand. "Expected you in my office," he said brusquely.

"I know you did," I said in my gentlest voice, and continued to smile.

"Svensdotter?" someone said. "Are you Star Svensdotter?"

"Why, yes," I said, and we were surrounded. They deserted Brother Moses, the community bulletin board, their deal-making, a few of them even came out of the bars to crowd around and shake our hands, stammer out thanks, and ask where Charlie was. I was pleasant in return, even charming, if I say it who shouldn't. Through it all I watched Takemotu out of the corner of one eye. He stood at the edge of the crowd with a blank expression. When at last we managed to break away, fielding invitations to obscure claims and camps all over the Belt, he led us into his office. He went behind his desk and sat down.

I remained standing. Caleb took his cue from me. Takemotu looked up, and as I was already at least a dozen centimeters taller it was something of a strain for him to maintain eye contact. With an air that would pass—barely—for civility he stood and gestured to the chair against the wall. "Sorry there's just the one chair."

I smiled at him again. "We can wait until you have another brought."

His expression didn't change. We waited. Takemotu called next door and a young woman in SOS black and silver toted in a chair. I waited until she left, moved both chairs to where they directly faced across Takemotu's desk, sat down, and smiled. "Traveling in vacuum is thirsty work."

Takemotu sent out again, this time for coffee. We exchanged civil if strained chatter until it arrived. He mumbled ungracious thanks for our help during their medical crisis. All three of us ignored the fact that Caleb had had to force his way into Piazzi City at gunpoint to secure shelter for the ailing. Takemotu seemed to notice for the first time that we overflowed the seats of our chairs and said, "Why didn't you leave your suits at the hatch?"

"No lockers were available."

He looked at us beneath heavy brows. "No need. It's a shooting offense hereabouts to steal someone's p-suit." Still, he made no offer to help us out of or hang up ours. The coffee came, tepid and tasteless, but at least it was wet. Sean and I were sweltering, which always makes me irritable. It may have been the reason I was less than tactful in opening negotiations with a request to rent space for the Sisters of St. Anne's boarding school, as well as a branch assaying office for the Terranova Expedition. Ceres had the strongest surface gravity in the Belt next to our as-yet-unassembled station. All that meant was that your food and your feet stayed down, providing they started out that way, but it was enough for the work we wanted to do.

Takemotu resisted the suggestion. It wasn't hard to see why; in his place I might have done the same. Terra-Luna Mines and Standard Oil and Solar had the prettiest little setup for price fixing it had yet been my privilege to run across. On the way down Strasser had told us all about it, in detail and embellished with curses freely bestowed on everyone involved. SOS and T-LM bought ore for a fixed, flat rate, agreed upon by the superintendents in advance and redeemable only in Ceres scrip. Virtually the only place to spend that scrip in the entire solar system was in the local bars—and in the Planetismal Trading Company, which I was willing to bet the *Hokuwa'a* had some familiar names among its founding officers. Belters in Ceres bars almost universally partied away their latest delivery, went into debt outfitting their next foray into the Belt, and never got out again. It was a good bet we weren't going to be paying for any ores delivered to us in Ceres scrip, or in Alliance dollars, for that matter, and we threatened the cozy arrangement now in place. If I were Takemotu, I might have taken a blunt object to the oxygen valves on our pressure suits myself.

I didn't say any of this, though. I examined my fingernails carefully and said instead, "I couldn't help noticing all the business one of the storefronts on the square is generating. Takemotu's Sublight Services, wasn't it, Caleb? Any relation to you, Mr. Takemotu?"

"Son," said the man behind the desk.

"Yes, indeed," I said dreamily, raising my eyes to the ceiling. "You're providing quite a humanitarian service there. I noticed a lot of miners sending messages home to Terra or Luna. Some of them didn't have to wait more than fifteen minutes for a return reply from their families. Collect."

He hesitated. "Our comm engineer has developed a wave-enhancing process that boosts transmission speed."

I lowered my eyes to his face and said gently, "I'd certainly be interested in meeting your communications engineer." I gave him a bland smile. "Perhaps if he is willing to adapt his system, the expedition could donate a viewscreen to your service. I'm sure seeing the faces of their loved ones would be a real morale booster. With no time delay in transmission, it would be the next best thing to being there."

I knew, and now Takemotu knew that I knew, that unless someone had changed the laws of physics when I wasn't looking it still took between twenty and forty minutes, depending on where Ceres was at the time, for a single transmission to travel between Terra and the Belt. Any replies those miners were receiving from their families in fifteen minutes had been written not by their families but by an industrious little elf in the back room of Takemotu's son's business.

It hurt him to get the words out, but before we left Takemotu's office the Terranova Expedition had the run of Ceres and lease-purchase options on some prime caverns adjacent to Piazzi City. I could tell from Caleb's expression that he would have preferred more direct action, but SOS and T-LM had got there first, no matter how sloppy their operation was now. Upon inquiry, Takemotu confirmed what Charlie had told me: that Ceres did not have anything as basic as a medlab. The bottom line had apparently blinded the organizers of the Belt Rush to everything but net proceeds. In a transparent effort to improve those, Takemotu inquired after our proposed transportation methods.

"Some robot processing ships to refine as they go," I said vaguely. "Some rocks are pure enough to start with that we can ship them whole. It's all pretty standard. I'm sure we don't have anything to teach you." I sat for a moment enjoying the expression on his face. If he disagreed with me he was committed to sharing information and he didn't know if I had anything he wanted. If he agreed, he would never know. "But enough shop talk. We were reading the notices on the bulletin board in the square. A lot of them use someone named Maggie as a reference. The miner Strasser also mentioned her. Who is she?"

Takemotu pressed his lips together. "She came out about three years ago, from Ellfive—Terranova it's called now, you say. She runs the biggest local whorehouse." There was a malicious flicker in his eyes. I wondered idly if he was going to draw an inference from the professional tendencies of Terranovan immigrants, but he didn't dare go quite that far. "And I think she prospects for silicates on the side."

Silicates. The other shoe dropped. "Maggie Lu!" I exclaimed, my memory finally clicking in.

"You know her?" Caleb said.

"She used to work in the Frisbee," I said. "She's the one who had that little problem with your predecessor."

A light dawned, and he said, "She the one who spaced the third security supervisor?"

Takemotu's eyes widened. I frowned at Caleb. "We don't know that." He raised an eyebrow. "For sure. Anyway, she's the one. Used to be a lab tech for Silicon Syndicates in the Frisbee. After the security supervisor disappeared, she left. She was a damn good chemist, too, especially in formulating explosives. They were angry when she shipped out. I didn't know she came in this direction."

I asked Takemotu for directions. He did not rise to show us out.

"I didn't notice the Ma Bell operation," Caleb said.

I pointed out the storefront with the long, patient line leading from its doors. "It's an idea as old as Jefferson Randolph Smith, and probably older," I said cheerfully.

"Shouldn't we do something?"

"Anybody dumb enough to believe they can talk to Terra sametime from here deserves to get ripped off," I said. "I don't know how some of these people survive in vacuum."

"Sometimes I think you are not a nice person," he remarked.

"Sometimes I think you are right."

We entered the bar Mother had gone into. Inside, the ceiling and the light were both very low. The noise of piano music badly played, shouted conversations, shattering glass, and falling bodies took up the slack. We hesitated in the doorway, waiting for our eyesight to adjust so we could see something. A squat woman shoved past us. She had dark hair that looked as if it had been hacked off by a blind samurai and a jumpsuit that had seen a better century. Neither had been washed in the last hundred million kilometers or so. Caleb looked at me and wrinkled his nose and I said, "Nature art disdaineth, her beauty is her own."

The crowd sensed an epic moment in the making and parted before her. She swaggered up to the bar. Her jumpsuit had pockets over each breast, upper arm, forearm, hip, thigh, and calf, all of them bulging with intriguing lumps and bumps. Coming to a stop center stage, she raised her right leg up and brought her heel down on the bar with a crash that jolted the glasses and brought silence to the room for at least two seconds. The seat of her well-worn jumpsuit promptly split open, to tremendous cheers and applause. Fortunately for our delicate sensibilities she was wearing long johns.

Oblivious, the woman ripped open the pocket over her right calf and out spilled what looked to my untutored eye like the same bunch of rocks earlier donated to Brother Moses and his evangelical crusade. The barkeep, wiser in the ways of Belters, reached beneath the counter for what proved to be a compact assay kit. He scooped up a few pebbles and shook them in a test tube filled with a clear liquid. After a few tense, expectant moments, the liquid turned a deep, glowing red, the color of rubies or a good cabernet.

A roof-raising shout went up. They crowded around to thump the woman on the back and shake her hand. She called for a round for the house, cause for another cheer. The barkeep put away the assay kit and produced a digital scale to weigh out the tab. Our drinks, when they came, weren't much more than watered-down molasses with a faint flavor of rubbing alcohol. "Gak."

"You said it."

A loud crack made us both jump and Caleb grabbed for his side arm. The piano player slowly toppled from his stool. Into the startled silence the bartender swore loudly. "Goddammit, Lyin' George, I told you the next piano player you shoot you replace! Now get on up there afore I take your own pistol to you!"

Lyin' George, a barrel-chested miner in filthy clothes and a sheepish expression, shuffled forward and sat down on the piano stool. A bad rendition of "Chopsticks" followed and Lyin' George barely made it through the door in front of a virtual hail of glasses and pitchers.

Caleb made as if to help the bartender haul away the piano player's body. The bartender waved him away. "Thanks, mister, I can handle it."

Caleb stood there with his arms dangling at his sides, one of the few times I'd seen him at a loss. "What're you going to do with the body?"

"Recycler in back," the bartender said matter-of-factly.

I looked from him to my glass. I set it down very gently on the bar and took a few unobtrusive steps away.

The squat miner knocked hers back in a single gulp, spied mine and finished it off, a third followed and she started on her fourth barely without pause. A grizzled Belter sat next to her with tears flowing unashamedly down his face and into his beard, fingering bits of ore still scattered across the bar. She noticed. She shifted her drink from one hand to the other and gave him a rough hug. "Don't worry about it, Mel boy," we heard her say.

"Don't worry about it?" Mel boy said through his tears. "I sold you that claim for sixty thousand and now you stand to take a half million out of it and you tell me not to worry?" He sniffled.

"More like a million five, in Alliance dollars," she said cheerfully. Mel boy sobbed outright. She patted his shoulder with a rough hand. "Hell's bells, Mel boy, I've took enough to see me through the next twenty winters, and in Belt time, too. I give you my coordinates and you work over the tailings, okay?"

"I think I'm in love," Caleb said.

"Control yourself," I replied, "there's Mother."

Mother didn't bother to look up from her interview with a man bigger than Tweedledum and Tweedledee, who had what looked like but could not possibly have been a bearskin draped around his shoulders. "I'm fine, dears. Go away, please," she said to us, and continued to the giant, "Three wives? And how many children did you say you have? Dear me. And yours is the only family on—what was that designation again? 8482Sultan? Of course it is."

Maggie's Place was reached by a good-sized tunnel about a half a kilometer from the entrance to Piazzi City. There was an almost discernible path worn between the meter-high posts cemented into the surface. Red lights glowed dimly from the tops of the posts and I grinned. We moved forward carefully; the surface gravity was like Luna's in that if you got going too fast you could find sheer inertia pitching you forward on your helmet, with a cracked visor to brighten your day. "I wonder if we could launch ourselves off Ceres just by jumping," I said.

Caleb's voice crackled over my headset. "Could we not find out today, please?"

We passed between the lights and found the tunnel entrance. The light from Sol dimmed and then vanished as we descended deeper into what was clearly a man-made tunnel. After about twenty meters it opened suddenly into a small cave. There was one vacuum vehicle grounded just outside the lock, with the large yellow pinwheel warning of nuclear fuel present plastered to its stern; we gave it a wide berth. I wondered what a REM badge clipped to the owner would read.

There was a hatch set deep into the rock wall, a rectangular airlock with another dim red light beside it. I chuckled and pounded on the door. Caleb, feeling around beside me, twisted a knob. After a few minutes the hatch cracked and we stepped inside the lock. The door closed automatically behind us. We waited for the lock to pressure up. When the hissing of air stopped the opposite hatch opened. We hunched down and stepped through.

A bald man in shorts, shirt, and a scowl patted down our p-suits, one hand on the shooter clipped to his thigh. Inasmuch as a normal-sized person in a pressure suit looks like a marshmallow the size of Rhode Island, our outsize suits made him wary. When I finally made it all the way out of mine, he was at first startled and then appraising. "You looking for work?"

When Caleb emerged from his p-suit he sucked in an audible breath and said, "How about you?"

"No," I said, trying not to laugh at Caleb's expression, "we're old friends of Maggie's. She around?"

He seemed undecided and looked us over again. "What's that you've got there?" he said, poking one finger at the bundle strapped against Caleb's chest. Paddy gave an angry yell and he jumped. "Fer crissake! What was that?"

"Our daughter," Caleb said, and pulled back the hood to show him.

The little man stared, slack-jawed.

"And our son," I said proudly, as Sean began to cry on cue. The twins settled down after a few soothing pats and went back to sleep. They were good that way. I asked again where we might find Maggie.

"Through there," the little man said weakly, and tottered over to collapse into a chair.

We entered a corridor and followed the lights and the noise until we emerged into a large room. It was decorated more like a suburban home than the only pleasure palace outsystem. Almost twelve meters square with a high, curved ceiling and walls with no corners, it was painted a soft cream in color. And—

"Windows?" I said incredulously. I went over to one and tried to draw the blinds, only to discover the cord was painted on the wall. So was the rest of the window. It was some of the best trompe l'oeil I'd ever seen. I gaped at it, and at Caleb.

"Whoever did this is wasting themselves out here," Caleb said, "when they could be ripping off New York art galleries big time."

The blind on this "window" was open and a bright yellow sun was setting into a lake between two forested mountains. Hidden lights mimicked sunshine and dappled the rug. There was actually a rug, a thin brown affair without any padding, not that any was really needed on Ceres—if you fell down you wouldn't bump that hard. Leafy potted plants and enormous floor pillows in pastels and earth tones completed the decor.

A bar against one wall, tended by a very young, very pretty blonde who looked very tired, did steady business. Perched on a stool on a tiny stage against the opposite wall, a man with a grimy bandage around his eyes and an unsightly case of sun itch played a concertina. He sang lustily with his head back and his mouth wide open. The working girls and guys, there must have been at least twenty of them crowded around him, sang along with enthusiasm, some of them even in tune. There were many shapes and sizes and races, some pretty, some homely, some thin, some plump, all young. The girls were wrapped like candy in bright colors. The garments floated softly around them in graceful folds in the low gee whenever they turned abruptly, which they did often for just that effect, especially on the tiny dance floor I saw in the back of the room. The guys looked clean and masculine in crisp blue jumpsuits.

The rest of the room was taken up by Belters young and old, a few female, more male. All had silly grins on their faces as they clutched their paid companions closer with one hand and drank with the other. None seemed in much of a hurry to race upstairs, or wherever the equivalent was located at Maggie's. They looked clean and smelled the same way, which after Piazzi City was a pleasant surprise. I saw the reason when one woman emerged in a cloud of steam from behind a door that said "Showers."

A nice place, all told, Maggie's. A place of business, true, but that business did not interfere with having a good time. I liked it. And then Maggie herself entered the room through a door in the opposite wall. Her eyes, and I didn't blame them, barely bothered to register my existence on her peripheral vision before fastening on Caleb. The strong, silent type never goes out of style, and tall, dark, and handsome don't hurt, either.

Maggie padded toward him, her interest and her intentions plain, and Caleb looked at me, registering mild alarm. I swallowed a giggle and took a smooth step forward, inserting myself between them. "Hey, Maggie Lu. Read any good books in the last million klicks?"

The annoyance she felt at being moved off target vanished when she looked at me again and recognized me the second time around. "Star!" she yelped, and threw herself forward. "It's about time!"

She gave me a fierce hug and Sean started to cry again. More than one incredulous eye turned our way and we had to bring out both babies and show them off, always a chore. We took the opportunity to change their diapers and the whole room crowded around to ooh and ah. I reflected that in the business she was currently in, Maggie must have one hell of a medtech working for her for babies to be that much of a rarity. I'd seen more than a few kids racing around Piazzi City.

Maggie calmed the hubbub and commandeered us. "Step into my office." We followed her, past one door opening onto a tiny theater with a tinier stage and another that opened into a kitchen where three cooks sweated and swore over pots that smelled of nectar and ambrosia, through a third, behind which was a large office. The giggles and curses and squeezebox arias shut off like a switch when the door closed. "Sit down, sit down," she said, waving a hand. I forgot and sat down too hard and bounced up again. Maggie grinned. Maggie had a great grin, wide and wicked; she reminded me of Charlie that way. I sat down, slower this time, and put Sean to my breast while Caleb got out a bottle for Paddy. "She gets the bottle, he gets you? Doesn't quite seem fair."

"We trade off." The wails shut up. Peace broke out. I leaned back and smiled at Maggie. She shook her head. "What?"

"You. With babies. I never thought I'd see the day."

"I baby-sat Ellfive for some seventeen years," I said dryly, "including two on Luna and thirteen on site. I used to go thirty hours without sleep and weeks without a bath and sometimes a whole month without an assassination attempt. I was exhausted, I smelled bad, and I was paranoid the whole time."

"So?"

"So what makes you think motherhood is any different?"

"You're still wearing it," she said, pointing. She pushed her dark, straight hair back from her right ear and displayed the one-carat diamond solitaire in her right earlobe. "Me, too. She ever tell you about that?" This to Caleb. "I'll never forget the expression on Sam's face when we broke open the nucleus on that comet and found all that crystalline carbon, but you should have seen Star when they told her they were making earrings for the whole team."

"Maggie, I—"

"One little hole," she hooted, "and you would have thought someone was taking aim at her with a twelve-inch cannon."

"You never told me this story," Caleb said to me.

"Maggie," I said, "as I have explained many times before, it is simply that I do not usually wear jewelry."

"Uh-huh. You had to that time. After what you put the trapper team through to make that gizmo work, you could hardly refuse." She smiled expectantly at Caleb. "I don't believe we've met."

"If I could get a word in edgewise," I said. "Maggie, this is Caleb O'Hara. Security for my little expedition."

"Her husband, too," he added. Maggie made Caleb a little uneasy.

She looked at the twins, raised one eyebrow, and said, "Well, I should hope so."

After we burped the babies and got them back to sleep, I leaned back and cast an appraising eye over her office. "What's a nice girl like you doing in a place like this? Are you—ah—working?"

She grinned again, as if I should have known better, and perhaps I should have. Maggie Lu was one of the freest people I'd ever met. She had discovered as a youth, she once informed me, that life was just one big fucking laugh. The realization was a strong and lasting one, so much so that she never got serious enough about anything to allow anyone to run her or her life. If someone tried, she simply downed tools and walked away. She was a wizard at R and D into adaptation of silicon and silicon compounds in vacuum, and she was never out of a job for long. But mention company loyalty or national pride or true love or anything involving a long-term commitment to a single cause in her presence and she was gone, all bills paid and all her belongings stuffed into an army surplus duffel bag that looked older than she did. If Maggie was afraid of anything, it was of staying in one place long enough to put down roots. "No need to be so delicate, Star," she said, still grinning. "No,

I just manage the place. I struck out prospecting pretty quick after I arrived. Processing silicates is one thing. Mining them is something else altogether." She grimaced. "So I found out."

"What went wrong?"

" 'Wrong'?" She looked straight at me, but I got the feeling she was seeing something else. "Nothing went wrong, not exactly." We waited. "It's black out there, Star. And quiet. You've never heard such quiet. After you've been out for a while, you realize you're the only living thing in an area the size of all Terra. You start wondering how you thought you could survive in this wasteland. You begin to fear death. To fear God, even if you don't believe." She shook herself and laughed a little. "Sorry. Didn't mean to make a speech. I guess you could say I found out I was mortal."

" 'Were you ever out in the Great Alone, when the moon was awful clear?' " I quoted softly. " 'And the icy mountains hemmed you in with a silence you most could *hear*?' "

"Yes," she said, almost eagerly, "that's it. That's it exactly. 'A silence you most could hear.' "

We sat quietly for a few moments before I said, "And then what happened?"

Her shoulders moved in something halfway between a shrug and a shudder, and she gave me a sheepish smile. "After I'd done pondering the mysteries of the universe, you mean? Well, I came in here one night to drown my sorrows. The guy who owned the place wanted to put me to work. He wasn't real polite about asking. I wasn't real polite about refusing. After he died, the girls offered to cut me in for a piece of the action if I'd stay on and run the place, and I thought, what the hell. It's a good little business. It's registered with the Magdalene Guild on Luna, and we make our own booze, so it's been profitable."

"This outbreak of Hudson's Disease couldn't have done you any good."

Her smile faded. "No, and I have to thank you for getting us out of that mess, Star." Later we found out that Maggie's Place had turned itself into a hospital for the duration of the disease, cycling its locks to anyone who could make it that far. She even had an old '02 Ford Flivver modified to run on raw uranium—the vehicle with the yellow pinwheel decals we had seen in the lock—that she used to haul in a group of Aussies from 8687Boomerang who were too sick to make it in on their own.

"We just came from speaking with Takemotu. From the way he talks you'd think there had never been anything wrong. No illness, no closed city, nothing. Butter wouldn't melt in his mouth."

Her eyes darkened. "So you've met him?"

"Today, for the first time. He doesn't seem to have enough on the ball to be running Piazzi City."

"He's only been in charge a few weeks," she said thinly. "Give him time." And then she pointedly changed the subject. "I've heard some interesting things about you, Star." I groaned and her hazel eyes twinkled. "Leading habitat revolutions against Terran tyranny. Establishing diplomatic relations with Galactic City Hall." She demanded a firsthand description of the Librarian and her ship. She was disappointed when I told her the Librarians were disinterested in returning to our backwater section of the galaxy anytime soon, unless somebody threatened Archy, but she accepted their appearance the same way most spacers did—"It was only a matter of time before somebody showed up. We're lucky we bored them." She cocked an eye at me. "I heard about Grays, too, Star. I'm sorry."

I shrugged. I was long over Grays's betrayal and death. Or I had been until Leif showed up. "He wanted Terranova to round out his personal fiefdom. He just wouldn't leave it alone."

"He couldn't," she said. "That was Grays all over. He saw something he wanted, and if it wasn't something he would inherit or could buy, then he'd just take it. Look at LEO Base. Look at HEO Base. He's lucky he didn't start a war when he moved in on HEO Base." She shook her head firmly and summed up Grayson Cabot Lodge the Fourth's career in two words. "Dumb fuck."

I just hoped it wasn't hereditary. "Charlie said about the same thing."

"Wise woman, your sister," she observed. "How is Charlie? And Simon?"

"Come on over and see for yourself."

Maggie's face lit up. "They're here, too?".

I nodded. "And Crip, and I think you know Roger Lindbergh. Actually, Maggie, I had an ulterior motive in coming to see you."

"Oh?"

"I remember you telling me, when you worked in the Frisbee, that you almost didn't sign up for the job. You were always conducting other people's experiments, you said, usually something typically idiotic dreamed up by Terran scientists."

She shrugged. "I didn't like it much, but I wanted to space. Everything's a trade-off."

"I was wondering—" I let my voice trail off artistically.

Her eyes narrowed. "Yes?"

"Well, I was wondering if you were at all interested in returning to your original line of work." I added, "We saw your notice in the town square. It had a kind of wistful ring to it, I thought."

Her feet slid down off the top of her desk. "Silicon teching? You mean it?"

"We can always use another silicon specialist, and you've actually mined it on Luna and worked with it in zerogee, as well as prospected for it here."

"I've processed it here, too."

"Well. That's more experience than most of the people I brought along have."

"What would I be doing?"

"We plan on shipping the silicon raw at first, but I want to see if we can't design some kind of simple solar refining process to take place on or inside the raw rock, a process that ideally employs the slag for propulsion while leaving the refined silicon in place for delivery."

"And that's what I'd be doing?"

I nodded. "With your experience you can run your own show. We're looking for ways to refine oh-two and hydrogen and nitrogen in transit, as well, so I think we can keep you interested." I smiled when she expelled a large whoof of air. "Sign on with us, Maggie. We're not much more than a couple of overgrown space trucks right now, and," I added, grinning, "I doubt if I can match your wages here, but you get board and room and a salary to start."

"Bonuses later?"

"Bonuses, my foot, you'll be getting a piece of the action eventually. I've put the word out that I will entertain any idea, no matter how bizarre, that anyone has for utilizing our assets and our location to start up anything that looks remotely profitable."

"Hell, Star," she said, "wages are the last thing I'm worried about. I told you the truth, Maggie's Place has a good gross, but I'm barely getting by." She waved a disgusted hand. "I keep grubstaking miners with hard luck stories and the bastards pay me back by eloping with my employees. I feel like a goddam dating service. Besides, I always knew I could run a research and fabrication department better than those nerds I worked for in the Frisbee." I opened my mouth and Maggie held up one hand palm out. "Stop. Put right out of your mind any thoughts of advertising for help. You don't have to ask me twice." I shut my mouth obediently and she bellowed, "Nora!"

Nora was a busty Irish woman with a loud, merry laugh, shrewd blue eyes, and a business sense like Andrew Carnegie. The two of them had it all arranged and ready for thumbprints in about ten minutes. Nora insisted the business keep Maggie's name. Maggie was appropriately touched. She packed a bag— still her old duffel—and we went out into the party room to baptize the birth of a new regime in alcohol.

Nora stood the room the first round. Everyone raised a glass in Maggie's direction and Nora led the group in a chorus of "For She's a Jolly Good Fellow." They sang a verse or two of "The Day Star Went Nova" just to make me feel at home. The squat miner in the filthy jumpsuit came in, Nora got out the assay kit, the test tube bloomed red. There were loud hosannahs and more toasts and I didn't think we were ever going to get out of there. At last sight the lucky miner was on her way upstairs (or wherever) with one of Nora's boys in tow. I only hoped for the sake of her companion that they'd detour by way of the showers.

— 5 —

Paper Tiger

The asteroid belt ... is a paper tiger. The material in it is strewn so widely over so vast a volume that any spaceship going through it is not at all likely to see anything of visible size.

—Isaac Asimov

At ten hundred hours the following day I looked down at my assembled crew chiefs, half of them off the *Voortrekker*. "So. Have you folks had enough of practicing first aid?"

The response was long, loud, and unanimously in the affirmative and I had to grin. "All right, then, it's show time. Perry, start working out a way to turn that rock loose in close orbit to Ceres. Caleb, you'd better detail someone to discourage any stray miners who might trip over it and try to sell it back to us. Crip, get the *Voortrekker* to moor parallel to us, and start the crew breaking out the companionway modules. You're in sole charge of curing the intestinal gas of this expedition."

"Lo how the mighty have fallen."

"Shut up, Archy. Claire," I said, "suit up your crew and get out the assay equipment. I want one medium-sized asteroid, thirty percent silicon minimum in composition, with significant trace deposits of either oh-two, hydrogen, or nitrogen, suitable for launch to Terranova within six months. I want similar rocks staked out for routine launch at four-month intervals thereafter."

Claire Bankhead, a Georgia belle and the only person I'd ever seen wearing makeup in freefall, gaped at me. "Medium-sized?" And then she said, "Did y'all say within six months?"

"Y'all heard me right." They were all sitting up straight and looking at me with expressions ranging from excitement to disbelief. "Terranova bankrolled this expedition, at not inconsiderable expense to themselves, specifically to facilitate the speedy construction of Island Two. Now we're going to demonstrate good faith by giving Terranova a return on their investment, and fast."

"How?" somebody said.

"How what?"

"How are we shipping the asteroids?"

"We're going to slap a pressure plate on them and give them a nuclear kick in the pants, same as what powers the *Hokuwa'a* and the *Voortrekker*. As soon as the cargo bay is clear, Whitney Burkette and his engineers will be setting up a fabrication shop for one-shot expendable pressure plates. In the meantime, those of us not actively involved in setting up the station will begin cannibalizing pulse units and modifying them to fuel rock shipment from Belt to Terran orbit."

"If we use up our pulse units to ship ore, how are we supposed to get home?" Perry Austin wanted to know. She was a small woman, with dark hair cut short in a fringe across her forehead and the alert, inquisitive expression of a terrier at a rat hole. She was dressed the way we all were, in a silver-blue jumpsuit that looked and smelled the worse for wear. On her collar was a gold pin, three rocket plumes encircled by an orbit and rising to a five-pointed star. Crip wore one just like it.

There was a slight but perceptible space around her in that crowded galley. Perry Austin was one of those people it surprises you to know are still alive, since they've already accomplished more in one lifetime than any ten other people you could name. Born in 1951, she received her doctorate in physics from CalTech in 1973, joined NASA in 1978 to fly shuttle missions twice as mission specialist, and then quit in 1986 after *Challenger*. She rejoined in 1992 after the Beetlejuice Message caused the creation of the American Alliance and eventually put the combined gross national products of the North, Central, and South American and Pacific Rim countries behind the newly created Department of Space. She was capcom when *Challenger II* went up on its fatal test flight. She flew second in command to Crip on *Enterprise II*'s successful test, after which she pioneered the revival of the BDR, short for Big Dumb Rocket, an expendable chemical-fuel rocket series that lifted essential Terran construction materials into geosync for Terranova for four grinding, nonstop years. I hadn't been all that surprised to see her show up at Ceres ahead of schedule with an asteroid in tow.

"We'll start worrying about that five years from now." I shifted Paddy's weight on my breast and peeked inside the baby bag. She was sleeping like—well, like a baby, with her tiny fist jammed into her mouth. I congratulated myself once again on my dazzling procreative capabilities and raised my head. "Shipping raw rock is only the start, people," I said. "It's always cheaper to ship a finished product than it is raw material. That's why—"

"That why there are oil and gas separation centers on the North Slope of Alaska—" Charlie said in singsong.

"—and pineapple canneries on Lanai—" Simon chanted.

"—and the Frisbee on Terranova," Sam chimed in.

"Well," I said, "I'm glad you guys have been paying attention."

"Only for five years," someone muttered.

I ignored her. "Now, obviously this expedition is not ready to begin refining and shipping pure ore. However, we do need to develop an interim plan, a compromise between raw rock and pure ore." They were intent, listening to every word. No one had actually said "Bullshit!" and stalked out, which I found encouraging. "Shipping ore raw, partially processed, or as a finished product—all these have different values to us, to the miners, and to Terranova. For example, it would be cheap for us to ship the rock raw forever, but eventually not worth the effort of refining on arrival at Terranova.

"To put it simply, the idea is to start out on this end with a chunk of mixed matter and to finish in Terran orbit with a mass of more or less refined ore, or at least a mass with a reduced amount of slag, to speed up extraction on the Terranova end. The process may be automated, it may have to be manned, we don't know yet. To that end, I'd like to introduce Maggie Lu, formerly of the Frisbee on Terranova, where she pioneered a lot of zerogee silicate refining techniques. She will be heading up research into this project, which means she will be looking over everyone's shoulders for the next year or so. Answer her questions and stay out of her way. Anybody who has an idea, feed it to her through—Archy, what shall we name Maggie's program?"

"How about Cortez?"

Charlie snickered and Simon looked offended. I sighed. A computer that can think for itself is a computer that will think for itself. "Thanks a lot, Archy, your opinion of the human race's motives and methods is always welcome. Call it Klondike."

"There's an asteroid with that name already, boss."

"I reckon we could call it Agricola," Claire said. "He was the first Terran mining engineer worth a spit."

"How about it, Archy?"

"Agricola it is."

"If we do come up with this process, and if it does have to be manned, who do we hire?" This from Perry Austin. She didn't seem so much skeptical as intent on nailing down every loose end. "We only came out with two hundred and fifty people, Star. We're going to need every one of them right here."

"Think about it, Perry. How many prospectors actually strike it rich? As compared to how many strike out?" From the corner of my eye I saw Maggie's rueful expression. "You ever study gold rushes? The provisioners, the outfitters, made out like bandits, but most of the miners died broke. And those were the ones with the hardest heads; the smart ones gave up and went home before they starved to death." I looked around the room. "We offer some poor slob who's had about all they can take of the Great Alone a free ride home, if they'll just do us these few little chores along the way."

"And if they don't?"

"If Maile's half as good a communications technician as she thinks she is, Terranova will have the rock's composition and the expected delivery percentages long before they show in Terran orbit." Maile gave her happy grin. "They'll be reimbursed on arrival by a prearranged fee per kilo of refined ore. The more ore refined, the bigger their paycheck. It'll be in their interest to push the process along."

"It's a long trip home at those speeds," Charlie observed. "Might want to make it a two-person operation."

"Good point. But that's way down the road. Right now, we're just looking for rocks with a payload worth more at Terranova than the fabrication costs of the pressure plate and the propellant charges it takes to get them there. Simon, you're in overall charge of transportation. Crip, Perry, and Sam are your seconds." I looked at Sam Holbrook.

"We're working on it, Star," he reported. Sam was a tiny Santa Claus of a man with a shock of white hair, twinkling blue eyes, nimble hands, and a boundless, childlike curiosity. "We're ready to test the program we blueprinted on Ellfive, excuse me, Terranova. When Claire okays our first shipment, Archy's ready to plot orbit, inclination, and eccentricity on a map showing relative course and speed to the *Hokuwa'a*. When we've nailed it down, we'll begin computing an interception and a course correction."

"You guys just aren't going to leave anything where you found it, are you?" Bob Shackleton said sadly.

"Burkette and Lobos in engineering have the specs and the hardware for the propellant system; check with them after Claire has registered her coordinates with Archy. Archy, run a separate snakeskin on individual incoming data, but no hard copies until you find a rock the three of you think Terranova might like to see rising in the east one morning. And, Claire? I want you to keep your assayer peeled for any uranium oxide deposits you might find. We're fine for fuel, but it won't hurt us to have a stockpile in reserve independent of what the miners may or may not bring in. Look at everything and I mean everything, staked or not, that you come across, and feed the data into Agricola. Any rocks you find with significant quantities of oh-two, nitrogen, and hydrogen, tag them for future reference. Although I imagine anything close in to Ceres has been pretty well exploited by now. Any rare or odd elements you stumble across, notify the chemists and me, in that order. Any questions?"

Claire blinked, shook herself, and pulled her way out of the galley. We could hear her muttering to herself as her feet disappeared up the companionway.

"Roger." He was floating in front of the galley viewport, his hand tightly clasped in Zoya Bugolubovo's.

"Roger," I repeated. He looked around. "The minute we have spin, break out the geodomes and get the meat and milk vats set up. Much more of that regurgitated slop out of the galley and Caleb's likely to go into a decline." At my breast Paddy burped agreement. "Remember, we are farming for sale as well as for our own consumption. I didn't see anything on Ceres but the standard hydroponics tanks"—I looked around at Caleb and he shook his head—"and none of the claims are big enough to support a really varied crop yield. By now, everyone in these parts is probably more than a little tired of manual pollination." I smiled. "Many of you come from Terranova. I'm sure you remember what the first years were like. Whatever we grow, we can probably sell for its weight in platinum."

"Couldya crack that whip a little louder, boss?" Archy said. "I think you mighta missed one or two people."

In a day the *Voortrekker* was dead in space across from us, nose to tail and tail to nose. 10849Perry's had let go its leash and been bumped ever so gently into a matching orbit well off the *Hokuwa'a*'s stern. It was marked with a claim beacon warning off inquisitive prospectors.

Aboard ships, we jettisoned our pressure plates and spot-welded them together so that they looked like a giant round clam. We applied fluorescent yellow pinwheels to both sides, tagged it with an eyes-and-ears warning flare, and nudged it off in the direction of Ceti Alpha Five. "Now the real fun begins," I said.

"Easy to say for you," Dieter Joop grunted. "All right, folks, it show time is!"

Working together nonstop, with time off for food but not sleep, under the fussy direction of Whitney Burkette, both ships' companies had the companionway modules broken out of the holds in fifteen days. During the following month the modules unfolded outside the parallel-moored *Hokuwa'a* and *Voortrekker* like the web of a large, tipsy spider. For the next six weeks, led by Dieter Joop's heavy-duty mechanics, a hundred riggers in p-suits played connect-the-dots with the triangular grid frames, looking like fat white flies caught in the web.

Right away we ran into one of those problems you pray you've planned for and usually haven't. I'd been EVA for

thirteen-plus hours, supervising—the unkind would say getting in everyone's hair—when I heard a small but nonetheless
distinct *crack!* I froze in place, floating halfway between the
Hokuwa'a and the *Voortrekker*. Small but nonetheless distinct
cracks! are the last thing anyone needs to hear in vacuum,
because the only sound you hear in vacuum comes from you
and your pressure suit. Small but nonetheless distinct *cracks!*
usually presage larger and more distinct *cracks!* that presage
suit failure and suit owner failure shortly thereafter. I wasn't
putting any more stress on my suit until I knew exactly what
had caused that unnerving little sound. "Archy?" I said softly
into my communit.

"Boss?" he responded, equally softly. "Why are we whis-
pering?"

"I just heard a cracking sound, like something in my suit is
splitting on me."

"Oh," he said, "probably we should do something about
that."

I was starting to sweat. "Could we do something about that
soon?" I said, almost singsong.

In the same singsong Archy replied, "I think so, boss, security's on its way, hang on now, don't move, stay right there."

"Where would I be going?" I sang.

"I don't know but they're on their way," he sang back.

"When are they going to get here?"

"They're almost there, okay, boss, there's the sled, okay,
the waldo's out, okay—*gotcha.*" I felt a gentle tug at the
back of my suit where the waldo remote latched on to the
emergency eyebolt and I felt myself being tugged rapidly
backward. In the blink of an eye I was stuffed into a lock,
the lock was cycling, and I tumbled out into the *Voortrekker*'s
galley. I made new time shucking out of my pressure suit and
thanked whatever the gods may be that the twins were with
Charlie.

"What's wrong, Star?" Perry Austin said, appearing from
the companionway.

"I don't know, I heard this—" The lock cycled again behind
me and Simon rolled in. Impatient hands yanked his helmet
off. He bounced it off a bulkhead and Perry had to duck the
ricochet. "Shit!" he bellowed. "Helmet polarizers never burned
out at this rate at Ellfive and there we were 150 million klicks
closer to Sol! What the hell is going on?"

I scrambled after my own helmet and examined the visor. Sure enough, I found a hairline fracture beginning at the top of the frame. "Is it just ours, Simon?"

"Hell no, it's not just ours!" he yelled. "Visors're cracking like peanut shells out there! What the hell's wrong with them?"

"I don't know but we'd better fix it and fast. Another five minutes EVA and I'd have been freeze-dried."

Marco Venezia jury-rigged a smelter to boil down silicates and alkali to make replacement visors while Sam Holbrook studied the problem. In the meantime the work went on at half-strength and half-assed, one companionway module at a time with a two-hour crew rotation and visor replacement, which was probably excessive, but better safe than sorry.

Marco got the smelter up and running. Then we had to wait around while someone went out and found the right kind of silicates, which with Maggie on board did not take as long as it could have. Turned out there were traces of various metallic oxides in some of the ore samples; Simon's new visor was a delicate chartreuse, which lent his five o'clock shadow an interesting hue. Whitney Burkette's was hot pink. His walrus mustache looked especially bristly behind it. A couple of days after Whitney had it fitted Sam came to me with a big grin and an electronic whatsis the size of a fingernail paring. "What's that?" I said.

"It's why the polarizers were burning out. It's the UVS."

"The what?"

"It measures and monitors UV. You can get them for five cents apiece on Terra; twenty-five for a buck."

"Are they all defective?"

"A good percentage. Somebody slipped up in quality control. I've ordered all UVSs in for testing and replacement on a rotational basis."

"Son of a *bitch*."

"It won't be that bad; I've pulled everyone off the line who has training in p-suit maintenance."

"How many replacement UVSs we got?"

"Almost enough."

"Can we make more?"

He squinted at the tiny part, dwarfed by the lines on the palm of his hand. "Eventually. In the meantime the glass visors will have to do."

"They're heavy, though."

He looked at me and said chidingly, "Dear darling Star, it don't matter a whole hell of a lot out here, do it?"

Two months and three days after we began our Herculean labors, the two ships were linked by curved tubular passageways to form a squarish circle about 130 meters on a semi-side. Another ten very brisk days fixing guy wires and stabilizers and we were ready to put on spin. Crip and Perry fired their verniers at precisely the same moment and everything we had forgotten to tape to a bulkhead slowly floated down to what was now the floor in our new one-half artificial gravity, enough, like Ceres, to keep our feet and our food down and, with proper care, our muscles in shape. "Silverware!" Caleb said at our first real sit-down dinner in months. "Forks, knives, and spoons! Who says there's no God?"

When we stabilized at twenty-four-hour halfgee, Charlie cut the crew's exercise requirement down to one hour per twenty-four. I started looking for ways to cannibalize excess treadmills into something useful, until Charlie extended her emergency treatment program for hypercalcemic Belters into a regular service. She advertised it in Piazzi City, charged a fee, and infuriated me by breaking even the third month she was in operation.

All was not sweetness and light once we had spin, of course. Artificial gravity has its down side, i.e. motion sickness. During the first few days of halfgee, not less than a third of the crew suffered nausea and disorientation. There was a steady stream of walking wounded into Charlie's inner sanctum until she found the right combination of drugs to steady the stomach until the inner ear caught up with the station's RPMs. At full spin the twins started to cry and kept crying for two days, three hours, and seventeen seconds, at which time they suddenly shut up and went back to sleeping and eating and blowing bubbles. I couldn't believe I'd ever wanted them to do anything else.

In transit, the ships had been pressured to one third of an atmosphere, and everyone had sore throats from yelling out what they wanted to say because sound does not travel well in less than a full atmosphere. It had been a dry trip as well and we immediately started pumping hydrogen into our air supply. The smell at one third had been bad but tolerable; at full pressure there was a strong and immediate necessity for the air-conditioning system to kick into high. It did, and worked fine, until a careless mechanical engineer ripped open a tool kit before we had full spin and the air was filled with nuts and bolts. We were picking them out of the air filters and our nostrils for three days, and Charlie had to do at least one emergency tracheotomy after a p-suit tech inhaled a washer the size of a dime. Maile thought it all quite hilarious.

The next step was to put out the photovoltaic array, and not before time as our batteries were beginning to run low. The nicest benefit of space industries is that, after the initial costs of setting up a solar power generator, the rest is gravy. A simple reflector, say a hundred meters square, weighs less than six tons and collects eleven thousand kilowatts per twenty-four-hour period. On Terra, similar output of KWH could use up seventy thousand barrels of oil a year, or forty-eight hours output of the F Pad wells in the ANWR#3 field in Alaska. No wear and tear from wind and weather, either, and solar receptors are notorious for their lack of moving parts, so nothing ever wore out.

With the hexagonal PVAs unfolded inside and outside the perimeter of the station, we took on the look of a flat Mitchell Observatory, or less like a spiderweb and more like a soccer ball before it is sewn together and inflated. We didn't have a cosmic anchor, and although we were dead in space relative to Ceres, we were still circling Sol within range of who knew how many other revolving bodies whose gravitational pulls would just love to screw up our orbit. Our position would be constantly monitored by Archy's "what I tell you five times is true" orbital position program and the autogyros hooked into the hydrogen peroxide–powered vernier jets. I caught Simon in Archy's stacks one day, pulling cards and poking at them with a tool that looked like a corkscrew. "Did you feel that?"

"No-oo-oo," Archy said doubtfully.

Simon swore and pulled another card. "George, check the autocontrol on the 3-north thrusters."

"I just did!"

"Then do it again!"

Mumble, mumble over the communit. "Oh. I guess it wasn't plugged in. Sorry, Simon."

"When all else fails," Simon said grimly, "read the directions." He plugged in the card. "How about now, Arch?"

"Aw-*right!*"

I left them to it.

The last thing we did was stockpile our propulsion systems outside the hull in a clump that looked like a silver beehive. With full spin and halfgee and atmosphere fully established, we put away the gray tape and the bungee cords and began extending spokes to a central hub. This would equalize stress on the rim and provide us with a zerogee hangarlock and a space dock and was where later we would build on a zerogee recreation center. Tridee basketball was fun, and it didn't matter how tall you were as long as the walls were padded.

The cargo bays were gradually being cleaned out, and there the engineers and various technicians were assembling tools and setting up shops to thread screws and smelt plasteel and pour Leewall. It was time to give some thought to crew accommodations.

As I've said before, an Orion Express looked like the bishop piece in a chess game, with an interior constructed of concentric rings of decks containing lockers, shops, cabins, controls, and one given over exclusively to a galley/recreation area. We'd packed everything we could think of into every available space, so on the way out there hadn't been enough room anywhere to brush your teeth. After the companionway modules were extended and bolted into place, after the PVAs and the heat radiators were deployed, and after the Fuller geodomes were thrown up like mushroom caps from every available section of hull, the ships were pretty well emptied out. We started getting back a little of the elbow room we had lost when we put on spin and were reduced from three- to two-dimensional living again. I put everyone to work on the interior, primarily building and insulating crew cabins. After the Sisters of St. Anne moved down to Ceres, there were 138 women to 103 men (I didn't count Leif) on board. Privacy was my number one priority.

In-flight conditions aboard the *Hokuwa'a* had not lent themselves to romance, and when we were stationary— gawd. The ship's bulkheads were thin to reduce weight and push price. At full pressure, the slightest sound traveled throughout the entire ship. During star sights or other kinds of navigational calibration, any and I mean *any* indoor activity was out of the question, since the slightest motion exerted against the hull of the ship could jiggle it and did register on the instruments and oh ho ho went Sam Holbrook. Romance was confined to meaningful winks. Take it from me, abstinence does make the heart grow fonder.

Neither was freefall beneficial to anyone's looks. Our bodily fluids rose upward, our legs got thinner, and our chests expanded. Our faces bloated up—"We look like a bunch of goddam chipmunks, for crissake," Simon said disgustedly.

"Chipmunks with the mumps," Caleb grumbled.

Chipmunks with the mumps and indigestion. Freefall encouraged a certain amount of flatulence as well. The ambience was less than arousing, a condition aggravated by the fact that taking a shower in freefall was a lot like going through a carwash on Terra, without the car. There were plenty among the crew who decided to hold out until the water streamed *down* again.

The only sure way to enjoy freefall is de-nosed and deaf. Everyone was less grouchy when we put on spin.

The ships had a diameter that would allow for two decks, so we built in a partition that became the floor of the interior deck and the ceiling of the exterior deck. We put living quarters on the outside and the work areas on the inside, turned the *Voortrekker*'s galley into a medical clinic for Charlie, and expanded the galley of the *Hokuwa'a* to feed and amuse the crews of both ships. We broke up the monotonous interior of the station by raising and lowering ceiling levels at odd intervals and putting doors and hatches and room dividers off center. We put down a roll of thin matting that added some texture to the visual look of the place, painted the multilayer ceilings and walls a variety of primary colors, and cut viewports into every bulkhead not otherwise occupied, oriented to receive sunlight reflected from mirrors outside. Roger and Zoya cobbled together window boxes and filled them with nasturtiums, marigolds, and dwarf sweet peas.

"Nasturtiums!" I said in disgust. "Marigolds! You can't eat sweet peas!"

"They're bright and pretty and they'll grow anywhere," Roger said, patiently for him.

I grumped and harrumphed but in the end I made no official protest. Between Caleb's orchids in our cabin and now the entire station decked out in window boxes full of inedible plant life, I was feeling like I was back in the Farthest Doughnut.

In August, our chef, Edith Inouye, set up her meat and milk vats with more help than she considered absolutely necessary from Caleb, and promised the station biobeef within the month.

We had a zoologist on board, one Domingo Esteban Santa Maria y Bravo from Los Angeles. He put his menagerie of halibut, oysters, and bees in neighboring compartments on the inside deck. For the first week everybody made excuses to stop by and see the flat fish in their plastigraph tanks swim cockeyed until they oriented themselves belly down to the bulkhead. Caleb introduced Paddy and Sean to each individual oyster, hovering over their pool every waking moment, until Steve managed to convince him that (a) their shells were too hard enough, (b) the water was too cold, and (c) red tide was unlikely to threaten marine life 1.8 astronomical units from its last known infestation. Charlie sweated whenever she got near the bees. Not me. They might have been a pain in the extra-Terran ass initially but after the help the honeybees gave Terranova in the One-Day Revolution, they and their descendants were welcome wherever I went from now on. I paid my respects often.

I divided the crew into ten-hour, six-day shifts, put two to a cabin, tried to pair day sleepers with night sleepers, and tried to make sure that the quality snorers weren't all roaring away on C Deck all at the same time. On the first day of spring in the Antarctic, researchers step outside and walk away in a straight line, without looking back, as far as they can on the ice, until they are out of sight of each other and their temporary homes. No endless icy landscapes on our station, but the privacy of the cabins was a good second substitute. I noticed that as soon as a cabin was completed the assigned crew member usually vanished inside it, neither to see nor to speak to another person outside of their jobs, until their roommate came off shift. It was a phase that seemed to last from about a week to ten days. They emerged looking rested and with their senses of humor restored.

Reconfiguring from ship to station took a while; our first twelve months in the Belt we were never without some kind of hammering from somewhere on board. Eventually, it stopped.

Caleb smiled at me, a long, slow smile. "Now all we need is a baby-sitter."

"Oh," I said innocently, "is love about to find a way?"

"Archy?" Caleb said.

"Yo."

"Ask Leif if he'll take care of the twins until tomorrow."

If Archy hadn't buzzed us at nine-thirty the next morning, I might still be in bed. Every woman should have her own Caleb.

About two minutes after we put on spin the miners began visiting the station en masse, bringing with them their ill, their lonely, and their ore samples. I'd been a little nervous about allowing them the freedom of the house, so to speak. These people had been away from home and civilization a long time. I didn't want to be unfriendly but I didn't want to be foolhardy either. Caleb took the problem out of my hands by securing all our airlocks but two and setting a twenty-four-hour guard on each one.

There never was a problem. We didn't cure the Hudson's epidemic to get the miners to sell their ore to us but the miners didn't see it that way. From the day Claire set up shop, they brought in more high-grade ore than we could handle, and contracted with Claire to explore for more. This steady, incoming stream made me wonder if the miners didn't feel as vengeful and vindictive toward Standard Oil and Solar and Terra-Luna Mines as they did grateful and appreciative toward us.

Down on Ceres I had accepted with outward equanimity the absence of a free market and a hospital but I have never demonstrated more self-control than when I did not comment on the lack of a library. The only thing that keeps humankind a step ahead of the chimpanzees is the library, and the station's library was usually any Belter's first stop after the assay office. Armed with a credit voucher issued to them by Claire or one of her assistants, they descended like locusts on our stock of book and filmtapes. No one left the station without a borrowed tape clamped beneath one arm. That was the rule, one tape to a customer at a time. The penalty for not returning it within the prescribed period (eight weeks, to allow for travel time) was a revocation of all library privileges for the period of one year. We didn't have a lot of trouble.

Correction: We didn't have any trouble, ever.

Archy, acting librarian, was making a lot of new friends and conducting a sample census of the Belt while he was at it. When Archy was done with them, the galley was the next stop. Roger's AgroAccel program had us harvesting coffee beans within a year of our arrival. Maile, who had grown up on a coffee plantation in Kealakekua, Hawaii, rigged up a vacuum bean roaster on one of the solar cells outside the hull, and soon we were selling as much Kona Premium as we were showtapes. Then a miner got loose in one of the geodomes and told the others about it and they all wanted a chance to smell the flowers and revel in the humidity.

Roger got wind of this and informed me, through clenched teeth, that he would space the next miner who crushed one of his delicate seedlings beneath a clumsy boot. I said in that case he couldn't be less than overjoyed that I was taking over one of his geodomes. Oh, I was, was I? he said. I was, and I was turning it into a kind of rock garden for recreation, to which, naturally, we would charge a small entrance fee. Roger said never mind the miners, I had better be careful how I stood next to airlocks in his company. I quoted him that bit from Thomas Brown about a garden is a lovesome thing, God wot. Roger said God wot eating was a lovesome thing, too, and how was he supposed to feed 252 people and God wot how many free-loading Belters if I persisted in turning every last square meter of his arable plots into frivolous parks? He also muttered something about starvation and famine and scurvy and general pestilence culminating in the end of civilization as we knew it, but being a large-minded person I ignored him. Central Park, as it came to be known, opened for picnics, parties, and two-by-two strolling on its tiny, winding path a month later. It paid for itself in six months, and at the very least it got all Caleb's orchids out of our cabin. If I have to be married to a closet gardener, why can't he grow something useful, like garlic for fried potatoes, or oregano for spaghetti sauce?

Caleb made a point of personally meeting every new face that came aboard. He took them down to the galley, filled them full of coffee and fresh baked bread, and picked their brains clean of anything they knew about the Belt. There were rumors of homesteaders farther downarm. We had yet to meet one face-to-face, however, and I was inclined to regard as dubious anything we were told secondhand. Knowing is always better than not knowing, though, and Caleb coordinated what he learned in the galley over coffee with what Archy learned in the library over showtapes with what Claire learned on the road in the Belt, and we began to have a more complete overall picture of life beyond our bulkhead.

The outbreak of Hudson's Disease had reduced the mining population by nearly twelve percent, according to Nora at Maggie's place, who was feeding us demographics for a fee she took out in luxury comestibles. The percentage of male miners to female miners was something less than three to one, lower than we had expected. The majority of the miners were independents who staked their own claims and kept themselves very much to themselves. Claim jumping was not widespread but neither was it unknown. So far as we could detect, Standard Oil and Solar and Terra-Luna Mines had not made the least push either to buy into existing mining concerns or to develop any of their own. Instead, they remained bovinely on Ceres, chewing the cud the miners delivered to them and never seeking out any new pasture on their own. Neither had they bothered to set up a spaceport or a traffic coordination center or a space rescue unit or, as we already knew, a hospital.

"I've seen this before, you know," I told Caleb one day. "Back home, the Outsiders came and fished all the fish, cut down all the timber, and sucked up all the oil, sold it, and then left without making the slightest effort to provide for the future."

"You think it was any different before the Revolutionary War in New South Africa?" he replied, aiming a spoonful of pureed spinach at Paddy's mouth. She rejected it with an indignation that splattered Caleb from breastbone to the scar on his eyebrow. "Dig up the diamonds and get out the gold and good-bye," he said, wiping his face on his sleeve. "Rape and run. It's the oldest human story there is."

"It's going to be different here," I said, strapping Sean into a new diaper. He watched my every move with enormous, thickly lashed blue eyes. "We aren't going to exploit the Belt and then leave it flat to die of disuse and neglect. We aren't leaving a ghost town behind us when we go. We are going to build an economically viable community that will be able to support itself and its children for generations to come."

"Congratulations," he said, and smiled at me. "We'll be the first."

"I'm sorry. Was I preaching?"

"Relax, you only sounded a little like Brother Moses." Paddy poured her milk over her head. It dripped down off her short black curls. She smiled blindingly up at her father. Caleb sighed heavily and reached for a sponge. Leif put one into his hand. "Thanks, kid."

"No problem."

"Want to feed her?"

"Sure."

Caleb watched him for a few moments. "Want to baby-sit tonight, Leif?"

"Sure."

"Caleb," I said reprovingly.

"What?"

"Don't take advantage of Leif. He might have his own plans for this evening."

Caleb looked at Leif. "Do you?"

Leif looked at me. "No."

"Oh," I said. "Okay, then. I guess."

Mother poked her head in. "Dears, I'm off."

"Where to?"

"I've heard rumors of a circus on Vesta."

Caleb laughed. "I've heard rumors of a circus on every claimed asteroid in the Belt, Natasha."

"No, dear, a real circus. With a tightrope walker and performing dogs. Under a tent."

"Natasha, you have got to be kidding."

"No, dear. I've talked to several gentlemen who claim to have attended performances. They're charging admission and you know Belters don't joke about money, so that leads me to believe the stories are true. Interesting to speculate if this circus arrived in a ship of its own, or if it evolved out of the current population on Vesta. Hmm, yes, and why." She shook her head and said briskly, "And Crippen tells me the station is as close to Vesta as we'll get for the next year, and you know how you are, Esther dear, about fuel consumption. So I do think I should take advantage of our present location to see for myself, don't you? Good-bye, dears."

"Mother!"

She waved. The door closed silently behind her. Caleb took one look at my expression and roared.

When Caleb and I were curled up next to each other in bed that night, he said into my hair, "I got an idea. Has to do with Patrolman Lodge. Every hear of Samuel Benton Steele?"

I tilted my head back to stare at him. "Every Alaskan has. Superintendent of the Northwest Mounted Police during the Klondike Gold Rush, 1899 or thereabouts. Kept the peace. Kept Soapy Smith's bunch on the American side of the border and out of the Klondike."

"Very good," he said, complimentarily.

"Thank you. Now quit stalling and tell me, what has the Lion of the Yukon got to do with Space Patrol Lieutenant Ursula Lodge?"

"Space Patrol," he said ruminatively. "Space Patrol. Means patrol of space, right?"

"It's not like you to belabor the obvious, Caleb."

So he told me, and the next time Strasser, who had constituted himself as a sort of Belt Representative at Large, was on board we put it to him. "Our in-house computer has a program, Hermann, called High Frontier. We're using it to register claims. It's tied in with our astronomical chart, a fax of which you receive upon registration."

Strasser had two friends with him and I watched them mutter together for a few minutes. The first time I had seen him, over the cockpit viewer the day of our arrival at Ceres, Hudson's Disease had had Strasser's body swollen up like a balloon filled with water and spotted like a Dalmatian. Today, his hair cut, clean-shaven, clean, he looked slim and dapper and maybe even perky. It's amazing how getting yanked back from the edge of the grave can brighten up your whole year. Strasser growled, "Anyone using the library has a shot at that chart, then?"

"Yes, and every miner who registers a claim."

"Then no thanks. I put my name on a rock, next thing you know I've got claim jumpers coming out my ears. I've got one of the richest neodymium strikes in the Belt"—one of his friends made a rude noise—"and the only way I'm going to be able to negotiate an exclusive contract as a sole source supplier to a laser crystal company is to hide what I've got until the ink's dry on the signatures."

"You may need the legal leverage of an established claim of record in the future, Hermann. And as for your fears of claim jumpers," I said, and hooked a thumb over my shoulder. "You know Caleb O'Hara, my security chief. This is Lieutenant Lodge, his second in command, seconded to our expedition from the Space Patrol. For a negotiable fee in raw ore they are prepared to guarantee your security."

He looked Caleb over critically, then Lodge, as if assessing their chances against Butch Cassidy and the Sundance Kid. Lodge looked affronted, Caleb amused. "And how will they do that?"

"For starters, they'll tie you in on a tight beam to our comm system so you will have access to us in an emergency. Maile Kuakini's already got half a dozen commsats in operation. She plans to double that number over the next year." I described a possible security route and assured him that our scoutship could pour on enough coals to reach him quickly in a real emergency. He still looked skeptical and I said, "Don't decide today. Think it over. Tell your friends, and talk it over with them. And, Hermann? Think about how much more time you're going to have for mining if you don't have to spend it in preparation for repelling boarders."

The Belters came around to it in the end. Shortly after the first one hundred miners signed on Lodge acquired the frazzled look of someone who spends a large part of each day fighting her way into and back out of a pressure suit. She and the rest of her people spent most of their time on solarsleds, checking up on the patrols she and Caleb had set up, cross-checking asteroid claims with the haphazard miner's registry on Ceres, and charting rock coordinates for Belt composites for Archy. The tridee map Archy generated from the registrations gave us a much clearer picture of the twenty or so degrees of the Asteroid Belt that had thus far been explored.

Crip test-drove the map eight months after our arrival. He left at noon on Monday for 7871No Return and was back before dinner on Wednesday. He went out with a hold full of trading goods. He came back stuffed to the hatch with nickel, an element we were in urgent need of for the making of the alloys necessary to construct our one-shot pressure plates. "Got there and back without getting lost once, thanks to Archy's map and my navigator here." He clapped Leif on the shoulder as Mother beamed proudly in the background.

I concealed my surprise. "Well done," I said. "I guess it's safe to let you off the leash now, Crip. Once the word gets out we've got a bona fide pickup and delivery service, the miners'll be calling us."

Leif.

He was an independent, self-sufficient little cuss, all over the ship at all hours of the day and night. At first I was inclined to put the brakes on his activities, but when I saw that he was genuinely welcomed wherever he went, I backed off. After Crip told me how he never got lost with Leif riding shotgun, I told Archy to work up an introductory course in navigation and run it by Mother. If I had to have supercargo on board the *Hokuwa'a-Voortrekker*, it was going to be productive, contributing supercargo.

I didn't try to force an intimate family relationship between us overnight. Maybe it was the easy way out, but we were, after all, total strangers. Mother and our DNA were all we had in common. There were only so many routes I could take in expressing my displeasure over her manipulation of my future, not to mention my body parts, and taking it out on a ten-year-old boy wasn't one of them. The truth was I didn't know what to say to the kid. I went into labor practically in his face the first time I saw him. And Grays was his father. Lodge was his cousin. Tigers breed true, so they say.

He did spend a lot of time with the twins, who adored him. And when he wasn't riding with Crip he followed Caleb around; that boy never turned down an opportunity to go anywhere, which all by itself was a character trait that convinced me he was my son, genetically at least.

We didn't spend a lot of time together, though.

— 6 —

Staying in Motion

Every body continues in its state of rest, or of uniform
motion in a right line, unless it is compelled to change
that state by forces impressed upon it.

—Sir Isaac Newton

Mining in its essentials is the same anywhere in the system.
Exploration techniques involve geological inference, remote
sensing, and drilling for samples. The tools, with adaptations,
remain the same. There are the core drillers, the thump trucks,
the spectroscopes. Loonies might use optic cannons where
Terran roughnecks use a rotary drill; the result is again the
same, a ten-meter length of cylindrical core sample extracted
for dissection and analysis by the resident geologist.

Each area of excavation does have its own local problems.
On Terra the high gee causes rock falls and the atmosphere per-
mits the seep of poisonous gases such as hydrogen sulfide. On
Luna, regolith, the powdery surface dust, gets into everything,
tripling maintenance and replacement costs and tech hours in
repair. In the Belt, there is no atmosphere, no regolith, and
more often than not little or no surface gravity. But because

Mother Nature always, *always* gets the last laugh, the human factor leaps in to fill this breach of natural obstacles.

Vacuum is cold, cold and black. Sol is a bright shiny ball somewhere over your shoulder, but it offers no warmth. A billion stars twinkle brightly all around you, mocking your craving for light, and it isn't long before the cold seeps into your bones, slowing your physical reactions, and the dark seeps into your heart, slowing your instincts and initiative. You're tired all the time.

And when you're tired or exhausted, fatigued or just plain pooped, then is not the time for you to handle a substance that seems almost malevolently human in its determination to put parts of you into orbit around Pluto. In the first year after our arrival in the Belt, Charlie handled over a hundred cases of trauma resulting from severed limbs, usually hands, caused by the careless handling of nobelite, TNT, plastique, Meltall, Nukite, Crackette, and any and all other explosives known to man, including a few original and frequently fatal concoctions indigenous to the Belt. It got so she could tell how long someone had been mining in the Belt by how many fingers and toes he had left.

If, after an accident, the claim's partners got the injured miner's suit to seal at the nearest joint immediately after the accident, there was a chance to save his life and the possibility of prosthetic replacement for whatever was missing. Charlie got pretty good at jury-rigging longshoring hooks for hands and waldo claws for feet. Faced with injuries more extensive, she got out the long sleep serum and told Archy to enter the miner's will into the station log.

I was in her clinic once when a miner died that way. He was one of the bad ones, with burns over eighty percent of his body, ruptured lungs, and three missing limbs. How he'd lived long enough to make it to the station was anybody's guess, and Charlie's skill and the machines were all that was keeping him alive now.

He coughed and wheezed. "Am I going to make it, Doc?"

She put her hand into his remaining one. "No, Bill," she said steadily. Charlie never lied to a patient.

"How long?"

"A few hours."

"Shit." He coughed again and spit up blood. She wiped his mouth. "I've got a wife. Couple kids. Downstairs. Haven't

seen them in ten years." I thought his eyes filled; I couldn't
be sure because I found it hard to look at him.

"Where downstairs?" Charlie said. He didn't answer immediately. "Where downstairs, Bill?"

His face twisted and he groaned. She reached for an injec-
tor. It must have been some kind of painkiller because his
expression eased. Panting a little, he said, "Missoula, Montana.
Shakespeare's the name. Elizabeth. Evan and Craig. My part-
ner on Caliban knows the split, he'll—" He began coughing
again.

"We'll get it to them, Bill," Charlie said soothingly.

As the miner's pain grew worse, Charlie doubled and tripled
his painkillers. She talked to him as long as he could talk. She
held his hand until it grew cold in her own. When he was gone
beyond all possible hope of reviving, she disconnected all her
useless equipment methodically, one tube or wire or needle
at a time. She straightened his torn clothes as best she could.
She smoothed his hair from his forehead. Lastly, she lay gentle
fingers on his eyes and drew his eyelids slowly down, and
stood next to his bed, her hands folded, for a few moments.

When she turned, her eyes were filled not with sorrow or
pain but with rage. Charlie was unlike Mother in that she could
hate, and unlike me in that she could hate only once. Charlie
hated Death. When Death had the temerity to snatch a patient
out from under her care, Charlie didn't think of it as fate or
karma or a destiny that shaped his or her end. It was Death,
using trauma or disease to cheat Charlie and Charlie's skill
and Life, in that order of importance. She fought him for her
patients claw and fang every step of the way, and she took it
personally when he beat her, which wasn't often.

It was almost more than I could bear, but I knew better than
to offer sympathy.

If the miner worked alone, and unlike Bill Shakespeare so
many of them did, after a fatal accident their bodies became a
part of Belt debris, drifting in space forever or until discovered
by some startled passerby. Later it would be standard operating
procedure for each claim to have a resident, accredited explosives expert, and when the miners formed a guild they made it
mandatory, but that was many years away. In the meantime,
Charlie worked long hours, Mother Mathilda held a lot of
funeral masses, and Brother Moses made a killing selling St.
Joseph medals. St. Joseph was the patron saint of the working

man and Brother Moses claimed to be plowing the profits on the sale of each medal into a Miner's Disability Fund, for disbursement to and support of disabled miners. Very few lived to take advantage of it.

It was a good thing I set up a schedule for delivery that I knew couldn't be met. During the testing period, the first rock we slapped a pressure plate on didn't go anywhere because the pulse unit detonated too close to it, blowing a neat hole right through the center of the plate and the rock. It was a tremendous explosion, quickly snuffed out in vacuum, oddly the more terrifying because we couldn't hear it. Two days later the remaining rim began breaking up. We ducked the debris for weeks, and Archy expressed his dissatisfaction with the extra load it put on the station's space anchor.

Intimidated, the transportation team cut back so drastically on fuel for the next attempt that the result was the tiniest possible puff of dust where the controlled-velocity distribution of slag impacted against the plate. There was no perceptible degree of movement out of the rock's plane of rotation. A week later we were still waiting. Two weeks later the rock had moved maybe half a meter.

Third time's a charm, so they say. The third time the pulse unit misfired. The fourth time it didn't go off at all. We waited for twelve hours as the fuse hung fire. Finally Crip said over his commlink, apparently to the Belt at large, "I'm not going down there to see what's wrong. Are you going down there to see what's wrong?"

The response was instantaneous and unanimous.

"Uh-uh."

"Nope."

"Not me."

"Not hardly."

"I don't rightly reckon so."

"Mrs. Lu didn't raise no dummy."

"I was born at night, but not last night."

Eventually, over Bob Shackleton's objections ("Oh, hell, there goes another milepost marker!"), we torpedoed the rock and its dud for the protection of any unsuspecting prospector who might wander into the area. By then we were getting crafty and were doing the testing downarm. The new test site was about ten million kilometers from the station on that ecliptic so the debris went wide before it got as far as the station. Which it never should, since we'd angled the detonations to erupt in the other direction. Theoretically. In the Belt, we were discovering Murphy's Law worked overtime.

The days and weeks slipped by and so did my six-month deadline for the first shipment. I extended it three months. It passed. I gave the rock-throwing team a third deadline and they missed it, too. I was unhappy and said so. "It's a damn sorry day when my own handpicked team of experts can't do a simple thing like start a little pebble moving through space on a preset course," I informed a staff meeting. "Get on with it, dammit. This is starting to look like the timetable for the old STS program."

"How about the Atlas rockets, when nine out of ten failed at launch?" Simon said brightly.

"It's just that we've never done anything like this before, Star," Crip said.

"What the hell's that got to do with it? People have been doing new jobs since one of us thought up the stone axe. So shipping ore from the Belt to Terran orbit is a new job. Get with it!"

Crip flushed a dull red and stamped out. He also whipped his team in line enough to run a series of three perfect tests on asteroids graduating upward in size. For the fourth, fifteen months after our arrival, we launched 10849Perry's, which had in fact assayed out at a twenty-one percent grade of that good old heavy stuff that made spaceships go. "Is that medium-sized enough for y'all?" Claire wanted to know.

"Well," I said grudgingly. "As long as it was *there*."

We estimated ETA Terranova in nine months, which meant they would be receiving their first shipment in just under twenty-two months from our departure. "Fairly well done," I said, and had to turn away from the team leaders' collective expression to hide my grin. "By the way," I said over my shoulder. "Mayor Panati promised us a bonus if they received the first shipment of ore in under twenty-four months. Twenty-five percent of annual salary in a lump sum distribution. It's being held in escrow at the First National Bank of Terranova, along with your salaries. It's not much, I know, but—"

Whatever else I might have been about to say was lost in the ensuing uproar.

You want to know the secret for getting the best out of your employees? Here's one formula for you:

A) Hire the best.
B) Cut them in on the take.
C) Tell them precisely what you want them to do.

Last, and most important:

D) Leave them alone. Or try to.

Works for me.

The next rock we sent off was much smaller but almost eighteen percent titanium ore, a lightweight metal that holds its shape up to very high temperatures, much in demand for pressure plate and spaceship hull composites. Although we launched it seven and a half months after Perry's rock, due to the asteroid/planetary lineup at the time of launch, we skipped it off a gravitational field here and there and it would arrive less than four months later. The third rock was essentially a whole bunch of technetium, which does not naturally occur on Terra, or on Luna, in any significant amounts.

Terranova needed it. Terranova needed everything we could throw at it. Island One had about run Loonie miners off their legs; Island Two, if not supplemented by material from the Belt, would leave nothing behind on Luna but scorched earth. And although the Apollo expeditions determined that Luna had oxygen to spare, she was poor in three elements necessary for human life: hydrogen, nitrogen, and carbon. This led to an accumulation of horrific lift costs from Terra, and upon completion of construction left Terranova heavily in debt to the American Alliance. That situation had prompted the frantic construction of the zero-gravity manufacturing module, the Frisbee, so we could start paying off some of that debt even as we were incurring more.

Island Two would be different. Analyzing the albedo of the asteroids from Mitchell Observatory had confirmed that the Belt was rich in carbon, nitrogen, and hydrogen. In planning our expedition we had calculated exploration and processing costs down to the last Alliance dime. When we added up the numbers, the general consensus allowed as how the trip might be worth it, if only we could find the right minerals in sufficiently large deposits to make recovery and transportation economical and rapid. No matter how much the astronomers and the exogeologists reassured us, we told ourselves, we weren't going to believe anything until we saw it, smelled it, tasted it our own selves.

But after we got there—zowie! The abundance of Terran-poor elements was staggering. Silver, platinum, copper, nickel, potassium, and uranium in quantities that, if Archy and Simon never thought us up a new star drive, would keep us beetling around the solar system for the next five centuries. Cerium and erbium went into metal alloys essential to life in space; they were present in abundance in the Belt and ours for the taking. Neodymium, holmium, and dysprosium were used to make laser crystals and Belters had struck them so rich that LCM, Inc. eventually sent a representative out to Ceres to open a purchasing office. We found one asteroid a hundred meters in diameter estimated at containing four million tons of nickel. If we could have set it down whole on Terra it would have paid for the expedition's trip out and part of its projected five-year stay.

Then one morning Claire tumbled into my office, tripped over the sill, bounced twice in the low gee, and fetched up with her chin on my instep. Her eyes were glazed. She was unable to speak, only gargle. By the time I stopped her hyperventilating and started her making sense most of the rest of the ship's crew had been attracted by the commotion and gathered around or tuned in to listen.

"Star!" she said. "Star!"

"What, Claire?"

"Gold, Star! Gold!"

"Gold?"

"Gold! The whole rock! There must be a hundred cubic meters of the stuff in that one rock all by its lonesome!"

"So what?"

"So what? So what? Star, y'all don't—Archy honey, what y'all got gold selling for on Terra now?"

"About eight hundred and fifty a cubic centimeter, Claire."

"Eight hundred and fifty Alliance dollars per cubic centi-meter—a hundred cubic meters—Star, do you realize I've just stumbled over a chunk of rock worth eighty-five billion in Alliance dollars?" She was almost weeping.

"On Terra," I said.

She raised dazed eyes. "What?"

"On Terra it's worth eighty-five billion. Out here it's just a chunk of metal, too soft to be any good to us."

"What!"

I led her over to a chair and sat her down gently. I raised my voice so the hundreds of listening ears could hear me loud and clear. Frank had foreseen something like this and had warned me in advance. I'd done my homework, which I proceeded to regurgitate whole from the *Encyclopedia Americana*. Gold is a soft, bright, yellow metallic element (atomic number 79), I said. It is the most inert of metallic elements, I said. It is also the most ductile and malleable of metals, I said. Twenty-eight grams of gold can be rolled out flat enough to cover twenty-seven square meters, I said. " 'Like gold to ayery thinnesse beate,' " quoth I, smiling.

Claire did not smile back. I noticed no one else smiling either, and I noticed I had started to sweat. "Gold," I continued in the same patient, sane voice, "is a good conductor of heat and electricity. Hardened by platinum we could use it in electrical relays, but since fiberoptics came in we just don't need that much of it." I smiled again. "If we were jewelers, it would be different, but we aren't."

I explained all this, and more, in detail, very carefully, to everyone I could pin to a bulkhead. None of it did one damn bit of good. Few listened, and those who did had their own reasons to sidestep the rush. Caleb's family sort of ran New South Africa and he viewed all Belt gold deposits and gold-mining Belters as potential rivals in an industry that supported the family business. Maggie had contracted her fever two years before, had recovered, and was now immune. Roger was supremely disinterested in anything incapable of sprouting, and Zoya was supremely disinterested in anything other than Roger.

There were a few others who held tenaciously to sanity, but the rest of the combined crews of the *Hokuwa'a* and *Voortrekker* went, to put it in strictly medical terms, bananas. Gold fever, as I learned only too well during those few mad months, is a virus that strikes like a cornered snake, spreads like butter over hot bread, and is about as curable as puberty. Unfortunately Charlie could find no suitable vaccine down in her dispensary. When she wasn't out prospecting herself, that is. For three months almost every single crew member spent every single off-duty moment they had in vacuum banging on rocks with ballpeen hammers, torqueless wrenches, and their p-suited fists. I wanted to use their heads.

A few shrewd entrepreneurs made out like bandits. Every person on board station had a pressure suit, it was one of the safety precautions I'd insisted on before leaving Terranova and hang the expense. In the general course of work there were always a couple of dozen out of commission for maintenance, so that a few forward thinkers rented their suits and jetpacks out by the hour. In spite of how crowded people think the Belt is, in a solar orbit conservatively speaking between one and four billion kilometers in diameter, there is a lot of space between rocks. A jetpack hour through vacuum from Ceres seldom produced a close-up inspection of anything but more vacuum. The p-suit excursions became longer and longer, and since the area five degrees to either side of Ceres had been pretty well exploited before we got there nobody made any major strikes. One or two made enough to pay their suit rental. It didn't slow anybody down.

What was I supposed to do? Forbid any extrastation activity? The most I could do, within the purview of the "freedom to pursue life, liberty, and pursuit of happiness" clause in the expedition's articles, was limit it. Should I declare all expedition pressure suits company property and forbid their use on off-duty time? Sure, if I wanted to preside over the first outsystem mutiny. I've never been one to piss into the wind, so I was willing to humor the madness long enough for everyone to get the gold fever out of their system.

And then one of Charlie's medtechs was killed in a fight over a glittering rock no bigger than a p-suit helmet that turned out to be nothing but silicates, and low-grade silicates at that.

Charlie called me from her clinic when Lodge brought the body in. "I'll be right down," I said. "Archy, impanel a jury and assemble them in the galley."

"Yes, Star," he said soberly.

I reached for my dress tunic and went down to Charlie's place of business to examine the body. It was a typical p-suit decompression death, not pretty, fortunately fatal. I gave orders for the burial service, recycling of the body and repair of the p-suit, and went down to the *Hokuwa'a*'s galley. Enlarged to feed the crews of both ships, it was the largest room on the station.

The seven-member jury was generated at random from the ship's roster. I handed out the jury armbands, one at a time, the last to Mother. She wouldn't look at me. She pulled the armband up above her right elbow and took her place on a bench sitting against one bulkhead. I presided from another directly across from it. The defendant sat in a chair in the middle of the room with Lodge standing behind him looking as grim as I felt, one hand on the laser pistol strapped to her side. Witnesses, by ship's law as many as could crowd into the space remaining, stood shoulder to shoulder around the room, and I knew everyone else had downed tools and was standing by their monitors and communits. The entire station was still, stiller than it had been since final assembly, the kind of stillness that was thick enough to choke on.

"Archy," I said, "load Orestes."

"Orestes program loaded and running. Hear ye, hear ye, this first ship's mast is now in session aboard Space Station *Hokuwa'a-Voortrekker,* Esther Svensdotter presiding. It is 2:30 pm Greenwich Mean Time, the sixteenth day of July, 2010, on this the five hundred thirty-second day of the Terranovan Belt Expedition. The jury will stand in the presence of the law."

The jurors rose to swear the oath of loyalty to the expedition's articles. The plain, unequivocal words strengthened and comforted, as linguist Helen Ricadonna had designed them to back on Terranova. When the jury resumed their seats, their backs were straight and they wore a united expression of grim determination.

The trial didn't take long. The defendant, one of Dieter Joop's engineers, waived counsel and admitted to striking the deceased, shattering his visor and causing suit decompression. Two witnesses corroborated his statement. The jury brought in a conviction without leaving the room. Their faces were a collective gray as they announced their decision in a vocal poll, each of them pronouncing the verdict one by one. Then it was my turn.

I was furious with myself for not acting sooner to put the brakes on the gold fever. I was angry at the engineer, too. A guilty-of-murder verdict was a hellacious burden to place on his shipmates; if his sense of morality couldn't or wouldn't do it, then simple good manners should have been enough to have kept him in line. I set my teeth, swallowed hard, and said, "Micah Reardon, you have been found guilty of the heinous crime of murder by a jury of your peers. How say you?"

Reardon, whom I was glad I knew only slightly, shook his head once. "Let's get it over with." His face was white and he spoke without raising his eyes.

At my breast Paddy stirred, her thumb in her mouth, her bright blue eyes alert. "Then rise and hear the sentence of this court."

He rose. His knees were shaking so badly that Lodge put a hand beneath his elbow to support him.

I swallowed again, trying to moisten my suddenly dry mouth. "Micah Reardon, having been found guilty of murder, this court sentences you to immediate execution. Lieutenant Lodge, take the prisoner in charge. Members of the jury, follow me."

Down in the cargo bay Lodge placed Reardon against a bulkhead. The jury was issued a sonic rifle each out of the locker placed there for that purpose. They lined up opposite the convicted. Mother's face was expressionless, her small hands on the sonic rifle deft. Lodge asked Micah if he wanted a blindfold. He said yes. We waited. When the cloth was tied round his eyes she stepped back and I said, "Ready, aim, fire," and it was done.

The sonic rifle was developed early in space colonization when the need for a weapon firing other than solid projectiles became evident in an environment precariously maintained against killer vacuum behind a quarter-inch titanium shell. It sent a jolt of laser-amped suprasonics to short-circuit the autonomic system. It was quick, clean, and quiet, and they say a painless way to die. There was only one way to find out for sure. Certainly Micah Reardon died easier than Charlie's medtech had.

"Are you all right, Mother?" I said after the sonic rifles were back in the locker.

"No, dear," she said, her voice strained, "I am not. Crippen?"

They left. Hand in hand.

I went back to my cabin and found Caleb and Sean waiting for me. He put the twins to bed, and then me.

"Did you know about Mother and Crip?" I said.

"Uh-huh."

"Nobody ever tells me anything."

"Possibly because they expect you'll see what's right under your nose."

"Possibly."

"Does it bother you?"

"It's none of my business," I said.

"True."

"She is eleven years older than he is."

"Also true."

"But it really is none of my business."

"No."

"I guess I just assumed, when Dad died, that that was it for Mother."

"Evidently she doesn't agree. When did your father die?"

"He went down off the Aleutians in 1996," I said. "I couldn't get home. It was right in the middle of the Cycle 23 flare incident."

Caleb caught at my hands. "Relax. You're going to tie that blanket into a knot."

"Come to think of it, I caught Crip whistling last week, charting coordinates into the flight plan program. I should have known something was up. I'm glad for him. I didn't think he was ever going to recover from Paddy's death."

"But it really is none of your business."

"Right. Crip and Perry have more in common, though."

"Probably why they never got together."

I lay there thinking about Mother and Crip. It was easier than lying there thinking about Micah Reardon. Caleb must have felt the same way. Later that long, long night I heard him mutter, " 'A half-dead thing in a stark dead world, clean mad for the muck called gold.' " I twisted around to stare up at him, and looking a little self-conscious, he said, "After you recited that bit at Maggie I got Archy to read me some Service. It fits, doesn't it?"

I don't know why it comforted me to know that, over a century before, the Yukon had had its own Micah Reardons, but it did. I burrowed deeper into Caleb's arms and willed myself to sleep.

The next morning I got up at six, bathed and changed Paddy, and went to breakfast. I ordered scrambled eggs and toast in the galley and sat down next to Simon.

"Business as usual, right, Star?" Charlie said from his other side.

"Shut up, Charlie," Simon said.

"How you could permit Mother, of all people—"

"Shut up, Charlie," Caleb said, forking scrambled eggs into Sean's mouth.

"I beg your—"

"Do shut up, dear," Mother said from across the table. Charlie shut up.

After the medtech's death and the Reardon execution gold fever abated aboard the *Hokuwa'a-Voortrekker*. One day Parvati Gandhi, in company with two engineers, one mining and one mechanical, came to me and said, "We got an idea." They spoke fluently for a half hour. They had answers for all the questions I asked. The result was that we hauled in what remained of Claire's asteroid, called 10863Ophir, and set up a solar smelter and a zerogee rolling mill. Parvati and Company began fabricating knickknacks and novelty items in their off hours. When they'd built up something of an inventory, they began selling it to Belters at an exorbitant price. Suddenly miners were sprouting hoop earrings so heavy they caused lower back pain and slave bracelets so enormous they couldn't fit beneath a pressure suit. When the practice spread to my people I thought for a while I was going to have to institute a dress code. My all-time favorite gold innovation was the twenty-four-karat thunder mug in the john at Maggie's Place, although I never felt really safe sitting on it—too soft and kind of slippery. It took weeks to talk Caleb out of the baby bottles and by then they were weaned and out of danger.

It was our first experience with industry for individual profit among the crew. Incorporating it into the station's bookkeeping was loads of fun. Belters traded raw ore for the finished item, after expenses the station took a modest percentage, and the remainder was divided between Parvati and her group, Parvati getting the largest cut because it had been her idea. We were in the market for as much raw ore in small amounts as we could get for experimentation and our own manufacture; the ore the station was shipping back to Terranova was in much larger quantity.

Maile was one of the blessed few who had remained happily immune from the gold fever. She methodically went about her business, which entailed setting out commsats and putting the station on a direct, dedicated skip band to Terranova. Her first priority, set by me, was in linking us up to the Hewie monitors surrounding Sol so we'd have a continual readout of solar activity. I'd lost too many Fivers during the Cycle 23 flare. The construction of the Helios Early Warning System had been a direct result of that terrible event, and the arrival of the Librarians' ship from a refueling stop on Sol had scared me enough to require continual and enhanced updates.

After Maile had a steady readout from the Hewies and had invented a course-speed-and-composition (CSC) schedule for outbound rocks, she turned to the news and other more personal matters. The lag in transmission both ways made it impossible to hold normal conversation with Terranova and messages received that way did lack a certain sort of immediacy. We settled for prerecorded weekly messages for business and monthly messages for personal. Savvy miners who knew their physics crowded into the radio shack with messages of their own to send—for a small fee, naturally.

After a few months of this, Maile came to me and said, "I got an idea." She talked for a while, I gave her my blessing, and she began compiling news from around the system and broadcasting it on Channel 9 each evening at nineteen hundred. Necessarily delayed, it was still more recent and more accurate than either the faxsheets on the bulletin board or the gossip around Piazzi City. From the first Maile had a loyal following. She bracketed her broadcast with two hours of rock and two hours of jazz, and after Charlie set up a yammer she extended the program with weekend symphonies and operas. After a while she began accepting advertisements. Before long, KBLT was paying its way. "And we might start thinking about a trivee station," she said cheerfully.

"Did we bring a trivee transmitter?"

"No."

"Can we build one?"

Maile thought about it, and shook her head reluctantly. "No point in it. We can't manufacture trivees yet."

Two and a half years into expedition operations Terranova had taken delivery of the first two rocks. We got better with practice; within the next year we had over five asteroids in transit. Once we got the proportions between mass to move and thrust to move it down correctly, and an alloy strong enough to stand up to the propulsion system and cheap enough to build throw-away pressure plates, it was simply a matter of moving both up and out of the Belt and lighting a match. Drop-kick propulsion wasn't what you'd call sophisticated, but it got the job done. Sam Holbrook, assisted by an enthusiastic Leif, plotted and schemed and sweated over ways to assist the propulsion process with gravity slings from any celestial body that happened to be even marginally along the route. Once he delayed a launch for three weeks until Mars was in the right place. It was just long enough for Terranova to get wind of it and Frank Sartre started firing messages down the communications network that ranged from aggrieved to agonized. Sam finally let the rock go, bounced it off the outer reaches of Mars's gravitational field, and moved up the rock's arrival in Terran orbit by six weeks. The messages from Frank stopped.

"Guess he's decided we know what we're doing," Sam observed.

I was satisfied enough with the operation to turn my personal attention elsewhere. I'd had this idea that had been nagging at the back of my mind since before we left Terranova. I hadn't meant to lay it out so soon but I was pretty certain it would complete the cure for gold fever and prevent its ever recurring, at least on board the *Hokuwa'a-Voortrekker*. I was mentally working out my sales pitch at dinner one evening when Mother said, "What is it, dear?"

Startled, I said, "What is what, Mother?"

"You're bursting with news, dear."

"You're like this little kid with a box of candy who's determined not to share any of it until the box is half gone," Charlie said unkindly. "I want some."

I grinned. It was useless to try to hide anything for any length of time from Mother or Charlie, another disadvantage in working with your family. "All right," I said. "Charlie, how are things in the clinic?"

She shot me a keen look. "Running smoothly."

"Any more cases of Hudson's Disease?"

"Nah, we've got it licked. The Sisters of St. Anne have started a vaccination program down on Ceres, so I think we've seen the last of it."

"Nothing else on the medical horizon?"

"Nope. Just routine. Until the next mutation."

"Crip?"

He shrugged. "The transportation department is pretty well running itself now, Star. I've got time for the next rabbit you pull out of your hat."

"Roger?"

Roger looked gloomy. It was his natural expression so I wasn't worried. "Geodome Five is up and running. One of the orange trees isn't taking hold too well."

"Throw a bucket of water on it," Charlie said.

Roger looked at her.

"Well," Charlie said defensively, "that's what I do for shocky patients."

"Throw water on them?" Simon said.

"Give them fluids," Charlie said with a dark look.

"Simon?" I said. "How goes it in your department?"

Simon stretched and cracked his knuckles. "Archy hasn't blown a card in weeks. I'm bored."

Everybody laughed. "Well, Simon, it is always an object with me to keep life interesting for you, so why don't you call a meeting of all department heads in the galley for tomorrow at noon."

"I've got an idea," I said the next day, looking around the crowded galley. "Let me start it off by asking you a question. What does Terra have most of?"

"Smog," Maile said instantly, and Charlie said, "Bugs," and somebody else said, "Brazilians."

"Seriously, folks," I said. "What does Terra have the most of. More than anything else, what does she most need a—a relief valve for?"

There was a brief silence, and then Leif piped up, "People."

"Exactly." I smiled at him. Leif had shot up in the most amazing way; at twelve-plus years of age he came up almost to my shoulder. "Now, what if there were a viable, off-planet alternative. In that case, would some of the minority, religious, ethnic, and any other special interest groups on Terra pay, and I mean really pay, for—say—a world of their own?"

A thoughtful silence followed my words. "All right, Star," Simon said at last. "You've hooked us. Go on."

I said, "Archy, what was the population of Terra, last count?"

"Nine-point-three billion at the 2000 census, Star," Archy replied promptly. "Speaking of rabbits."

"Are Terrans starving?"

"Noooo," Archy said carefully. "The air is pretty foul and the quality of life literally stinks. The greenhouse effect is starting to take a real toll on the productivity of the North American breadbasket, and it feeds the world. People aren't actually starving, no, but they are getting thinner. And there's the ozone depletion, too. Gotta wear hats and sunscreen outside all the time."

"You would not describe life on Terra as pleasant, then."

"No."

"Not something you would like your kids to inherit."

Archy chuckled. He was getting more human every day. Scary. "Definitely not my kids, Star."

"Thanks, Arch. Okay, boys and girls, here's the deal." I looked around the room and took a deep breath. "Multiple-family dwellings, mass produced for lowest cost, sold on site or delivered upon request at extra charge."

Simon said, "What, you want to go into the prebuilt home construction business now?"

I said softly, "Try the prebuilt *world* construction business."

"What's the deal, you want to build everybody their own Terranova?"

"I'm thinking more along the lines of a sphere maybe one and a half klicks in circumference. A seven-to-two ratio of shell thickness between the axis and the equator to resist atmospheric pressure and centrifugal force. Then, Terranova has, what, a meter of solar-ray shielding? Let's build in a safety factor and make it two. So, a two-meter shell, with a transparent area around one axis through which sunshine enters via a circular reflecting panel. The panel adjusts for day and night the way the reflecting cape does on Terranova."

"A Bernal sphere," Sam Holbrook exclaimed.

"Got it in one. But my way we start out with an exterior and shielding already in place."

Sam stared at me, before his puzzled expression cleared. "Rocks?"

"Right again. The first criteria for selection will be size. The model calls for one that supports a population of ten thousand people, with about forty-five square meters of living space per inhabitant, which puts it at about four hundred fifty meters in diameter. We can provide earth-normal gravity at the equator with a one-point-ninety-seven per minute rotation."

"How many asteroids with that diameter y'all think we can hunt up?" Claire said.

"Enough to turn a profit," I said. "And nobody says they have to be that big."

"Yeah, ten thousand?" Simon said. "Isn't that setting our sights just a little high?"

"Probably," I admitted. "This project will likely wind up being overengineered and twice as big and ten times as expensive as originally projected. Think of the TransAlaska Pipeline, the Chunnel. Atlantis. Orientale Base." I smiled then, and it was not a nice smile. "But, Simon, how many Luddites do you figure are on Terra? Who would like to get as far away from Terran technological corruption as possible? Who would pay any amount of money to see that they did?" He didn't answer, in fact no one said a word, and I went on. "How many Amish? Sephardic Jews? Palestinians? Nudists? Born-again Baptists—we're talking real money, there. Speaking of money, how about Las Vegas? Think they might go for an orbiting casino, off Terra and away from all those awkward Terran laws restricting gambling and drugs and prostitution? They practically underwrote Atlantis. How about retirees—think about Sun City on Luna for a moment, and then tell me you think this wouldn't pay. Ten thousand is piddly for what I want to do."

"Which is, specifically?" Simon said.

"Which is to offer a whole new world, a world of their own, to groups of people bound by similar political beliefs or utopian social dreams or even paranoid delusions, who can't find peace on Terra or Luna or Terranova, or in any habitat that causes them to rub up against competing faiths or constrictive political systems."

"And individual ecosystems for each one," Roger said.

I grinned. This was going to appeal not only to Roger's imagination but also to his vanity. "With free and unlimited solar power, a habitat sized for ten thousand is within the limits of our present capability here in the Belt. The key is how fast after R and D we can turn these suckers out. We need a planetary—a minor planetary assembly line." I paused, dazzled at the prospect, and Charlie rolled her eyes. "So, Sam, within those physical parameters, what are our chances of finding enough asteroids of the right size to turn us a profit?"

Sam rubbed his head with his hands, as if to stimulate his thinking processes. When his white hair was standing straight up all over his head he dropped his hands and said slowly, "The profit I don't guarantee, but a four-hundred-fifty-meter diameter isn't that odd a size. Shape will narrow our selection down a bit, as some rocks are so oddly shaped that they will obviously not be suitable, but there are enough spheroids to give us a discretionary selection. And," he said, suddenly excited, "nothing says we can't compress smaller rocks together to form the right size!"

"We could buy played-out claims," Simon suggested.

Sam's eyes lit up. "Hell, yes! That way half our work might be done even before we climbed aboard!"

"Claire? Composition?"

She stirred and said, "Nitrogen, hydrogen, oxygen—we can make anything if we got those, and I reckon we got plenty."

"Star?" Crip said, frowning. "Are we going to chip out the innards of these prospective new worlds or what?"

"Or what," I replied. "What I want someone to invent for us is a Little Bang."

"A what?"

I turned to Whitney Burkette. "Can you produce a controlled explosion that set off in the center of an asteroid will shove matter outward, toward its rim, without breaking the rim?"

He rolled the idea around, fingering his mustache like Snidely Whiplash. "What you want is a kind of a melting process?"

"What I want is something like a controlled atomic explosion, without the fission, so that lets out employing pulse units. And after the initial clearing we go inside with MeekMakers to finish off the interior."

"Meekwhats?" somebody asked.

"MeekMakers, magnetrons that focus microwave energy on slag or soil to fuse particles. When the surface cools, you can use it for roads or slice it into blocks to use for building materials. For a year we didn't use anything but MeekMakers on Luna."

It took another moment for Burkette's next comment, which was a characteristic blend of caution and optimism. "The charge would have to be reworked for each individual rock, depending on composition and shape."

"But you could do it?"

"If there were charges fired on the outside of the rock at the same time to produce a centrifugal force. Which, if we did it right, would also provide the necessary onegee across its equator."

We all looked at Crip. He shrugged. "One-time propellant charges on timers, maybe even reusable vernier thrusters. Simple enough in theory."

We turned back to Burkette. "So you could do it?"

He deliberated some more. "So," he said at last, "we put on spin through exterior application of force, heat the interior with one blast, and allow the centrifugal force of the rotating sphere to sling the matter outward toward the rim. But only so far, or we'll melt through the shell, defeating our purpose. When it's cooled off we send in crews with MeekMakers to ensure sealant to trap an atmosphere." He cocked an eyebrow at me. I nodded. He thought a while longer, through the growing buzz that was filling the room, and said finally, "I'll need to run some tests, and I'll need a free hand in experimentation."

I said patiently, "But you think you can do it."

"Perhaps," was as far as Whitney Burkette would go, but that was like "Absolutely!" from anyone else, and I was satisfied.

"Then what?" Roger said, his usually hangdog face alive with interest.

"Then you move in, with your AgroAccel program," I told him. "Ever wonder why I threw all that money at you back on Terranova, so you could do that experimentation with accelerated growing cycles? Now you know it wasn't just so you could impress Zoya with your expertise." Roger reddened and Zoya, amazingly, grinned at me. We hadn't exchanged more than two words since we'd met, largely because I thought her English wasn't good enough yet. And maybe a little because I was afraid she might blame me for breaking up her marriage. Not that there was a word of truth in it.

"And a self-teaching computer that automatically monitors, runs, and repairs the life-support systems, the way Mehitabel does now on Terranova," Simon said.

"Step three," I said, nodding.

"Timetable?" he said, with the remote look on his face that indicated he was really somewhere else, running calculations, probably with dollar signs in front of them.

"Oh, I think we could have a working model ready to show by the end of next year. Just a little one, say a hundred meters in diameter, plenty of room to make and correct our mistakes." Someone gasped. I looked around the galley and added wickedly, "Let's make it something flashy. A water world maybe, say a fish farm. I'm open for suggestions." The crew sat in stunned silence and I said blandly, "Well? Conjecture? Speculation? Any theories going cheap?"

"I'm beginning to feel like a third-century Egyptian magician," Simon murmured, "looking for the philosopher's stone to help me in the transmutation of lead into gold."

"Attempts at alchemy led to the science of chemistry," I pointed out smugly, "which has in fact accomplished the transmutation of elements."

Claire looked at me solemnly and said, "I think y'all've lost your mind, Star, but it'll be fun looking for it."

The room was suddenly full of competing ideas. I shouted, "I want one person dedicated full-time to overseeing and collating ideas. Archy—tag a new program—call it—what? World Builders?"

"Ugh. We'll call it Star's Rabbit." For a computer Archy had a really horrible cackle.

I shuddered. "Fine. Mother's in charge."

"But, dear!"

"Yes, Mother, it's time you contributed something concrete to the expedition." She bridled defensively. I said, "With your help, Archy will be investigating our market, identifying the personal habits of individual groups, and working out ways to customize each habitat to suit the needs of future inhabitants. Mother," I said, as she still looked unconvinced, "your whole life you've been studying the way people live. Now you've got a chance to influence the way they *will* live." She brightened a little and I knew I had her. "Archy, when someone commissions us to build A World of Their Own, what do we do first?"

"Check their credit rating," he replied promptly.

"Attaboy."

"For example," I heard Simon explaining to Charlie, "we won't have to build in a domestic power system for the Amish since they don't use electricity. We won't have to plumb for heavy industry, either."

"And no poison ivy growing in the nudists' habitat," Roger said, actually grinning.

Burkette added dryly, "And of course no technology later than the wheel for the Luddites," and the fact that the Britisher had made a semi-joke was enough to shut everybody up, but only for a moment.

"Luddites?" Charlie said doubtfully. "Living in a world that was made and not just happened?"

"Why not?"

Charlie looked at me askance. "Well, for one thing, they tried to kill you seven or eight times. Why should you want to build them a home? For that matter, why would they be inclined to let you build it?"

"It was only six or seven times," I said, "and according to Caleb's sources on Terra, it wasn't the Luddites, it was a splinter group, the Rifkinites."

"Now I really have heard everything," Simon told the ceiling. "Star Svensdotter, Luddite apologist."

"Who says fanatics have to make sense anyway?" I demanded. "For centuries the Luddites have been trying to make Terra over into their own image and have failed miserably at every attempt. We build them their own world, to their own specs, they can build exactly the kind of life-style they want."

"And deserve," Simon added.

"And who cares anyway, as long as their check clears?" Archy said.

"That's my boy," I said. "What do you want for Christmas, Archy?"

"Another pentillion megabytes worth of storage space," Archy said promptly. "I'm going to need it if this project pans out."

"There's the possibility of a certain symmetry there," Mother said to Burkette. "Advanced technology providing a back-to-basics, Mother Earth world. What they once tried so hard to stop may give the Luddites the world they have always dreamed of."

"And why not tandem worlds?" Crip said, grabbing Caleb's arm and spraying him and Paddy with enthusiasm. "Ten thousand inhabitants to a world—hell, we could set a ring of worlds in orbit around each other—a real space community!"

The meeting broke up into excited, chattering groups. I regarded the room with benevolent satisfaction. Charlie sidled up to me and said softly, "When were you planning on letting Helen in on the big idea, Star?"

I scratched my head. "Actually, she already knows." I looked at Charlie and nodded. "Yup. We set this up back on Terranova."

"And Frank?"

I confessed all. "He doesn't know. I guess now would be about the right time to tell him."

"I guess," she said with a smile. "How do you think he'll take it?"

"What can he do? We're almost two AUs away, and we're more than fulfilling our contractual requirements in raw ore shipment. Maggie's come up with an in-flight processing plan that Archy is de-bugging now. If it proves out—and Sam and Claire both think it will—in another two to three years the silicon will be arriving at Terranova ready to use."

"You think he'd try to stop us?"

"No," I said. "No, I don't think Frank'd try to stop us. But he's not getting the chance, one way or the other."

We stood in silence, our thoughts on the spinning cylinder so far away. "I wonder how she'll tell him."

"With Helen, you never know."

"Still, Star. You're going to be spending a lot of Terranovan dollars on this project, and without prior approval. They may think they have some say in how you expend man hours and supplies."

"It's that kind of geocentricity that will keep us tied to Terranova or even, God forbid, Terra's coattails forever, Charlie. It's not money at stake here; it's our independence."

"I thought you liked working for Helen and Frank," Simon, who had been listening, said in surprise.

"I do. But there's no guarantee they will always be in charge. How would you like to work for the new mayor of Terranova, Simon, or for some Terran who has never even spaced?"

He shuddered. I had my answer.

Claire, Whitney, Crip, Roger, and Simon put their heads together and came up with a sign that read "Quiet—Alchemists at Work," and posted it on a partitioned section of the cargo bay. Smaller lettering beneath read "Starbuilt Mobile Homes, S. Svensdotter, Prop.," and "Astrocondos, Inc." Someone else penciled in, "The Cheapest Habitat Rates Per Square Meter for Multiple-Family Dwellings in the Solar System."

And beneath that someone else had scribbled, "The *Only* Habitat Rates Per Square Meter for Multiple-Family Dwellings in the Solar System."

— 7 —

Bacteria and Blue Whales

> Galaxies and stars, planets and moons, bacteria and blue whales, they are all merely arrangements of ninety-two atomic elements. . . . Give me the ninety-two elements and I'll give you a universe.
>
> **—Chet Raymo**

Three years after our arrival in the Belt we threw a party, a combination celebration of the fifth successful launch to Terranova and a sort of inaugural party for Homemade Homes. I got out my guitar, Charlie brought her keyboard up from the dispensary, and Simon beat percussion with a pair of drumsticks on the bottom of a couple of empty pots, one large, one small. We missed Elizabeth's flute. At that time I felt we had established enough of a routine to ease up on the constraints I had originally placed on alcohol, drugs, and the noxious evil killer weed. I had Caleb pass the word that such substances would now be tolerated in controlled amounts so long as they did not affect performance, whereupon I was obliged to view with at least the appearance of equanimity the materialization of a dozen illegal vacuum stills and the harvest of what I in my innocence had thought were tomato plants in

Geodome One. "You haven't been lying to me about the urine checks, have you, Charlie?" I shouted as the party went into overdrive.

"We've been straight on the job, Star," she shouted back, and I was satisfied. There wasn't a thing I could do after the fact anyway.

If you took your poison in liquid, powder, or gas, the party went a long way toward easing the tension we'd all been working under. The galley was so crowded I was convinced the atmospheric pressure was up by half a kay. No one seemed to mind, and at least this way no one had room to fall down and hurt themselves. I saw Perry Austin with a genuine thirty-two-tooth grin on her face as she listened to Maggie, listing precariously to starboard, tell lies about the madaming business. Whitney Burkette, whose normally immaculate exterior was looking slightly mussed, was drinking with one hand and drawing complicated diagrams on a bulkhead with the other for Leif, who was holding a lab beaker full of what I most sincerely hoped was fruit punch. Ari Greenbaum was talking New Yawk Bronx to Claire and she was coming back with pecan-pie Southrun. I couldn't understand a word either one of them was saying, but they looked like they were enjoying themselves. Bob Shackleton was making a move on Ursula Lodge, which made me think better of both of them. Roger and Zoya were nuzzling each other in one corner, Crip and Mother vanished before the evening was half over, and Charlie and Simon were working up to one of their better fights. The kids—there were over ten resident on the station by now—had long since sacked out. Caleb was looking yearningly toward our cabin and nudging me in that direction when somebody decided that Belt Station *Hokuwa'a-Voortrekker* needed a better and shorter name.

The festivities turned into a christening party as everyone advanced their choices—Fort Apache, Homestead, Frontier Fanny, Baby Belter, Botany Bay, Providence, Plymouth Rock, Sagres, Resolution, Santa Maria, et cetera, ad infinitum, ad nauseum. I never called it anything but the station so I didn't really care. We settled on Outpost, which was short enough and evocative of living on both a physical and social frontier.

"I got an idea," Maile said, and incorporated the new name in a weekly newsletter, the *Outposter*. The lead article of the first edition concerned our plans for redesigning the interiors of asteroids. I took the coward's way out and blipped a complimentary copy to Terranova in care of the American Alliance ambassador. It wasn't long before we had Frank breathing heavily down the commnet to find out what was going on. We responded with a sample demographics study Archy and Mother worked up on every social, economic, political, and religious splinter group ever assigned an acronym by the *American Times-Post*. Frank waited a week, during which time I had the distinct feeling Helen was talking hard and fast, and then replied with two symbols, a dollar sign and a question mark. I responded with a dollar sign and an exclamation point. Six months later we received two crates via a Truax Volksrocket. Caleb got out a crowbar, I got out my self-control, and we opened them up. One was filled with cryohed silver salmon roe, the other with milt. They were accompanied by an unsigned note that read as follows:

Put these up a creek or I'll put you there.

"Salmon!" Roger said as if it were a four-letter word. "Salmon! I thought we were building a freshwater fish farm! I'll have to change every plant in the place!"

"Now, Roger," I said soothingly, "you know since the Greenhouse Effect caused the Ten-Year Drought in the Pacific Northwest—"

"A saltwater aquarium? Really, Star," said Whitney Burkette with a calm even more icy than usual, "does Dr. Sartre have any idea of the effect of salt water on moving metal parts? It will be necessary to effect a complete redesign of the aerators."

"—during which time the creeks were so low the salmon couldn't get upstream to spawn—"

"Creeks!" Ari Greenbaum exploded. "Creeks! The river was hard enough to design and now she wants creeks yet!"

"—and there was no escapement and the three- and five-year schools have yet to restock themselves to predrought levels—"

By then I was talking to an empty room. "—so fresh salmon is now worth more per pound downstairs than starstones. How is it," I asked Charlie plaintively, "that Frank can cause a near mutiny from one-point-eight AUs away?"

"Talent," she said. "Also cussedness, and jealousy that it wasn't his idea in the first place."

Fortunately for the mental health of my crew the same Volksrocket bearing roe also bore an acting troupe. They settled into quarters on Ceres and began staging plays and musicals in Piazzi City Square. They scheduled performances for every night except Wednesday and a matinee on Sunday so as not to interfere with Brother Moses' evening services. The anticipation with which this news was greeted stationwide, even after the blowout christening party, forced me to realize just how hard we had been working and how much in need all my people were of rest and recreation. Just because, lacking a skating rink or a zerogee flight habitat, my only hobby is work, doesn't mean everyone else's is. I gave half the station leave Friday and the other half Saturday, and in a burst of generosity I immediately regretted, both sections all day Sunday off as well. I attended the first performance myself, holding Paddy on my lap, sitting next to Caleb with Sean on his. The initial production was *Les Miserables*.

The thing is, you have to remember when you're reading a Victorian novel or watching a play based on one that in Victorian novels people drop like flies, and I always forget. Characters fade gracefully away from consumption and are beheaded at the guillotine and stab their lovers and poison their husbands and fling themselves beneath trains, and a deathbed scene that lasts seven and a half pages in the novel and twenty minutes worth of dialogue in the play can go on for two solos and a production number in a musical. I managed to control myself through the deaths of Fantine, Eponine, Enjolras, and even Gavroche, but when Javert went off that bridge, and in the low gee he took a long time falling into the Seine. . . . It didn't help that I was sitting front row center. Or that I laughed so loud I woke up both twins. Or that our tickets were complimentary. They never were again. "I can't take you anywhere," Caleb said after the show limped to its finale.

It was the thin end of the wedge; the troupe's arrival in the Belt seemed to act as some sort of signal and hard on their heels came a series of performing groups, including the Duke Ellington Orchestra. "This is more like it," I told Caleb. For their finale they played Jelly Roll Morton's "Smokehouse Blues" slow, low-down, and dirty, with all five saxophones up front. I didn't bother to wait around for the encore. "I really can't take you anywhere," Caleb said in our cabin afterward. "Where's my clothes?"

"I don't know. By the door."

"Where's the kids?"

"I don't care. Stop talking and come back over here."

"Could I have maybe five minutes to catch my breath?"

"No."

"Help. Help?" And he laughed.

Jelly Roll Morton and saxophones. You're talking *real* music, there.

As our social and cultural lives picked up, the fatigue and enervation of the crew began to alleviate, and they turned to R and D into asteroidal worlds with a will. The basic structural requirements would never vary all that much. No vehicles faster than a bicycle, so no transport hassles. Low gee swimming pools. Hangars for low gee flight gear up close to the axis, walking to them the equivalent of climbing a gentle hill four hundred feet high, take about twenty minutes. Separate the sphere into three villages of four thousand people each. Make each village's day independent, and you had a round-the-clock work shift.

The individual adaptations, however, would change from world to world, depending on the prospective client. For example, how does a Moslem bow five times toward the east from a kneeling position inside a world that is 1.8-plus astronomical units from Mecca? In a world 450 meters in diameter, for a population of 10,000 people, Roger estimated a growing area of about 600,000 meters, but how many square meters must be given over to agriculture if that population is vegetarian? In such a vegetarian society, if an increase in arable land is called for, does that require a comparable decrease in living space, and what does *that* do to our baseline ten thousand population allowance? The design for such a world does not have to allow space for mycoprotein meat vats, but if they happen to be the kind of vegetarians who drink milk it does have to be plumbed for fixed-bed-enzyme synthesis equipment. If they didn't eat meat or drink milk, they might eat eggs and the design must incorporate a chicken farm. Some vegetarian sects, I was pleased to discover, eat seafood, which elevated our saltwater aquarium from a flashy showcase to necessary research for future products, and quelled the lingering rebellion among Messrs. Lindbergh, Burkette, and Greenbaum against all creatures great and small nourished on salt water.

But if the New England Territorial Penitentiary wants to explore the possibility of maximum security prisons in orbit, does the promise of a gargantuan federal grant for study purposes mean you can tell Frank to go piss up a rope? After he records a message in a tone of voice marginally below that of a primal scream to inform me that Terranova is not never was and never will be into criminal rehabilitation, which phrase he considered an oxymoron anyway? "We are not building whole new worlds so Cyrus the Second can tuck away renegade Bedouins and other of his political mistakes a nice tidy billion miles from New Persia!" ran one bitter bulletin.

You could always tell Frank was upset when he shifted from metric to oldstyle. But, as Simon pointed out, "At least it's 'we' now, instead of 'you.' "

An added benefit to my idea was that Claire's people were prospecting farther and farther afield for the perfect test rock. They went up- and downarm, trailed by a doggedly persistent Bob Shackleton, cataloguing and surveying and assaying and evaluating and finally plotting the orbits of all the asteroids they encountered. Some they flagged for future study, a very few they claimed outright. Our knowledge of what was where increased daily. Sam Holbrook said, "I got an idea," and with Bob Shackleton began publishing an updated map a month, incorporating the new discoveries we were making. They sold them for $100 Alliance or equivalent apiece, and the miners snapped them up like lottery tickets with a $1,000,000 Alliance jackpot. Finally, Shackleton's presence was showing a return. The day the map-selling business paid him a personal profit and he realized for the first time the possibilities inherent in a free market society, he became suddenly less concerned about the expedition's rock-moving and mining activities in the Belt. Every discovery, every shipment, every artificially induced movement out of natural orbit by an asteroid, meant the sale of a new map. Shackleton turned into a capitalist right before my very eyes. Now if I could only talk Mother Mathilda into charging a small fee for services at her free clinic on Ceres.

And then one day one of the geologists ranged even farther afield than usual, was out of range for three days, and just when Caleb had decided to go after her, she called in a contact with the long-lost *Conestoga.*

"Just the *Conestoga*?" I asked Archy.

"Parvati says the *Tallship*'s nowhere she can see it."

"Tell her to return to base, Arch. We'll take it from here."
I cut out of the link and looked at Caleb.

"What's the *Conestoga*?"

"Remember? We saw them on Luna that night we spent with Jorge." He still looked blank, and I said impatiently, "It's one of two ships sold by Space Services to a group of Terran geneticists. We saw them parked inside Copernicus—"

Caleb snapped his fingers. "I remember. They were part of that BioScience Engineering and Ethics Committee the American Alliance formed when genetechs started to grow little blond boys."

"That's the ones. Their chairman—what was his name? Leander? Lafayette? Lavoliere, that's it—Lavoliere led them out on strike, and then to Luna. They launched for the Belt right after the One-Day Revolution, and no one's heard from them since."

"Do we care?"

"Not much. Although Deke at SSI asked Helen to ask me to keep an eye out for them."

"Why?"

"He wants to know how SSI's ships held up in service."
Caleb frowned, and I said, "What?"

"I think this family is owed a bit of time off, don't you?"

"What have you got in mind?"

"Oh, a little rock hopping. See some new faces and new places. What do you say?"

"You want us to leave Outpost all by itself? Leave the lunatics in charge of the asylum?"

"Yes."

I considered it for maybe five seconds. "Okay."

He laughed and hugged me. Affronted, Paddy demanded, "Want down. Now!"

"Yes, ma'am," Caleb said. "I'll call Leif. Make this a real family outing."

"Oh. Okay. If we can tear him away from Mother and Sam and Archy." I added, "We'll make Mom and Pop's our first stop. Check out that rumor you heard about a chromium find."

He gave me a look. "I might have known you'd figure out some way to work a little business into a pleasure trip."

"And we'll turn Archy off."

Caleb whooped and grabbed me up in a bone-crusher of a hug.

"Star!" came Archy's indignant protest. "You can't do that!"

Caleb stilled. "We'll be out of range most of the time anyway, Archy. You can keep track of us on the Cub's locater."

I looked at Caleb. He smiled approvingly at me and I wriggled all over like a petted pup.

Caleb, Leif, and I and the twins set out two days later in a souped-up Piper Solar Cub. Caleb drove, Leif navigated, and I prayed. Travel through the Belt was always interesting, if confusing. Our first stop required a jump "up" from the plane of Outpost's rotation. When we'd moved three hundred thousand klicks (about three fourths of the distance from Terra to Luna) in that direction we hit the brakes, slowing to dead in space relative to Outpost orbit. We had to slow our orbital velocity to allow our first stop to catch up with us. That meant rotating ninety degrees and kicking into reverse, again relative to Outpost orbit. All this was accomplished with Sol burning brightly on our left, and it was a relatively easy navigation drill.

The second stop was a rock over twenty-seven degrees out of the ecliptic with an eccentricity of .25563 percent. Landing on it required a corkscrew maneuver that made me glad we had Archy and a three-man engineering team designing and redesigning inertial guidance systems for space compasses for Outpost's Transportation Department. Our third stop we had to catch up to. That required one long, grinding boost on a direct trajectory.

Because all these objects were moving closer to or away from each other as they pursued their own individual orbits, as did Outpost, the return trip would require an entirely new set of coordinates and a revised flight plan. When you add a third dimension to travel you complicate the act of getting from Point A to Point B by a factor of ten. Million. Ask any pilot. At least in the Belt we had little to worry about in the way of traffic, although we did need a collision alarm for those as-yet uncharted planetismals too small to eyeball.

We took a geodomepak with us and camped out on 6789Cribbage and 6012Black Rock. At Mom and Pop's on Cribbage, Mom, a tiny little fireplug of a woman with a long gray braid, and Pop, a muscular young man with skin burnt brown from working EVA, had more kids crawling around their dome home

than we did on Outpost. "This is Betty," Pop said, displaying
the latest addition proudly. Mom, who didn't look half as tired
as I thought she should, said, "Isn't she sweet?"

"Adorable," Caleb said, and hauled out the twins.

Mom clicked her tongue and said, "My, haven't they
grown!"

They had. They were taller, they could walk and talk, and
they still looked exactly alike, café au lait skin, blue eyes, black
curls. I looked at them through Mom's and Pop's admiring
eyes and my heart turned over. I cleared my throat. "What's
this I hear about a chromium strike, Pop?"

A group of miners stamped in from the warehouse. "Hey,
Mom, where's our order?"

"Just a minute, Bob."

"We're in kind of a hurry, Mom, 9722Lodestar's at Cribbage
perigee in an hour and a half, we've got to load for the jump
now if we're going to make it."

"Well, I got visitors, boys, so you get on in there and help
yourselves. The price list's on the clipboard next to the scale
and the assaying kit's hanging on the wall at the back of the
room. Add up your bill on the ten-key and weigh out your
payment and leave it by the lock."

"Okay, Mom, thanks."

"Now, Star, let me pour you out a little refreshment. This
batch of hootchinoo's not half bad." She bustled back to her
kitchen and lifted the lid from a fifty-liter drum and stirred
the contents with a broom handle. I thought about going over
and taking a closer look but my courage failed me. I sat where
I was, watching wisps of fog float up from the dry ice packed
around the drum.

"Hey, Pop." Another miner came in from the warehouse
with a small bulging bag. "Take a look at this."

Pop opened the bag and pulled out a fistful of loose ore.
He ambled to the back of the room and pulled out a jeweler's
loupe. The miner came up behind him. "So, whaddya think?
Is it worth the effort?"

Pop pulled off the loupe and dropped the rocks back in the
bag. He handed the bag to the miner and said, "Come on, Jim,
give me a little credit."

"That's just what I was going to ask you for."

"Funny, very funny. That's nickel from Jolly Jack Tarr's
claim on 9872Fortymile; it was played out months ago. Now

get outa here, and don't come back until you've got something worth trading."

The miner stood where he was, twisting the top of the bag in his hands. Pop shook his head and swore disgustedly. "All right, take a year's supplies out of store. Leave your marker."

"Thanks, Pop. I owe you big time."

"Bet your ass you do. See you, Jim."

"So long, Pop."

Mom gave the barrel a last vigorous stir and produced a ladle, with which she filled four large mugs. She put drinking spouts on the mugs, the mugs on a tray, and the tray into the oven. She nuked them for sixty seconds, and handed the ominously smoking mugs around.

I held mine out at arm's length, my elbow locked. "Gee, thanks, Mom. You shouldn't have."

"Damn straight I shouldn't have, a liter of Mom's hootchinoo retails for an ounce of fifty-grade U-235. Drink up, girl, drink up, it'll do for what ails you."

Or for what didn't. "I'm sure glad I'm still a child," Leif muttered to Caleb. My eyes met my husband's and I knew we were both remembering the recycler in the back of that bar in Piazzi City, but Mom was looking at us so expectantly that I couldn't bring myself to refuse. I took a deep breath and held it, closed my eyes, and drank.

Now I know what the old Roman emperor felt like when somebody poured molten gold down his throat. My teeth dissolved. My nose hairs melted. My toenails peeled back. I coughed and choked and wheezed and tears rolled down my cheeks and sweat broke out all over my body. When I could I gasped, "Jesus, Mom, what's in this stuff?"

"Well now, that would be telling, wouldn't it?" she said, winking at Caleb, whose dark skin had turned a deep winey red. Pop must have been used to it because he drank his down like it was only wood-grain alcohol and went back for a refill. "Molasses to start, sugar and dried fruit when I can get them, a little sourdough starter for fermenting. But you're not drinking, Star."

I closed my eyes and took another gulp, which now that I was braced for it was better than the first but not by much. Mom sipped and rolled the stuff around in her mouth like the sommelier for Ma Maison. She frowned. "Little light-handed with the garlic this time, wasn't I, Pop?"

"Oh, I don't know, Mom," Pop said, starting on his second mug. "Tastes just fine to me."

The miners on Black Rock were glad to see us but they were up to their ears in a new vein of molybdenum so we only stayed one night. We felt like tourists, and with Archy offlink it was like a vacation. Our seventh day out Jupiter was so close we could practically warm our hands by the Great Red Spot. The afternoon of our arrival on 7871No Return we suited up and went outside to watch the jet streams and cloud forms roil around in the red giant's atmosphere, a billion stars providing a spangled backdrop. The beauty of it hurt me so I could hardly breathe.

The twins were less impressed. "Orange ball, Mommy."

"Yes, sweetheart."

"Big ball. Want to play with it. Want out."

"We'll go inside soon, Paddy," Leif said. "You can get out then."

"Leif play with me."

"Okay."

"Leif play with me, too!"

"Okay, Sean, I'll play with both of you."

"How did you know which was which?" Caleb said to Leif. "I can't tell them apart in person, let alone over a commlink."

"I don't know, Caleb. They sound different to me."

Caleb grunted.

"Look," I said. "See that? Ahead of the Red Spot. Which one is that?"

"Europa," Leif said.

"Io," Caleb said.

"Oh," I said. "I thought maybe Ganymede." Jupiter has too many moons. We watched the red giant in silence for a few moments. I said dreamily, "You remember Sam Holbrook telling us that if you mix methane with ammonia and pass a spark through it, you can form organic matter?"

"So?" Leif said.

"So Jupiter's got methane and ammonia up the wazoo," Caleb told him. "Your mother figures if she studies on it long enough, she can grow clover for cow feed on the Great Red Spot."

"Oh." Leif paused, evidently thinking it over. "Isn't Jupiter's interior temperature something like ten thousand degrees absolute plus?"

"Uh-huh."

"That'd kill anything organic."

"A shame," Caleb said solemnly.

"Unfortunate," Leif said.

"It probably won't stop her."

"I doubt it."

"Maybe we should yank her air hoses now, save the human race from a fate worse than death."

"It might be the only merciful thing to do."

"Thank you, gentlemen, for your support and encouragement," I said. "Shall we go inside?"

The No Return miners were a rollicking bunch with an overwhelming sense of hospitality. They were led by one Hatsuko Matsumoro who, she explained engagingly, had woken up one morning in San Francisco and had been unable to face even one more day of her mother-in-law telling her how to cook rice. "I couldn't get it right," she told us, "it was always too sticky or not sticky enough." That particular morning, instead of washing out the rice cooker for another try, Hatsuko stuffed some clothes into a briefcase and lit out for Onizuka Spaceport on Hawaii. There, she signed on a TAVliner as a purser's assistant. By way of LEO Base and Copernicus on Luna, she worked her way to the Belt and to 7871No Return where, from what we could see, she was building up a sizable little nest egg from an obligingly productive streak of silver. "Every year or so I get a message from Hiroshi and the kids saying all is forgiven and to come on home," she confided. "The day he tells me that bitch has croaked, I'll do it, and not before."

At our appearance she and her four partners downed tools, broke out the homemade sake, and did everything up to and including handstands to entertain the twins. Leif, with his shy grin and his willingness to sit still for any tall tale no matter how outrageous, was an instant hit. We added to the festivities by spreading around some of the luxury items we were carrying in the Cub's freight compartment. I was afraid for a moment Hatsuko was going to have an orgasm when she spotted the coffee. It was four days before we were allowed to go on our way, and at that only if we promised to stop off again on our way back.

The *Conestoga* was less than six hours travel time from No Return. Up close it looked pretty much as I remembered seeing it at Copernicus Base, a smooth, slender ship a third the size of an Express, with a closed bow and a spheroidal pressure plate that made it look like the bulb of a lily. It toiled not, neither did it spin, it simply floated dead in space, next to a rock about three kilometers in diameter. I didn't see the *Tallship* anywhere.

Inside the *Conestoga* was the standard Space Service Industries ship's interior design, functional and utilitarian with the bare minimum of creature comforts. On a cylindrical ship the decks are usually divided into pie-shaped compartments around a central circular passageway; the *Conestoga* was no exception. Oddly, there was no color separation of floor and ceiling to give the Terran-bred zerogee traveler a sense of orientation. Everything was white, not eggshell or cream but a glaring, flat white, top, bottom, and sides. Each room was lit indirectly with a monotonous white glow. It felt like the inside of a jar of mayonnaise.

The second odd thing was the smell. There wasn't one.

Belt communities were distinguished by location, by size of rock, by amount and quality of population, by kind and quality of ore mined, but most of all by smell. It was said you could sit down solarwind of 7310Achorn and *see* the smell of burning hair headed your way. 9203Heaven smelled like sour milk, 9204Hell like old, unrefrigerated green olives, and not the gin-soaked kind, either. You forgot your own smell in time, which made visits to other communities a real strain on the olfactory nerves, until you got used to their odor. Then you returned to your own rock and had to become accustomed to your own aroma all over again. Outpost, with required daily showers (Section III, Paragraph 1, Expedition Articles) and an air purification system second to none this side of Terranova, smelled better than the inside of a pressure suit. Further than that I was not prepared to go.

There was no smell aboard the *Conestoga*. None.

We were met at the lock by one man alone, a courteous gentleman with chocolate skin, a mane of white hair, and a calm demeanor that reminded me of Mother. "Ms. Svensdotter, of course," he murmured as I was about to introduce myself.

"Have we met, sir?"

He smiled a gentle smile. "No, but you are not unknown in the Belt. And is this your daughter?"

"No—"

"Yes," Caleb said. "Yes, Star. I've got Sean today. Star has Paddy, sir."

"I knew that," I said.

"And this is?" He smiled at Leif.

"My name is Leif, sir," the boy said.

"How do you do, Leif." The man looked from Leif's face to mine without comment.

We clambered out of our pressure suits. In the *Conestoga*'s zero gravity the twins would have floated away, but after all the off station journeying we had done with them we were prepared with tow ropes and tethered a toddler each to our belts.

The gentleman chucked them under the chin and exchanged greetings. "Natural conception, of course."

Caleb and I exchanged a questioning glance. "Er, yes."

He shook his head. "Amazing."

Leif opened his mouth. Caleb caught his eye and gave a slight warning shake of his head. Leif closed his mouth. Caleb said, "And whom do we have the pleasure of addressing?"

"Oh, pardon me, I am Dr. Orlando Lavoliere. And you are?"

"This is Caleb O'Hara, sir," I said, "my security chief. Where are the rest of your shipmates, Doctor?"

He gestured vaguely. "About ship on their duties. May I offer you some refreshment?"

I said that would be lovely. Lavoliere led the way to a room off the lock, sparsely furnished with couches and tables bolted to the bulkheads, and sent down for coffee. When it came it was brought by a little girl perhaps ten years old, with olive skin, fair hair, and big brown eyes, towing a covered tray behind her. She seemed taller than her age would warrant but that might only be the effect zero gravity has on one's perception of size and shape. "This is my daughter Elaine," the doctor said.

Elaine clipped the tray to the table. She saw the twins and exclaimed with pleasure. She saw Leif and blushed. The four of them pulled themselves over to a corner.

"Sugar? Creamer?"

"Thank you."

Another little girl, the twin of the first except that she looked even longer and thinner, pulled herself into the room. "Father?"

"Yes, Eleanor?"

"Mother Eve says perhaps the visitors would care for some fresh-baked cookies?"

He gave a slight smile and a nod, and she swarmed into the room with a covered plate, regarding us with such a wide-eyed, unwavering stare that she missed the table clip entirely. The edge of the plate hit the edge of the table, the lid popped off and pale, round sugar cookies floated everywhere. The little girl's olive skin blushed a fiery red and I said quickly, "What fun—look at the twins snagging them out of the air!"

The little girl gave me a grateful glance and then turned to her father with a fearful one. He stared at her for a moment, his lips tight, and then waved his hand in a dismissive gesture. She went into the corner to play with the four other children. Leif was telling a story about Orion and Artemis.

"Either I'm seeing double or you have twins yourself, Doctor," Caleb said.

"Um, yes," Lavoliere said. "What's this I hear about the Terranova Expedition going into the world building business?"

I looked at Caleb. "I'm constantly amazed at how quickly news travels downarm."

"When you consider most of it is disseminated over nothing larger than pressure suit transmitters," Lavoliere agreed, smiling.

We chatted for a while about the homemades, and then the conversation shifted toward new arrivals at Ceres, which gave me an opening. "We didn't see the *Tallship* as we came up, Doctor."

Out of the corner of one eye I saw Eleanor and Elaine freeze with their hands stretched out flat. The twins, unabashed, beat on their palms with enthusiasm. Leif wasn't looking our way but he was very still. "The *Tallship*?" Lavoliere said blankly.

I exchanged a glance with Caleb. "Yes. You left Copernicus together in 2007, didn't you?"

"Er, yes, of course we did." He hesitated, and then smiled his sudden, charming smile. His smile reminded me of someone, but for the life of me I couldn't remember who. "We—well, the fact of the matter is we came to a parting of the ways once we achieved Belt orbit. We haven't kept in touch. Yes, Eugenia?" This time there was a definite edge to his voice. "Another daughter," he explained to us apologetically. "I'm afraid you're the—er—star attraction today, if you'll forgive the expression. The E Series always has been a little forward," he added, and then looked as if he wished he hadn't.

"Truly, Father," the little girl, a carbon copy of her sisters—triplets? I thought—said earnestly, "I did not mean to be rude. Mother Juliet asks if the visitors will be staying the night."

Lavoliere hesitated for a moment with an odd look in his eyes, and I must say I was a bit miffed. We'd come hundreds of thousands of kilometers to pay a social call. I wasn't exactly expecting a parade, but anywhere else on the Belt the red carpet would have been rolled out and most likely the captain of the ship or the principal miner of the rock would have surrendered their beds to the visitors. Lavoliere stirred and said with forced heartiness, "Certainly they will be staying, daughter. Instruct Mother Juliet."

"We appreciate your hospitality, Doctor," Caleb interjected smoothly, "but we are already late in returning to Outpost, and the people on No Return are expecting us back this evening."

I stared at him, my mouth half open. I never play poker, either. His eyes as they met mine were totally expressionless, but the nape of my neck prickled. Caleb's instincts were never at fault. "Uh, yes, certainly. Caleb is entirely right, Dr. Lavoliere. We don't want my people sending up flares."

"No, we most certainly do not." I turned my head and caught a genuine but fleeting flash of alarm in Lavoliere's eyes. Now that we had said firmly that we could not stay he was eager to convince us to do just that, and in the resulting protestations of undying hospitality found ourselves invited to stay for lunch at least. We could see he regretted it as soon as the words were out but in the Belt you don't give the boot to people who have traveled twenty-three degrees and fourteen minutes specifically to make your acquaintance. And we had his daughters on our side. Leif was turning into some kind of Casanova, even if he wouldn't give the time of day to a female who couldn't handle a laser torch in vacuum. Caleb signified his assent with a tiny nod, and I accepted for the five of us.

"Eleanor, tell Mother Juliet there will be guests for lunch. Say, in a half hour?"

"Yes, Father," the little girl said. She smiled shyly at us and pulled herself up the companionway.

We all sipped new cups of scalding coffee substitute through straws with varying degrees of relief. I was dying to take

Caleb aside but until we were safely out of range of possible *Conestoga* pickups private conversation would have to wait. I set my cup down in its clip. "What brought you to the Belt, Doctor? What is your special interest?"

"The usual. The choice to live life as we choose, and not as it is chosen for us." He smiled. He smiled almost as much as Maile, but it wasn't her he reminded me of. "I'm sure the originator of Ellfive independence can comprehend a desire for freedom."

I grimaced. "So you've heard that story, too, have you?"

"We've been reading what issues of the *Outposter* come our way," he said.

"Allow me to send you a complimentary subscription via optishot, sir."

"Why, thank you, my dear. I admit that it is pleasant to receive news of Terra occasionally." We chatted about the One-Day Revolution and the new Terranovan government and the Librarians, and agreed pessimistically on the possibility of Terra coalescing behind a single world government. Then it was time for lunch. "Perhaps the children would care to eat in the nursery?" Lavoliere suggested.

I hesitated. "May we take them there?"

There was an almost imperceptible pause and then he inclined his head. We followed him downship to a large airy room that seemed to be overflowing with babies, all taking full advantage of the zerogee. They all seemed to be too thin, and they were each tethered to a section of bulkhead that included a fastened-down sleepsack. None of the babies were sleeping. The din was tremendous. "David," Lavoliere said, and had to raise his voice. "David!"

A boy a few years younger than Leif popped up from the middle of a bundle of babies. "Father?"

"Can you manage two more for an hour?"

"Always room for two more babies, Father," the little boy said. He had red hair and freckles and intelligent green eyes. He too seemed overly tall for his age.

I said in an undertone, "Is he old enough to care for all these children? He's little more than a child himself."

Lavoliere shrugged and said, "We trust him with our own." I looked at Caleb, and he nodded slightly. When in Rome. Still, I was uneasy.

"I could stay with them," Leif offered.

Eleanor's and Elaine's faces fell, and I hid a grin. "It's okay. Come on."

We adjourned to their galley, which had a long narrow table bolted down the center with benches along each side and footslings beneath every place. Elaine, Eleanor, and Eugenia jostled for a place next to Leif, calling for a reprimand from Mother Eve, who with her olive skin and pale hair looked like their older sister. Mother Juliet sat between her four daughters Jane, Juliana, Joanna, and Joyce. All five of them were slender with fair skin, long dark hair, and blue eyes. In between appetizer and entree, David and what appeared to be his twin brother arrived.

"So who's minding the babies?" I inquired.

The two boys and the man exchanged an uncomfortable glance. "I'm not David, I'm Daniel," one boy said, "and this is my brother Douglas." They took their seats. "David is still in the nursery."

"Oh," I said. Suddenly I was very, very glad Caleb had refused the hospitality of the *Conestoga* for the night.

Lavoliere said uneasily, "It is confusing, isn't it? Sometimes I can't tell them apart myself."

"Pardon me, Doctor," Caleb said, "but I see only you and the two—er—mothers here. Are there no other adults aboard ship?"

"Good heavens yes," Lavoliere said.

Caleb waited. Lavoliere did not elaborate. Caleb smiled a friendly smile and said, "Where are they?"

Lavoliere gestured vaguely with a fork. "About ship on their duties, or asleep, or EVA on 7877Tomorrow. On a ship this size we must work and eat in shifts to accommodate our crew, you see."

I have never enjoyed freefall and neither has my esophagus. I was trying not to gag over a second bite of tofu gyoza spicy enough to clear out an elephant's nasal passages when I said, "What precisely are you working at?"

There was a sudden silence around the table. I swallowed, painfully, and looked up to see everyone else looking away. "A topic for after lunch," Lavoliere said smoothly.

After lunch the children and the two mothers, who had said nothing much beyond "pass the salt, please" and "thank you," cleared the table and disappeared up and down various passageways, leaving us alone with Lavoliere and more coffee.

"So, Doctor," I said, "what precisely are you doing here? You seem to be dead in space, and that rock you're moored to doesn't look as if you've gone in for mining in a big way."

"No, only a little silicon and some nickel, enough to trade for such supplies as we need."

"Then what?"

Lavoliere seemed to be thinking it over. Appearing to come to a decision, he met my eyes squarely. "Have you ever heard of the BioScience Engineering Committee?"

"I believe I have," I said calmly. "Ah, on Terra, the American Alliance formed such a committee in 1995 to explore research ethics into genetic engineering. The committee was to form patent laws, mediate disputes between academia and industry, and act as a clearing house of information to prevent overlapping studies and mistakes in research."

He smiled. "It was formed in 1994, actually, but for the rest your memory is remarkably good." He paused.

"I remember there were all kinds of experts on that committee, genetic engineers, lawyers, philosophers, entrepreneurs. I think they even included a few members of the general public."

"Again correct."

"Were you a member of that committee, Doctor?"

"I was, for a time. I resigned."

"Why? Seemed pretty worthwhile. They were even working on giving it the legal clout to make private industry and the Alliance government toe the line in . . ." My voice trailed away as I saw his expression.

Lavoliere inhaled and held it for a moment. "The specialty of our community is genetic research. What with the restrictions applied on Terra to splicing and cloning, we wanted room for intellectual freedom and experimentation. My own specialty is botany, and I think I've come up with something that will be of special interest to you in your current endeavor. You're calling them homemade homes, are you not?"

"Until a better name presents itself."

Lavoliere smiled again, his gentle quality tempered this time with indulgence, as if I were a child to be congratulated on the acquisition of a new toy. "We've adapted a plant to grow in vacuum. It's a genetically engineered weed with warm sap and a layer of superinsulating fur. We—"

"A comet creeper," I said.

"You've read Freeman Dyson, then?"

"Some," I admitted. "Have you been keeping abreast of the work the UER is doing in orbit around Venus?"

"I wasn't aware of the existence of a Venusian probe."

"It's not a probe, it's a manned station."

"Really."

"Yes, they're doing some very advanced work there in cause-and-effect atmosphere manufacturing." I caught Caleb's ironic eye and added, "Or so my meteorologist informs me. I'm not all that up in atmospheric dynamics. Any chance of taking a look at your work on Tomorrow?"

"Certainly. Would you like anything more to eat? No? Then, Elaine, you may return this tray to the galley." We detoured through the nursery to pick up the twins, who were fussing a bit. We pulled ourselves back down to the lock, suited up, and stepped out into space, Caleb and I crowding together to make room in the Cub for Lavoliere.

At close range Tomorrow looked like a bald coconut a hundred meters across. "We're hoping to create a cover of adequate thickness to produce enough oh-two to provide an atmosphere on the surface of the planetoid," he told us. We circled the surface a few times, noting several p-suited technicians working at what looked like mining pure and simple to me. None of them looked very busy. We thanked Lavoliere for the tour, extended an invitation to visit Outpost, and dropped him off outside the lock of the *Conestoga*.

As we were streaking away from the *Conestoga* Caleb said, "Intellectual freedom, comet creeper, my ass! They've been practicing gene splicing on each other! Those—those *litters* of children, all carbon copies of themselves!"

"The stuff of human life is very easily made," I said. "Lavoliere believes that the stuff of human life at its primary level is interchangeable with that of all other life."

"So?"

"So he thinks there is nothing wrong with gene manipulation for the betterment of the species as a whole."

"But we could engineer our own extinction. What was it the BioScience Engineering Committee said? That when we eliminate bad genes, we narrow our gene pool?"

"What about treatment of genetic disorders by altering genes in sperm and egg cells? Caleb, survival of the fittest and natural selection may no longer be the only factors influencing the evolution of human life. We have reached the point where we can control our evolution and change the world we live in without waiting for natural forces to operate."

"That sounds scary. And boring."

"What's boring about universal twenty-twenty vision? What's boring about eradicating dental caries? What's boring about eliminating Hudson's Disease in utero with genetic surgery?"

"What happens to subsequent generations?" Caleb responded. "And when we perfect these techniques, do potential parents then have a responsibility to turn out perfect children? I don't like it, Star. I don't like it at all."

"It's their business, Caleb."

"Where's the *Tallship*?" he asked bluntly.

"I don't know," I admitted, and sighed. "Caleb, like it or not, we came here for the same reasons Lavoliere did. Elbow room, freedom from government restrictions, unlimited raw materials and unlimited power with which to shape them. We came to make a future different from what we would have had on Terra or Luna. I want to build astrocondos. Lavoliere wants to build better genes. He's not interfering with my astrocondos. We're not going to interfere with his genes."

"Star, it's just—those kids, all those kids."

"They look well fed," I said, but I knew what he meant. "None of them looked unhappy or abused."

"But who asked them what they wanted?"

"Time enough to find that out when they grow up. For now they are their parents' responsibility. Not ours."

Into the dead silence one of the twins said, "Daddy?"

"What, honey?"

"Arm owie, Daddy."

It wasn't until we were ashore on No Return, where the inmates were surprised but pleased to see us again so soon, that we discovered a patch of shamskin on each twin's right forearm, covering identical square patches of missing skin.

I tackled Caleb heading for the lock.

This was the man they called the Iceman behind my back, the man whose voice I'd heard raised to a shout once in my life, and that was before we were married. He wasn't shouting now, he was moving, fast, toward the airlock and his pressure suit and the Cub, to hoist sail back to the *Conestoga* and eviscerate Lavoliere. I knew it as surely as I knew my own name.

I kicked off from one wall and drove my shoulder into the backs of his knees. We went tumbling end over end before fetching up against a bulkhead. Before we could bounce off I hooked one foot beneath a sling, wrapped my arms and other leg around Caleb's body, and hung on. Every time he managed to free a hand or a foot I grabbed for it and wrapped myself around him again.

I'm not much of a fighter; when it comes right down to it I'm big enough to scare away the faint of heart, and I hire people who take care of whoever I can't talk out of combat. Caleb was one of the people I'd hired. Under normal circumstances, he could have slapped me like a gnat and that would have been the end of it. This time his opponent had the advantage, because however angry he was I knew he wouldn't hurt me. All I had to do was wait him out. The low gee helped. Leif watched, white-faced, from the companionway as Hatsuko and her fellow miners placed bets behind him.

"Caleb!" I said urgently. "Caleb, take it easy. Ssshhh, take it easy, take it easy, love. It's all right, take it easy. It's all right now, it's all right." I clung to him grimly and kept talking, saying I didn't know what. After a long time, I felt his big body slow against mine.

"Caleb?" Leif's voice came from behind me.

Caleb didn't answer.

"Caleb?" Leif said. "I grew in a test tube. Do you hate me, too?"

The thin, shaky question hung in the air. Caleb stilled. I waited, unmoving. Finally Caleb relaxed, the breath sighing out of him. "I'm all right, Star."

"Sure?"

"Get off me."

I pulled myself away. I was shaking and I felt bruised all over. Caleb's face was taut with a tenuous control. I looked at him once and then looked away. "I'm going back to the *Conestoga*."

"I'm coming, too."

"No," I said without turning. "No, you are not. I'll deal with this alone."

"Star!"

"No! I can talk to Lavoliere as head of Outpost. You can barely talk at all. I'll handle it." He opened his mouth and I looked him straight in the eye. "That is an order, Chief. Do I have to call up the station log to make it official?"

There was dead silence in the inner lock. Caleb's green eyes, usually as impassioned as glacier ice, burned with barely suppressed rage. We stared at each other for maybe a full minute. It felt more like an hour. Then he turned abruptly to snatch up the twins. He shouldered his way into the corridor and out of my sight. I swallowed, and said, "Hatsuko?"

She came into the inner lock, looking wary. "Star?"

"I need a copilot."

She relaxed a little, and nodded. "My pleasure."

"I'll go with you," Leif said.

I put one hand on his shoulder and said, "No way, boy. You got off the *Conestoga* once with a whole skin. Let's not try your luck."

He pushed his chin out. "Either I'm part of this family, or I'm not."

"It's not a question of whether you're a part of it—"

"Elizabeth was ten and she fought for Terranovan independence."

"That was a question of circumstance, not choice."

"Baloney. She blackmailed you into letting her go with you on that mass capsule and you caved in. Archy told me all about it." He met my eyes and said firmly, "You're the one who's always talking about responsibility, and everybody contributing. I've been driving a solarsled for Emaa since we got to the Belt, and Caleb's checked me out on small arms. Plus, I'm a Petri kid, and I've got a better handle on the way these people feel than you ever will." He surveyed my frustrated expression with open satisfaction, and added, "And this is family business. No offense," he said over his shoulder to Hatsuko.

"None taken," she replied. I glared at her and she looked back at me with big eyes and a wounded expression. I looked back at Leif. He was thirteen now, and tall for his age. Irrelevantly, I remembered reading in the p-suit maintenance log that he'd had his suit in for upgrading the week before we left. Upgrading and enlarging; the kid had broad shoulders. "All right, Leif, suit up."

I got Hatsuko to remove the PVA cables from No Return's two flivvers on our way out. We took them with us. I wasn't taking any chances with Caleb.

We boarded the *Conestoga* for the second time that day. Leif took charge the moment the lock cycled. He pulled himself into the passageway, and with a disconcerting dignity said, "Dr. Lavoliere? I believe you have something that belongs to my sister and brother. We'd like it back, please. Now."

Lavoliere did not waste our time or his by attempting to deny the obvious. Lavoliere was, indeed, charmingly and anxiously apologetic. He said an overeager biotech had overstepped his authority in acquiring the samples. He said the tech would be suitably disciplined. Leif said that as a Petri kid he quite understood, and Lavoliere said was Leif indeed a Petri child, and seemed to relax a bit. They chatted while we waited. Soon Elaine (or Eleanor or Eugenia) arrived and handed over a thin, flat lab box that contained the sections of the twins' skin, Lavoliere said. I accepted it with an involuntary shudder. "And I do hope this unfortunate incident will in no way affect any future relationship the *Conestoga* may have with Outpost."

I busied myself with the oh-two feeder inside my helmet.

One of the very first things on-the-job training in Terranova's school of command taught me was that Thou Shalt Not Allow Thyself The Indulgence Of Saying What Thou Really Thinkst. Or showing how you really feel, in the face of those who manifestly, diametrically oppose those feelings. Individual beliefs, personal ethics, ethnic pride, and national patriotism are all subordinate, firstly to the safety of the crew, and secondly to the successful completion of the mission. One-point-eight astronomical units from Terranova, it was even more imperative to work the brakes on my instincts. It would be all too easy to start shoving my way through the crowd, instead of leading it.

I believe in freedom of choice. I believe everyone has the right to life, liberty, and the pursuit of happiness—old words, I know, some would say old-fashioned, but I don't. I believe implicitly in the right of a like-minded people to determine their own destiny, so long as that determination is not achieved at the expense or to the danger of others. It is a rule I try very hard to live by. It defines what I am.

I saw Leif looking at me with barely concealed apprehension. I forced myself to remember that the twins were alive and mostly well. When I was sure I could speak with some degree of composure I raised my eyes. I caught the gaze of the leader of the *Conestoga*, and I said, slowly and distinctly, so there could be no possibility of any misunderstanding, "Lavoliere. Do not attempt to trade with Outpost. Avoid contact with my people. I'll make that easy for you. The moment I return home, I am going to place the *Conestoga*, its crew, and 7877Tomorrow under my personal interdiction. If you or any member of your adult crew attempts to board our station, I will burn you down in the lock, myself."

His dark eyes widened and his face paled. Beside me I felt Leif freeze in place, hardly breathing.

"However. Should your children, once they are grown, wish to escape this, this *Brave New World* hatchery of yours, I will be only too glad to welcome them on board with open arms. I trust I have made myself clear."

We left. Halfway to No Return Leif said suddenly, "That's why you never touch me."

Lost in a pleasant contemplation of several different methods of bringing about Lavoliere's slow and painful death, I did not respond at once to that remote voice over my commlink. Leif said more loudly, "That is why you never touch me."

"What?"

"You think I'm like them. You never touch me." He was silent for a moment. "You think I was hatched, too."

"What?"

"It's true, Star. You never wanted me anyway."

I was still raw from the confrontation with Lavoliere or I never would have said what I did then. "Wanted you? I never knew you existed. You're something Mother dreamed up out of a frustrated grandmother complex."

There was a brief, weighty silence. Of course I couldn't see his face. Then his young voice said hardily, "I know."

I swallowed. My mouth was dry, and I sipped a few mouthfuls of water from the nozzle inside my helmet. "I'm sorry, Leif. That wasn't very tactful."

"It's true." Still that hard little voice.

I hesitated. "Yes. But so what? You're here now. You're a fact, you're a person, you're working your way up to being needed, to contributing. And you've always been wanted by someone, you've always had Mother. The situation between you and those children is completely different—they're experiments in gene splicing, for God's sake, not children created out of love and need. As for my never paying any attention to you, that's nonsense. You can't say I don't listen to you, and monitor your progress, and—"

"Oh, yes," he interrupted me. "I'm fed, housed, educated, disciplined. You'd do the same for any member of your crew."

Stung, I said, "It was your hands I pulled on when the twins were born."

"Only because Caleb wasn't there."

"He's my husband."

"And I'm your son. Whether you like it or not, whether you want it or not, I'm your son." He paused and then said, "Would you do that for me? Would you confront Lavoliere like that for me?" I opened my mouth to blister him and he said, "Of course you would. You'd do it for any member of your crew."

We left it like that, for about nine thousand kilometers, the longest and quietest nine thousand kilometers I'd ever traveled. Leif broke the silence as we were approaching No Return. "You know what that business back on the *Conestoga* was, Star?"

"I don't know, Leif, what was that?"

"That was an admission of failure of their reason for being here. They need a bigger gene pool, so they figured they could swipe a few cells for new DNA starters, and the twins would never miss them."

I thought about it. He was probably right. I put it to Caleb when we arrived back at Hatsuko's. Sometimes I think I have no tact. The thought of dozens of little Seans and Paddys running around the *Conestoga* busily cloning themselves into the millennium did not sit well with Caleb. He still wasn't speaking to me when we left the next morning at 0600 sharp over Hatsuko's protests; I wanted sanity and I wanted it now and I wanted it in my own home with my own people around me. We burned the sails off that Cub and caught our first glimpse of Outpost thirty-seven hours out of No Return. The squarish circle, revolving about a domed hub and cluttered with geodomes, reflectors, radiators, PVAs and antennae, the original lines of the two Express ships all but obscured, was developing a little halo from escaping atmosphere through lock ventings. It looked impossibly dear to me. In pressure suits in a Solar Cub traveling through black vacuum it is impossible to tell what a fellow passenger is thinking, but I imagined I felt an infinitesimal relaxation of the motionless figure sitting pharaohlike in front of me. I nudged the chin switch inside my helmet. Archy came through in his usual exuberant fashion. "Hey, Star! We missed you! How was the trip?"

"Interesting, Archy. Everything okay here while we were gone?"

Archy sounded a trifle disgusted. "You always think the place is going to fall apart without you, Star. Of course we're all right. We did have a little excitement yesterday, though."

When I docked the Cub outside the main lock I saw what Archy meant. Across the main personnel airlock, broken in half by the crack of the lock but still readable, someone had stuck a rectangular yellow sign with black block printing on the hull of the station. Inside I shucked out of my p-suit, vented it into the station's waste disposal system, and turned it over to a maintenance tech for its five-hundred-hour check. I ducked into the nearest shower. Paddy didn't want to get out of the soothing, heated spray, and pouted a little when I insisted. Charlie was waiting in the dressing room with clean jumpsuits for five. Caleb and Sean merged from the next stall and Leif from a third. We dressed quickly and followed Charlie into the galley, where the scent of fresh coffee drove me into a feeding frenzy. The hospitality of the Belters was legendary and overwhelming, but none of them had fresh coffee, or F-B-E equipment for fresh milk, either. It was Simon's turn for Alexei that day and the twins pounced on both of them with squeals of glee. I stretched and began to relax for the first time in what felt like months. "So, pray tell, who is this Save the Rock League slapping signs on our hull?"

Charlie smiled and Simon, emerging from a tangle of arms and legs, snorted. "It's a branch of the Divine Brethren, as near as we can figure."

"So what are we now? The first stop on the Hallelujah Trail?"

"It's better than that. They've decided Outpost is endangering the livelihood of the average Belter by hogging all the good rocks. Not to mention the prospects of future generations of miners. A few of them seem to be worried that there won't be enough asteroids left to show our great-great-great-grandchildren the Belt in its natural state."

"That's ridiculous," I said. "Why, our farthest probes haven't progressed much more than twenty degrees downarm in either direction. We haven't even catalogued half of the Sutter Cluster, much less mined it. Nobody's even looked at the Carmack yet."

"Who said it wasn't ridiculous?" Simon grinned. "The League wanted to picket the station, I understand, but Brother Moses made the mistake of convening the meeting in Piazzi Square. He couldn't get enough miners with transport out of the bars in time to form a line. So he came over himself, with half a dozen loyal followers, in an R-bus that looked like it came out on the *Sagdeyev*. They would have run into the station if Crip hadn't gone EVA to take the controls. He brought them back down safely to Ceres."

"How'd that sign get there if Crip waved them off?"

"Crip put it there for them."

"He what?"

Charlie giggled, and Simon shrugged. "Well, they'd made such an effort, come a hell of a long way for nothing. He thought it was the least he could do. They went away happy."

"Crip says he even got a blessing from Brother Moses," Charlie added.

I stared at Simon. He stared back blandly.

I suppose I was tired. I started to laugh, and once I started I couldn't stop. Paddy, bouncing up and down on my chest, thought it was all in fun and laughed, too. The next thing I knew the tears were running down my face and I could see Charlie visibly downshifting into doctor.

Gasping, I said, "It's all right. I'm all right. Wait a minute." I fought for control. "I'm sorry," I said, wiping the last of the moisture from my face. "I'm afraid it was a—somewhat tiring trip." I dredged up a smile. "I must be getting too old for two weeks in zerogee."

Caleb, speaking for the first time, said, "Charlie, the twins need a checkup. Let's go down to the dispensary."

"What? Why, what's wrong?"

"Let's go down to the dispensary," he repeated. He tucked Sean beneath one arm and held the other out for Paddy without meeting my eyes. I gave her to him and he left the galley, Charlie right behind them.

"What's wrong with him?" Simon said, looking after the four of them.

"Everything," I said wearily.

"That sounds fairly comprehensive. Tell Brother Simon all about it."

So I told him about Lavoliere and the *Conestoga*, about Mother Juliet and Mother Eve, about Elaine and Eleanor and

Eugenia, about David and Daniel and Douglas, about the barren, creeperless plain of 7877Tomorrow.

There was a brief silence while Simon assimilated all this. Finally he said, "And Caleb is angry that you insisted on dealing with Lavoliere."

And for pulling rank on him, I thought, but said only, "Yes."

Simon said shrewdly, "What did he really want? For you to blow them out of the sky?"

"He didn't say so."

Simon said firmly, "If you'd let Caleb go back breathing fire, he would have gotten himself killed."

"I thought so. He didn't."

"And if you let him go back now, you'll be advocating an act of deep-space piracy that would run contrary to everything Terranova and this expedition represents. The miners would shun us."

"Agreed."

Simon sat back, frowning. "I don't like the idea of turning that *Conestoga* Frankenstein loose on unborn generations any more than you do, and Caleb is right to be furious about what happened to the twins, but you handled it the only way you could."

I hadn't realized until that moment how much in need of approval I'd been. I was afraid for a moment I was going to start crying again. "Thanks. Thanks, Simon."

"No charge. We'll put the word out, make the *Conestoga* off limits for the crew." I looked toward the hatch that led toward the dispensary, and Simon said soberly, "Caleb will get over it, Star."

I stretched again, and groaned. I was sore from so many days of isometrics in little or no gravity. Any minute now Charlie would be harassing me to take a turn on a treadmill. "I don't care what they manage to grow on that rock of theirs, Simon, we don't trade with them."

"Understood and agreed, Star," he said. "But there'll be plenty who will. Think of it, a slice of immortality for a slice of skin. That will sound like an attractive proposition to a lot of Belters." He paused, and added, "I wonder what the *Conestoga* is going to be offering in trade?"

"So far all they're growing is kids." The silence stretched out between us, becoming heavier by the moment, and finally

I blurted, "Don't, Simon. Don't say it. Don't even think it."

And then I remembered who Lavoliere reminded me of, with all that smooth charm and that disarming, infectious smile. He reminded me of Grays.

— 8 —

Buckaroos and Bluenoses

Day after day for more than a month the international parade of boats continued . . . They brought sundowners, shantymen, sodbusters and shellbacks, buckaroos and bluenoses, vaqueros and maquereaus, creoles, and metis, Gaels, Kanakas, Afrikaners, and Suvanese. They brought wife-beaters, lady-killers, cuckolded husbands, disbarred lawyers, dance-hall beauties, escaped convicts, remittance men, cardsharps, Hausfraus, Salvation Army lasses, ex-buffalo-hunters, scullions, surgeons, ecclesiastics, gun-fighters, sob sisters, soldiers of fortune, and Oxford dons.

—**Pierre Berton**

In the three years following our arrival in the Belt, SOS and T-LM Volksrockets arrived at irregular intervals, one approximately every three or four months. They docked in orbit around Ceres, into whose less than enthusiastic embrace they spilled payloads of prospective miners before loading payloads of refined ore and beating the solar winds back to Terra. Hundreds and eventually thousands of these prospective miners flooded into Piazzi City and bid fair to crowd out the original settlers. The old-timers did not take kindly to this influx, but they would have put up with it, grudgingly, if it hadn't been only the first minuscule trickle of an overwhelming deluge.

They came on the ugly and trustworthy one-shot BDR, the ugly and powerful Kenilworth space tug, the utilitarian Boeing VLOCs, in sleek new SSI Skywagons and aboard tired old Ford TriDrives. It was the most bizarre and diverse flotilla ever to set sail, on land or sea, in air or space, and unquestionably the most hazardous. Outfitters on Terra with little or no experience in space travel underwrote bands of prospectors and underestimated what it would take to feed them. They starved in transit and in some cases resorted to eating each other. One inventor long on imagination but short on practicality put a hundred paying passengers into cryogenic sleep and stacked them like cordwood in a DC-110 Spaceliner designed for traversing low earth orbit. Three of the one hundred survived the trip. Some ships made it halfway and had to turn back because of low food stores, overcrowded passenger accommodations, or outright mutiny. Poorly maintained pusher plates gave and entire ships were lost in a single puff of nuclear dust. Life-support systems failed and asphyxiated whole crews and left floating coffins drifting in space.

And still they came. One morning I woke up to the reported sighting of an old STS shuttle, limping into Ceres orbit with a solar drive hanging off the stern. It looked like one of Rube Goldberg's better ideas, and it leaked so much atmosphere that they were moving beneath a kind of cloud of dirty vapor. As soon as Perry Austin heard the news she commandeered a solarsled and paid a social call. "It's a shuttle, all right," she said when she came back, shaking her head. "The *Resolution*. I flew a mission aboard the *Resolution* twenty years ago. I thought they'd scrapped her for parts."

"Who's got her now?"

"A couple of The Seven's kids went into business together and bankrolled this trip. They've been twelve months on the road here. The crew are all ex-Express and BDR." She shook her head again. "I can't think why they haven't killed each other before now. Do you know how much space there isn't on the middeck of an STS shuttle?"

"What are they doing here?"

"What's anybody doing here? They're looking for a way to make a quick buck. With thirty thousand kilograms of payload they may just do it, too. If they can hold her together long enough to get back." She shook her head again. "Her interior bulkhead is covered with graphplex fixative and gray tape and they're leaking so much oh-two they've got four AtPaks working twenty-four hours a day just so they can breathe without passing out." And she shook her head a third time. "I don't even want to know what their CO_2 count is."

Some of the new Belters were driven by the lust for gold or platinum or silicon, some by the lure of adventure, some by a quest for power. Others sought escape from nagging spouses, from collection agencies, some simply from the overall grayness of present-day life on Terra. A tenured professor of English at Harvard lost everything she had in the crash of '99 and was seeking a quick return so she could go back and lose it all in the next. One man was fleeing seven wives on Terra and an eighth on Terranova, where they take a tolerant view of such things, but mostly a ninth on Luna, where they do not. Another man, an actor primarily famous for having been plucked clean in two successive palimony suits, had thrown up his career and come to the Belt where, he said acidly, he could pay someone to shoot him if he fell in heat a third time. He bought out a silicon claim on Vesta, sank a shaft next to the producing vein for living quarters, and put in a connecting shaft between the two. Whenever he ran out of vodka he strolled next door and hacked off another piece of ore to trade for his next liter. So far as I know he's still there.

One woman went to work for Nora the day she arrived and proceeded to set an in-house record that stands today for volume of customers serviced per twenty-four-hour period. She returned to New York in two years' time to open an Art Vieux furniture store catering exclusively to the very rich. She later became the much-revered patroness of a born-again sculptor who specialized in swaddling the Venus de Milo and Michelangelo's *David* and suchlike in silk draperies.

They came with stardust in their eyes, what they owned on their backs, and the stub of a one-way ticket in their pockets. Maybe one in a hundred could tell a core driller from a leather punch. For some, the journey itself seemed to be the culmination of a dream—they were glad and proud to have made it that far, and they didn't really care if they ever saw so much as an ounce of salable ore. In a backhanded kind of way, these turned out to be the smartest and luckiest of the bunch. Other optimistic new Belters upon arrival immediately staked out the nearest rock, oblivious to or contemptuous of any previous claim beacons, and where it may be said they were almost immediately buried. A third kind, according to Caleb, were the kind of people who are always caught out with forks when it's raining soup—no food, no shelter, no money, no plans, only a dream of wealth and plenty, which all too often turned into a nightmare of starvation and death.

The smart ones sized up the situation quickly and went to work for SOS or T-LM or Robber Joe in the casino or Nora at Maggie's. A few with a little capital tried their hands at grubstaking their less fortunate fellows, always for a percentage, and did fairly well. Half a dozen off the *Columbus* went partners and formed a taxi service that folded in less than a year. "No market and no product," one of them explained laconically.

"No travelers and no place to go," translated his friend.

"Your biggest problem is you were too early," I told them. "Try again in ten years. There'll be a fortune to be made in cheap, scheduled transportation out here." I bought out their rolling stock and turned it over to Claire, and for the umpteenth time wished I had brought somebody from Boeing along. We could have used a trained, experienced transportation engineer.

Of all the oddities I saw come into the Belt, what we came to call the Love Boat was surely the strangest. It arrived in July of 2011, an old Express to her shame and embarrassment converted into a luxury liner. She settled into a parking orbit for a long stay. Aboard were Lady Margaret and Lady Melisande Arundel, two very short, very plump dames of the UER state of Britain, who claimed kinship with Charles III. With them, they brought two Great Danes, both snappishly spacesick, a parrot and several canaries that were more than snappish, a pair of hens but no rooster, a Pioneer octophonic sound system that at full volume caused the hull panels to vibrate ominously, AtPaks enough to supply the needs of half a dozen Express ships, a library larger than Outpost's, two maids, a housekeeper, a butler, and twin braces of Purdy shotguns with a thousand rounds of ammunition. What big game they thought they might find to hunt in the Belt, I had no idea. I knew they must have had a pilot and crew but I never saw them. Probably not allowed abovestairs.

As chiefs respectively of Outpost and Piazzi City, Takemotu and I were invited to a state dinner. We were offered pâté de foie gras, salmon en croute, and fresh broccoli with hollandaise sauce, with raspberry mousse for dessert, all served on Royal Dalton china. It was all washed down by Tattinger's 1999 served in Waterford crystal stemware. The Lismore pattern, Lady Margaret was pleased to inform me. I was too busy trying to calculate the lift cost of one Continental Champagne Glass to pay much attention.

Our hostesses were attired in flowing silk gowns with long trains that provided the unwary with unexpected glimpses of acres of dimpled flesh. All too often said trains wrapped one or the other lady about the neck. When this happened, a little man stationed unobtrusively next to the hatch kicked off from his handhold, disentangled his mistress, and returned to his post. After dinner, the ladies strapped themselves into hammocks, stretched out languid arms for the French horn and oboe hanging conveniently nearby, and tootled out a mournful duet. They finally dozed off in mid-toot, leaving Takemotu and me to make friends with the Great Danes and effect an escape. At least I found out Takemotu could laugh. "Aw hell, Star," he said, wiping tears away, "come on down to Piazzi City. The beer's on me."

Well, there hadn't been much reason of late for me to rush home after the day was done, so I followed him down on my sled. We went into the OK Corral, the same bar Caleb and I had followed Mother into the first time we set foot on Ceres. We had to dodge a Salvation Army band thumping out "Bringing in the Sheaves" to get in, but on the inside the bar itself hadn't changed, except that the bartender was advertising home brew. I cocked an eyebrow at Takemotu.

He nodded. "The real McCoy. Somebody imported a Volksrocket full of malt and hops and bought into the Corral with it. They—"

A waiter bustled up. "What can I get you folks?"

He was short and stocky, with sharp eyes and a way of cocking his head that made him look like an inquisitive sparrow. "Wait a minute," I said, "I know you." He looked at me, his eyebrows raised. "Sure," I said, "a while back you were trying to sell me a cigar out in the square there."

He smoothed his mustache that for some reason made him look even more birdlike. "Ah yes, those cigars. Well now, that was some time ago."

"Couple years," I agreed. "Did you manage to sell them all?"

"Yes indeed, and by the end of that business day."

"I hope at a fair profit."

His expression turned cautious. "Fair, yes, I would say fair."

"And with that profit you bought yourself in here?"

He looked shocked. "Good gracious, no indeed. With the profit on the cigars I invested in city lots here in Piazzi City."

"I see. How long did it take you to turn them over?"

He smoothed his mustache. "Oh, I think about six months. Yes, not longer than six months. Once I laid my hands on a sonic excavator, it didn't take long to dig out the lots."

"I see. And the profit on the lots? Was it fair, too?"

"I'd say it was fair," he agreed, still cautiously.

"And with them you bought into the Corral."

"No, with the profit on the lots I invested in a shipment of yeast."

"Yeast? For—" I gestured toward the bar.

He looked shocked again. "Good heavens no. Fleischmann's Active Dry Yeast. For the baking of bread."

"So you sold the yeast."

"Certainly not. I used the yeast to bake bread, and sold the bread."

"At a fair profit," I told Takemotu, who was grinning next to me.

"Fair," agreed the cigar salesman, "and with the profit on the bread, I bought into the OK Corral. Two beers? Certainly. Oh—and, ma'am?" he said, turning back for a moment. "About those cigars?"

"Yes?"

"There *is* no smoking in the OK Corral. I'm sure you understand. The atmospheres of space habitats do tend to be somewhat volatile, do they not?"

The beer, when it came, was crisp, clean, and cold, and tasted like beer. One-point-eight AUs out, I couldn't ask for more. "Kevin," I said after another pull, "I don't get it."

"What don't you get?"

"How you could lock out the miners that time when they were sick."

He drained his glass and waved his hand for another round. He belched and said, "Hell, Star, that wasn't me, that was Lowell."

"Lowell?"

"Yeah. Lowell was mayor at the time." He grinned at me. "I was too busy running Takemotu's Sublight Communications Services to be running anything else."

"So what happened to him? Lowell."

The cigar salesman brought the next round through the increasingly crowded room with the air of Pheidipedes making it into Athens from Marathon against a stiff wind and a rocky road. When he left again, Takemotu swallowed half his glass in one gulp and said, "Ask Maggie Lu."

I didn't, of course. I didn't have to.

After their premiere performance, the Ladies Margaret and Melisande extended their welcome to all and sundry in true Belter fashion. Most Belters deemed the endurance of an after-dinner concert a small price to pay for the kind of dinner they had seen in the Belt only in their dreams. The flow of guests in and out of the Love Boat's airlock was unceasing. Six months later, the Love Boat departed in as stately a fashion as it had arrived, Lady Margaret and Lady Melisande informing me that they had run dangerously low on truffles and trout. There was deep and sincere mourning Beltwide on the day of their departure.

Some of the new Belters, it quickly became evident, were on the run from various law enforcement agencies on Terra, Luna, and/or Terranova. Caleb's rent-a-cop service was booming, so much so that Piazzi City itself had put out feelers. Caleb, Lodge, and Perry came to me one day. Perry said, "We got an idea," and told me what it was.

"We thought we'd call it the Star Guard," Lodge said.

Caleb said nothing, and left with the others when I gave them the go ahead.

Using Lodge's Patrolmen and Caleb's security people as a core group, Lodge and Perry began interviewing. Caleb established a rigorous physical that would have a washout rate of eighty-seven percent. With the remaining thirteen percent, they went to work.

The thirteen percent of applicants that survived the training were a breed apart from the rest of us ordinary mortals. We'd thought to recruit some of the vets who had fought in the Eur-asian War, but most of them decided they'd seen enough close order drill to last the rest of their lives and passed. "And recruit-ing from the Patrol is out, other than the detachment that came with us," I said. Lodge looked at me sideways but didn't object.

Even within those limits we never lacked for applicants. Surely it was coincidence that so many of our first recruits turned out to be the younger children of wealthy Terran families, seeking after the adventure that was nonexistent on civilized Terra in the vast, rowdy reaches of the Belt. In our first graduating class we had a Hawaiian alii, the second son of a Norwegian duke, the great-niece of a former chief justice of the Supreme Court of the American Alliance, the fifth daughter of the king of Thailand, one Kennedy, and two Rothschilds.

"Noblesse oblige?" Mother suggested.

"What about those triplets from Orem, Utah?" I said.

"Not exactly royalty, are they?" she agreed.

"Well, they do come from a long line of heavy-duty mechanics."

None of the recruits had seen any military service and most were fresh out of school. There wasn't a size requirement but I noticed that nine of the first ten cadets topped a hundred and eighty centimeters. Six of them massed over eighty kays. It was a pain for the maintenance technicians who had to modify their pressure suits, but it paid off in presence. Just the emergence of one of those young behemoths from an airlock, made twice their actual size by a red-badged pressure suit, was enough to quell riot in the most ardent soul.

Sitting in on one of the training sessions I noticed that one of the exercises involved the mock boarding and taking of a manned ship in space. "Planning a hijack?" I asked Caleb.

"A man can dream," he said coolly.

"Downstairs they'd call that piracy."

"We're not downstairs," he replied in that same cool voice.

"Men," Charlie said comfortingly and comprehensively when I stamped down to the dispensary.

"Mommy mad at Daddy again?" Sean asked intelligently, and then abandoned me to play jacks with Alexei. In half a gee the ball took longer coming down and their fat little toddler fingers had time to scoop up more jacks. Sean, not eight weeks older than Alexei, had only recently learned not to eat the jacks after he picked them up and was intent on imparting this useful piece of knowledge to his younger cousin. Sean already had a well-developed sense of family responsibility. Like his father.

"Where's Paddy? With Caleb?"

"Where else?"

"How's that working out?"

"The twins are going on four and you want to know how our child-care arrangements are working out?"

Charlie, bless her heart, didn't go all Hippocratic and evoke the "state of the mission depending on the state of the commander's mind" on me. Instead she said gently, "I want to know how it has been working out lately."

I fidgeted. "We're not fighting in front of the kids, if that's what you mean. Caleb is usually awake before I am. He snags whatever twin comes to hand and is gone by the time I get up."

"And in the evenings?"

I didn't answer.

Charlie persisted in that doctorly voice of hers that manages to be gentle and implacable at the same time. "I haven't seen you together as a family very often during the last month. You haven't been playing basketball lately, or picnicking in Central Park, or double-teaming Archy on Zork X in the game room. Caleb used to cook gourmet for you once or twice a week. I can't remember the last time I saw the four of you in the galley at the same time."

"What is this, a survey? May I remind you that Mother is supposed to be the sociologist in this family?"

She raised her eyebrows and waited.

I tried very hard not to sound defensive. "We've all been pretty busy."

Charlie said inexorably, "Busy with Outpost at the expense of your family?"

I remained stubbornly silent. She gave a tiny sigh. "Are either of you showing any special preference in which child you take for the day?"

"How? We can't tell them apart yet without changing their diapers." I reflected. "And they don't wear diapers anymore."

She smiled broadly. "You must be the only parents I know who are looking forward to adolescence." I grunted. "How do the twins take to being separated twelve hours each day?"

"They haven't complained. Why?"

She shrugged. "I've always been curious about twins. This is the first chance I've had to study their development up close. How do they communicate? Anything special?"

"They're almost four, of course they're talking," I said slowly. "Sometimes Paddy will hand a toy to Sean before he asks for it. Sometimes he'll finish a sentence she started." I paused. "Once Caleb took a bad fall in a training session with one of the Guards. It knocked him out. He had Paddy with him that day. I was on 4Vesta with Sean, doing a deal with Valhalla Lode over some industrial diamonds we needed for drill bits. The next thing I knew, Sean was absolutely insisting that we get back to Outpost, that Daddy and Paddy needed us. He wouldn't take no for an answer." I shrugged. "The usual."

"You consider that kind of behavior usual?"

I gave my sister a level look. "Nothing about children has struck me as unusual since Elizabeth signed hello to me from her crib at seven months."

I think I wanted to hurt her into shutting up, but she surprised me with a half smile. "I remember." There was a short silence. "It's every person's fantasy, you know."

"What is?"

"Having a twin. The perfect companion. The ultimate confidant. A soul mate. We're all looking for it, or something close to it. We all pray we'll find it."

My chest hurt. I took a deep breath, held it, and let it out slowly. "I thought I had."

She toyed with the aseptiwand in front of her and said softly, unconsciously echoing her husband's words, "He'll get over it, Star. There's not a problem in the world that can't be solved by two people sleeping in the same bed every night."

Yes, I thought, Caleb's got his side of the bed, and I've got mine. "It's just—"

"What?"

I said slowly, thinking my way through it, "Charlie, any man I marry—"

"Yes?"

"He has to be for *me*. He has to put me first, put my job before his, before his feelings. He has to put my goals first. If he doesn't help me in going after them, then he has to at least stay out of my way while I do. I come at a high price. I can't help it. It's what I do. It's what I *am*."

I'd put it badly, but she understood. "And you're thinking that Caleb's not exactly typecast as your basic follower."

"I thought it was going to be okay," I said miserably. "I thought they were both working, the marriage and the job. Now—now, I just don't know."

She sighed, and repeated, "He'll get over it, Star. Wait and see."

Like I had a choice.

• • •

They really did call it the Star Guard. "Oh, please," I said. "It's not you," Perry said, "it's euphonious."

"And accurate," Lodge added. "Guards are hired. Cops are sworn in."

"Oh."

When the Star Guard took over security on Ceres, Caleb decreed that no prospector could leave the rock without a year's supply of food and oh-two. At the main locks of both Piazzi City and Outpost, he instituted another rule: Every vehicle had to carry a serial number prominently displayed on the hull and registered with the Guard, as well as an automatic transmitter that broadcast that serial number at twenty-four-hour intervals when the vehicle was in motion. Each outbound vehicle had to file a flight plan including the crew roster and their next of kin with the nearest Guard checkpoint. If the ship, sled, buggy, flivver, or whatever they were driving didn't check in on schedule, the Guard would trigger its emergency locator beacon, another requirement for registering with the Guard, and go looking for it. If found alive and in trouble, the survivors would be billed for rescue. If found alive and well, they'd be billed the same for forgetting to check in. If found dead, the crew would be decently cremated and the vehicle and equipment towed back to Ceres for auction, the proceeds to go into a fund opened at the First Terranova National Bank, from which eventually the value of the equipment could be recovered with interest by the crew's heirs. In the meantime, that fund plus billings paid the Guard's salary, and would steadily recoup the original outlay Outpost had made on the Guard's behalf.

They contributed an imposing appearance. Caleb and Lodge trained them as close to physical and mental perfection as it was possible to come, Perry Austin provided a living legend to follow, and the first ten Star Guards lost no time in making their own reputation. In Piazzi City they never interfered with the casinos, drugstores, saloons, or whorehouses springing up around Paradise Alley, but anyone found and convicted of cheating or robbery was turned over to Lodge, given a speedy and public trial, and, if convicted, a blue ticket to Terra on the first available ship.

When the Patrol fanned out into the Belt, their task increased literally by geometric proportions.

The first scoutships of the Department of Space's Surveying and Mapping Division divided the Belt into 360 degrees, which was easy for them to say. The prime meridian of this arbitrary longitudinal carving up ran through Ceres. The orbit of Mars, more or less the inner shore of the Belt, is approximately 1.4 billion kilometers in circumference. Jupiter, the Belt's outer shore, has an orbital circumference of almost five billion kilometers. This means, without even leaving the plane of planetary rotation, that one degree of Belt can be equal to anything between 4 million to 13.4 million kilometers.

But of course one must leave the plane of rotation, for many asteroids are inclined to that plane, some to the tune of forty and more degrees. 944Hidalgo travels forty-three degrees out of the plane, and at aphelion approaches the orbit of Saturn to boot, which brings up the problem of elliptical orbits that I refuse to go into. To make the game even more fun, there are the Hirayama families, groups of rocks traveling together in similar orbits that may be the remnants of gigantic collisions among asteroids. Then there are the Kirkwood gaps, caused by Jupiter's immense gravitational field, the eccentricity of the Apollo asteroids, and the Trojan asteroids, traveling fore and aft of Jupiter and on which the first big uranium strike had been made.

Faced with these statistics I said, "You know what we need?"

"A faster solarsled," Perry replied laconically.

"I knew we should have brought along just one transportation engineer!"

"And Bob Shackleton his own solarsled," Lodge grumbled.

"He take off on yours?"

"For only the two hundredth time."

Of course the main body of the Belt is more compact than what I have just described, considerably inside the orbit of Jupiter and outside the orbit of Mars, and the average velocity of asteroids relative to each other is only five kilometers. But the rarest ore with the highest grade had a distressing habit of being discovered inconveniently distant, out of plane and sideways to Outpost. After a while the Guard measured each new strike and every new registry for Guard service by how long it would take to get there.

Ten, twenty, thirty plus degrees downarm, millions of klicks from headquarters, more often than not completely cut off from

Outpost and their officers, the Star Guard was all the law there was. Sometimes individual Guards were obliged to assume the roles of judge, jury, and executioner at one and the same time. They helped mining partnerships gone sour divide their outfits, adjudicated disputes over mining claims, and acted as executors to the estates of miners who died.

No quarrel was too small or too large to arbitrate. When 6423Emmie Lou declared war on 5291No Moss over a missing kilo of Outpost Kona Premium, it was tiny Star Guard Bhumibol Dila who stepped in to mediate before a fifth life was lost. When strife erupted between two claims on 2Pallas over a missing shaker table, it was Star Guard Kleng Qvist who found the table under a disguising layer of paint and forced its return. He then fined the thieves a hundred times what the table was worth, not so much for the theft, he informed them, as for the time the altercation had taken away from his regular patrol. When two miners on 4Vesta decided to split the sheets and then couldn't decide how to divide up one AtPak, Star Guard John Smith took it outside and threw it into orbit, with the heartily expressed approval of neighboring claims.

When the baro of the Manouches on 7683Gypsy accused the baro of the Frinkulescheti on 8102Rom of raping his daughter, produced half a dozen witnesses and pictures of his battered child as irrefutable proof, and was ready to launch a war of retribution and genocide, it was Star Guards John, James, and Joseph Smith who stepped in and proved the whole thing was nothing but a setup for extortion between Gypsy vitsas who had been bitter enemies since before Columbus sailed. The three Guards managed to achieve a workable truce where no gold changed hands, voluntarily or otherwise. "Well, not until after we left, anyway," Joseph said later. "With the Romany, gadje never really know what's going on."

"What the hell's a gadje?" a mystified Charlie wanted to know.

"Anyone who isn't Romany," he replied.

"Oh."

When 7011Lucky Strike was ready to tranship a load of processed plutonium, it was Star Guards Caleb O'Hara, Perry Austin, Sandy O'Connor, and Kelolo Kamehameha who escorted the ore and the ore's twelve very nervous, very trigger-happy quarrymen from refinery to Terra-bound Volksrocket, across eighteen degrees of black, lonely, and for the most part uncharted Belt, through two ambushes, three equipment failures, one life-support malfunction, and a mutiny. Every kilogram of ore made it in to Ceres and so did eleven of the miners, although two of them were a little battered. The ore was later valued by the Terra-Luna Mines assayer at Piazzi City at a little over five hundred million Alliance dollars. At the time, O'Connor and Kamehameha were pulling down something in the neighborhood of five thousand Alliance dollars a month. Perry, as usual, took out her biggest bonus in accrued mythology.

Most of the Star Guards were no more than kids of twenty-five or younger, but I never saw one of them take sides in a fight, or reveal to one miner the location of another's claim, or overstep the lines of his or her authority in any way. The biggest problem they had to face was what happened as a result of cabin fever, a combination of lethargy, boredom, and scurvy (a result of the Belter's typical three-B diet, beans, bacon, and bread) that could result in the breaking of lifetime friendships, the onset of madness, and frequently death, often self-inflicted. The Star Guard contributed a humane conscience to a frontier whose first settlers only too often were devoid of morality or scruple.

How did it happen? Well, you could say Caleb and his crew had made an inspired selection of personnel and had devised a excellent course of training. You could say these kids were aware that they were building a legend and for pride's sake lived up to it. You could say that since most of them came from money in the first place they weren't likely to be seduced from their sworn duty by that particular temptation, at least.

You could say all those things, and all of them would be true, and none of them would be true. The fact remained that after the first year the Star Guards seldom had to raise their voices to ensure compliance, almost never had to give an order twice, and only rarely had to recharge the ammopaks on their sonic rifles. Four years after our arrival, the Belt boasted a constabulary force that in a moment of weakness Lodge admitted was superior in execution of duty even to the Space Patrol.

"Of course, the Patrol has an entire world and a planetary satellite with a couple of dozen settlements and four space habitats to monitor," she added hastily, as if she expected her uncle's ghost to roar in outrage at such heresy.

"Of course," I agreed, poker-faced.

"With billions of people to answer for."

"Indeed," Perry said without expression.

"And entire nations to answer to."

Caleb almost smiled.

Whitney Burkette and Claire Bankhead, with Simon poking his nose in occasionally, were developing a "Little Bang" explosive designed to meet all my specifications, "and brush your teeth with besides," as Simon put it.

"We call it pahoehoe," Claire reported.

"Pa-what?"

"It was Maile's idea. It's what they call a ropy, fast-moving kind of lava on the Big Island, she says. Sort of melts down everything that gets in its way. It fits."

"How soon before we can test it?"

Whitney lifted one eyebrow ever so slightly and tilted his head back so he could look down his nose at me. "These things really must not be rushed, Star."

"How soon?"

Whitney looked disapprovingly at me for another moment before condescending to reply. "We may conceivably be ready to test a model, say, possibly in six months time. Perhaps."

The design program was moving ahead more rapidly. For a population of ten thousand people, Roger was estimating six hundred thousand square meters of arable land, along with water, soil, and nitrates in proportion, and a whole bunch of sunshine. For those worlds—everyone was calling them worlds by now—which would want light industry, it would be carried on within the habitat. Heavy industry would make use of zero gravity at the world's poles, and the sphere must be plumbed with power and connecting corridors accordingly.

Forty-five degrees up from the "equator" of our sphere, gravity on the inner surface would be reduced to seventy percent of onegee, and we would not build homes any higher—Charlie decreed that once the settlers determined their physiological tolerance, they could build higher if they wished. "After all, they can do whatever they want after they move in," she said.

"And their last check clears," Archy added.

Simon's design for "The First New World" called for a shallow river to circumnavigate the sphere, and that meant beaches and swimming holes. Windows for feeding solar rays into the habitat would be placed at both axis. With complete solar shielding, venting the heat of ten thousand people would be essential, and Whitney and Archy designed axial passageways fifty meters in diameter through which heat would disperse through external radiators. Coincidentally these same passages would provide access to vacuum and transportation.

"What about the test model?" Simon said one morning.

"What about it?" I replied. I was playing jacks with Paddy, and losing.

"We wanted something small and flashy," he said. "An aquarium that Frank changed into a mini-ocean by sending us those damn salmon."

"So?"

"So," he said, sitting down at the galley table and rolling out a blueprint. "Look. We've got a hundred-meter sphere, see?"

I gave the drawing a cursory glance, and slid the pigs in the pen three at a time. "Nice. I like the world inside a world concept. I take it the zookeepers will be working inside the interior sphere."

"That's the idea, but the stresses involved with putting spin on that much water, keeping the interior sphere stable, and providing complete access for the maintenance technicians have got us stumped. One axial passageway's not going to cut it."

"Hmmm." Four pigs in the pen. The ball bounced off the back of my hand and Paddy giggled. I sighed and pushed the ball and jacks over to her. She was on round the world already. I watched her tiny hands for a moment, and then I snatched a jack out of her reach.

She was indignant. "Mommy! You're cheating!"

I held the jack out to Simon. "If one passageway won't do it—"

His eyes narrowed as he looked from my face to the jack. He took it gingerly between a thumb and one finger and set it between us on the table. I reached out and gave it a spin, and it twirled around on point for a few seconds before coming to rest on two arms. "One, two, three, four, five, six," he muttered. "Four at right angles on the equator, two axial if you start counting from the center, we could run the creek substitutes in spirals up the outside of them and seed from the top." He was roughing it in on the blueprint. "Access hatches at all levels and that way we can get at the king crab on the outer rim—"

"King crab?" I said. "What king crab?"

"Umm," he said absently, rolling up the blueprint and getting to his feet. "Frank sent us some eggs." He went away, muttering to himself. Paddy rescued her jack, completed round the world, and went on to sheep over the fence.

The sphere for those of us without gills would rotate once every thirty-one seconds, providing onegee for everyone in their homes along the tropical degree latitudes. When at work, people would be moving in and out of various degrees of gravity, but Charlie worked up a chart and ruled that the one-gee at home should maintain muscle tone and strength without special exercise.

"By the way," Simon said one day. "Who's going to run these microcosms of humanity once they're finished?"

I stared at him. "We're looking at one hundred percent owner occupancy here, Simon. Who do you think?"

He said smugly, "Who's going to teach them how?"

So I put Archy to work designing a short course in World Maintenance and Repair. Mother fretted over the slanting of the planned curriculum toward the physical sciences. "Well, Mother," I said, not nicely, "perhaps Ari will let you teach Ecology of a Closed Environment 101 in Latin."

She looked hard at me, looked hard at Caleb who, miracle of miracles, was actually conscious and in the same room as myself, and did not reply. But her silence was very eloquent.

When we had the final draft of specs for Homemade I, what we were looking at was a structural mass of three and a half million tons, which made everyone swallow hard and tiptoe around my projected date of model completion. The original designs called for the habitat to produce whatever Terra needed to buy; our design was to make the habitat self-supporting, even keeping in mind the reasonable supposition that like-minded worlds might group together to form a community. "We're supposing most of these worlds are going to want to remain in Terran-to-Belt orbit," Simon said one day.

"Yes."

"Chances are, when the technology becomes available, they'll be moving them wherever they want to go within those parameters."

"Yes."

"What kind of perturbation are all these new worlds going to have on Terran orbit? On Lunar orbit? On the orbits of Ceres and Ganymede?"

So there was something else to worry about. Sam put Leif to work on it.

Leif was up to it, young as he was. He was an open and uncomplicated person, sturdy and curious with no prejudices or preconceptions. He had an air of pleasing placidity that could trick you into believing he was just a little slow, something I had discovered on the *Conestoga* trip to be a kind of protective coloration to disguise his almost ferocious intelligence. I talked Mother into letting him attend the Sisters of St. Anne's boarding school as a day student. He went for a week and at its end flatly refused to return. "Sister Margaret is nice but I can learn more from Archy."

"Aren't you ever lonely for someone your own age to talk to?" I asked him.

He gave me a look I could only describe as indulgent. "Only one out of those twenty kids is even close to my age and she thinks I'm weird because I came out of a bottle."

"What?" I said indignantly. "What's her problem? The little bigot."

"Ah, Naomi's just dumb. All she wants to do is stay home and cook and read." He snorted. "She's afraid of pressure suits, mostly because she doesn't understand how they work, and when I tried to explain she looked at me and said, 'Would you like to share a bran muffin? I made them last night.' "

"Where is Naomi's home, dear?" Mother, who was listening, said.

"Um, Apple Pie, Emaa. Seventy-four twelve, I think."

Mother nodded to herself. Later she told me, "I've been on 7412Apple Pie, dear. Albert and Victoria Hanover. The last time I visited, they had stockpiled enough ore to finance a small revolution in Central America, and had produced enough children to man a football team. He never lifts a finger inside the lock, she never stirs a step outside it. The boys never so much as wash a fork, the girls never lift anything bigger than a cooking pot. All the children are named after Old Testament figures. I'm surprised they allowed Naomi to go to school at all, because after all, dear, you never know what kind of strange ideas children pick up in foreign parts." When

I laughed, Mother said apologetically, "But really, dear, they do seem very happy."

"Ours is not to reason why."

"No." Mother was silent for a little while. "How are things between you and Leif, Esther?"

"Fine." She looked at me. "Well, they are."

"He's trying so hard, dear."

"So am I," I said, trying not to sound defensive.

"He's barely fourteen. You're forty-four."

"Forty-five." I sighed. "Is this going to be one of those oblique Mother-type conversations where I have to chase down blind alleys and up switchbacks for what you really mean?"

"I don't know what you're talking about, Esther," Mother said. "I have to go, I'm meeting Crippen in the galley at five. Good night, dear."

So Leif reenrolled in the Archy Academy of Higher Education, and Mother continued to take him with her on her various excursions to collect interesting Belt settlements. The three of them seemed content with the arrangement, and I left them to it. By then we were up to our ears in, of all things, an advertising campaign.

We'd always had Helen on our side with the homemades, and Frank was coming along, but it took the two of them some time to convince the Terranova Assembly that Star Svensdotter had not gone completely off her rocker. I found out later Helen dropped some hints about retiring Terranova's American Alliance indebtedness within the next decade; I'm sure glad I didn't know about that at the time. In spite of my carefully maintained can-do attitude, the whole project was just too iffy to be tying Terranova's entire future to it. But then Helen's nature was not exactly conservative, and the selling of homemades to the Terranova Assembly was no exception.

Unbeknownst to me, innocently and industriously plugging away some 1.8 astronomical units outsystem, Helen had orchestrated a media blitz.

Advertising, according to the dictionary, is a message designed to promote a product, a service, or an idea.

"Which means convincing people to buy something they didn't know they needed," Simon said.

"For a price they know they can't afford," Charlie said.

On Terra, Luna, and Terranova, advertising had been regulated by the government and by Madison Avenue itself.

Restricted to the truth, it lost in power, but the truth had never stopped Helen before and there was no reason to think it would now. Generally speaking, advertising campaigns are designed around ads placed in newspapers, magazines, on the trivee, and through direct and/or mail solicitation. Novelty items such as calendars, matchbooks, key rings, and pens serve to keep the product in mind.

The first thing Helen did was come up with a logo, the outline of a cozy brick cottage with a circle drawn around it and a starburst overlay. Smoke curled from the chimney and there was the suggestion of a lawn. Then she took our half-jesting slogan, *A World of Your Own*, and translated it into a concrete idea. Remember those little glass balls filled with water and a little house or a little Santa Claus? You'd shake them and they'd fill with swirling snow. There's a long German name for them that translates as "snow globes" or "snow balls" or something like that. Well, Helen designed one of those, only this one was a graphplex ball with a tiny translucent city in the middle of a dark green forest molded around the inside. Turn it and lights went on in the city and a very blue miniature river circumnavigated the equator. It fit in the palm of one hand.

Helen had the Terranova machine shop make up a couple thousand of them and took one with her to an interview on *Time Marches On.*

"Helen gave an interview?" Charlie said incredulously.

"That's what it says." I reread the relevant passage in the document scrolling up the monitor screen just to be sure.

"Whose idea was that?"

I squinted at the printing. "It says here Helen volunteered."

Charlie wasn't convinced. "To give an interview to the *press?*"

"To a *Time* trivee newsie."

"And she volunteered?"

"Read it yourself."

Charlie took my seat and read the entire article from start to finish. She read it again a second time, just to be sure. When she finished, we sat together in awed silence. "She really believes in this project, Star," Charlie said finally. "We better make damn sure it works."

The little graphplex balls became the favorite toy of every child in Terran orbit under the age of seventy-five. In spite of a generous offer from Mattel, Helen refused to sell the patent on them or give them out except as a bonus to the information packet she sent in response to an inquiry about the homemade.

When the first campaign began to run out of steam, Helen designed another snow ball, larger than the last one, that could be taken apart and reassembled, with tiny houses and trees, and came up with a new slogan, *World Enough and Time*. When that pitch showed signs of slowing down, she hit the market with *That Untraveled World* and a lilliputian aquarium, and then *A World to Win* and another aquarium model, this one with live fish. And we had yet to perfect our pahoehoe, or complete our demonstrator, or come up with a solid, workable architectural design for new world housing.

"You know what we need?" I said suddenly.

"What, besides a *Bartlett's Familiar Quotations*?" Simon said grumpily.

"We need a Roberta McInerny. She could whip out a plan for a bridge over the river Styx." I made the suggestion to Helen in the weekly report. Three months later the chunky, no-nonsense figure of Roberta McInerny debarked from a T-LM container ship and sat down at once to design a blueprint for housing that provided forty-five square meters of living area per person, divided inside the sphere into three communities of thirty-five hundred people each. The homes we would build for those settlers who wanted a turnkey contract would include terraced apartments below latitude 45, with a private garden six by ten meters for each residence. An industrial community would have the option of running the villages in separate time zones eight hours apart to provide the world with a twenty-four-hour work force.

The rest of us barely had time to catch our breath when Roberta plunged into plans for what she called her playpen design, which included half a dozen luxury hotels, two convention centers, a casino, a dog track, and, the pièce de résistance, a horse racing track. She called this potential world's three villages Kentucky, Belmont, and Preakness, and named the world itself Triple Crown. The only thing Roberta actively disliked about spacing was the distance it put between her and her father's bluegrass breeding ranch in Kentucky.

And lo and behold, Helen's advertising campaigns began to generate interest, a lot of it. She started feeding us inquiries.

I set Mother and Leif to sifting through the applications. The first thing we did, as per Archy's astute suggestion, was to check out their credit rating. We weren't looking for a group able to pay cash on the barrel head for an entire new world. Except maybe for the New Mafia and a few trivee evangelists, we weren't expecting anyone to have that kind of cash in a lump sum ready to hand, so we tried to tailor a payment program to suit individual needs. A group of engineers and technicians with specialties in vacuum construction, say, would come out to the Belt in advance and work on their world and others to reduce their debt with man hours. A group specializing in medical research might pay off their balance due in zerogee pharmaceuticals, a group of farmers in produce, a computech world in zerogee-grown gallium arsenide crystals for superchips. We encouraged everyone to think in terms of paying their way, of identifying a market they could supply prior to the decision to resettle, and then adapting the design of their world around that specific industry. We weeded out a lot of wishful thinkers, in particular one man who said he was the head of the IRA in Northern Ireland. Upon further investigation, we found that he wasn't looking for himself but for the Protestant Northern Irish opposition.

"Certainly that would be one way of solving the Troubles once and for all," Whitney Burkette commented. "What did he suggest we use for a model? Dante's *Inferno*?"

The International Olympic Committee, tired every four years of trying to find a location for the Games that didn't mortally offend ten or twelve Terran nations and threaten a continent's worth of boycotts, inquired as to our snow- and ice-building capabilities. "Maybe they'd let you carry in the torch," Leif said, reading their letter over my shoulder. "It's always a local athlete who does it. Or maybe you could compete again."

"Zerogee events," I said.

"Huh?"

"They're flying in the Bats' Cave on Luna and off Wilbur and Orville in Terranova."

A cartoon cockroach appeared on the monitor in place of scrolled text and Leif said indignantly, "Hey!"

The cockroach shoved his derby to the back of his head and shifted his cigar from one side of his mouth to the other. Simon had decided Archy needed a visage and had taken unilateral action in the matter. "New events, you mean?"

— 9 —

Ghosts

The breezes have nothing to remember and everything
to promise. There walk, as yet, no ghosts of lovers in
Canadian lanes. . . . It is possible, at a pinch, to do
without gods. But one misses the dead.

—Rupert Brooke

It took us a long time to find the right rock for the first new
world. What with the prospective success of the aquarium after
the axial passageways were designed, and Helen hounding
us, and inquiries bombarding us nonstop from Terran orbit,
we didn't want to mess around with a time-consuming orbit
correction. Our first new world had to have a reasonably
circular and noneccentric path. The orbital velocity had to
be comparable to that of the station, or slow enough to be
correctable without vaporizing the entire rock. Its diameter,
to meet the one-hundred-meter finished design prerequisite,
had to be of the proper size and density. It had to have a high
concentration of the right elements and a low concentration
of the wrong ones, in particular anything that might after
prolonged exposure cause a human being to glow in the dark.
It had to be close enough to Outpost not to eat up too much

travel time for the construction crews to get there and back, but it had to be far enough away to be as yet unexploited by Belt prospectors.

With fifty-thousand-plus asteroids to choose from, even within those parameters, we did not think the search would take as long as it did. But it was over a year from the time we first put the plan in motion before Caleb, registering a new claim for the Star Guard patrol on the fringe of the No More Gold Cluster, eventually stumbled across the perfect rolling stone.

He almost missed it when he turned aside to arbitrate an arms race between 8687Boomerang and 8688Lone Star. It seemed the Aussies had stolen an optic cannon from the Texans, who had retaliated by stealing an ore dredge. Next, a core sampler disappeared from Boomerang, followed by a centrifuge separator from Lone Star, a case of nobelite from Boomerang, and a gravity feeder from Lone Star. The thefts continued. The Aussies went out and bought laser pistols. The Texans sprouted scatterguns. The Aussies mined a kilogram or so of plutonium and built a primitive but functional nuclear device, at which time one Aussie, Missy Gulagong, had the good sense to yell for help. Caleb took one look at the setup and yelled for help of his own. Guards Jo-jo Kennedy and Eloise Rothschild responded, and nobody died, or at least not of radiation poisoning.

Caleb went on to register the new claim with the Star Guard, and on the way home came across this rock. Claire sent Parvati Gandhi out to make an assay and it proved up to the tune of fourteen percent oxygen and enough nitrogen to keep the airtechs giggling for years, and no prior claim beacons.

Best of all, 12047Peggie Sue, so christened by Claire, was moving at a speed and trajectory that with a gentle nudge and three months time would bring it virtually alongside Outpost, a mere three million meters off our portside, between us and Sol.

In the meantime, Claire and her geologists were sorting through the mass of samples brought on board Outpost for classification and cataloguing, and then the Belt's miners got in on the act. We hadn't made any secret of our plans and they were more than happy to trot core samples and albedo snakes and seismic readings of every real and imagined rock they had ever stumbled across, for a small fee in the form of

Kona Premium or a picnic in Central Park or a tape out of the library. There were cylinders of core samples everywhere, lining the passageways, piled up in the galley, and the neatly tied paper rolls of snakes and spectroscopic readings threatened to choke Claire out of the office she maintained in her cabin. She took to sleeping in Perry's cabin, until Perry made it clear that three was a crowd.

"What?" I said. "Nobody tells me anything. Who?"

"One of the Smiths:"

"Which one?"

Claire scratched her head. "No one's been able to tell."

I thought about it, feeling more than a little awed. "With Perry, and given the Guard's rotation schedule, I suppose it could be all three."

She nodded sagely. "This is true."

The twins and Alexei were playing in the galley. One twin, I was pretty sure it was Paddy, had a construction paper feather stuck in a band round her forehead and was being staunchly if shakily withstood by the boys from behind a core sample stockade. She let out a bloodcurdling whoop the likes of which would have struck fear into the heart of Daniel Boone and made a running assault against the front of the stockade. It came crashing down and rolled in seven different directions across the galley, knocking down two agrotechs and one stray miner in search of ice cream. In the halfgee bodies and rock sections alike bounced pretty good.

Paddy made triumphant preparations to burn her prisoners at the stake, at which prospect the younger settler began to cry. "This is not the way the West was won, kids," I said, coming up behind them. I picked up Alexei and sat down with him on my lap. "Yuk. What on earth have you been into?"

The kid was covered with a black, sticky mess that at a distance I had at first mistaken for chocolate, the cacao beans having been harvested from Geodome Three the past month, with a subsequently very heavy run on milk, ice cream, cake, and cookies.

Close up, the stuff did not look like chocolate. It was too thin and greasy. I touched one finger to the mess and sniffed. "Phew!" I said. "I haven't smelled anything this bad since—" I stopped. I held my hand back up to my face and inhaled deeply. I looked very hard at the three of them. Sean and Paddy stared solemnly back, unafraid, but my nephew looked as if he might burst into tears again. "It's all right, sweetheart," I said, gathering him into my arms. More of the black slippery stuff came off on my hands. I touched my tongue to my palm. The taste was acrid, bitter.

I reached out one arm and snagged a twin. "Where did this stuff come from?"

The three of them froze and looked at me out of wide, innocent eyes. "What stuff?"

"Don't give me that," I said, giving the one twin I had a gentle shake. The other took a few prudent steps out of reach. "This black stuff you've got all over you. Where did you get into it? Have you been messing around in the fab shops again?"

Paddy said in a very small voice, "Promise you won't get mad?"

"I promise."

"Okay, Mommy," she said. Sean walked over to a table shoved against one wall, and disappeared beneath it. I heard some scrabbling around, and then he reappeared with several sections of a core sample fractured into several pieces. He brought them across the galley and deposited them on the floor at my feet with the unequivocal air of one taking no further responsibility.

I sat Alexei down on the bench beside me and picked one up. The exterior was smooth from the optic driller but the interior was rough and almost sandy. It oozed a viscous black substance that smelled distinctly of sulfur.

"My God," I said.

"What, Mommy? What's the matter?"

"Auntie mad," Alexei said in a gloomy voice.

"This is crude," I said, not quite believing it even after I'd said the words out loud.

"What is what?" Simon said, coming up behind me.

"This is crude," I said in a louder voice, and shoved one of my dirty palms under his nose.

He drew back, wrinkling his nose. "Gak! What is that stuff?"

"It's crude, you dimwit." He continued looking blank. "Crude oil, Simon. Dinosaur piss. Petroleum."

He stared from my smeared black palm to me and back again. "Do you mean—petrochemicals? Hydrocarbons?"

"Yes, that's what I mean!"

"Well, that's all very interesting, of course, but—"

"Simon, you ass, wake up! *The presence of hydrocarbons in this form presupposes the existence of organic life in the Belt!*"

The organic theory of petroleum and natural gas—on Terra—has it that the substance was formed from the remains of tiny marine plants and animals that died millions of years ago. Sedimentary rock subjected the remains to great pressure that over several million years broke the substance down into hydrocarbons, which formed pools to be tapped several million years after that by the human race, to be used for everything from making plastic to manufacturing smog. That was no tiger in your tank, that was Tyrannosaurus rex.

There was no, and had never been, organic life in the Belt. Therefore the stuff smearing all over the five of us and the galley could not possibly be crude oil. Simon had just finished explaining this to me when Parvati came in. "I could hear you yelling all the way down to Central Park," she said. "What's going on?" I seized on her with both filthy hands. "Hey! Watch what you're doing!"

"Parvati, you're a geologist, right?"

She looked at me suspiciously. "What is this, a trick question? You know I am."

"Look at this stuff."

"This stuff you've just rubbed all over my clean jumpsuit?"

"Yes. What do you think it is?"

Parvati, a slender, dark-haired woman with a round caste mark between strongly marked brows, rubbed the greasy mess between her fingers and sniffed at it distastefully.

"Well? Well?" I fairly danced around her in my impatience. "What do you think it is?"

She sniffed at her fingers again, and her heavy brows snapped together.

"Well?" I demanded.

She shook her head decisively. "It's just not possible, not here. Where's the sample it came from?"

Alexei and the twins displayed the broken pieces mutely. Parvati's mouth went down at the corners. She got down on her knees to manhandle the pieces of cylinder until she found a number chalked on a side. She switched on her communit. "Gandhi here, log Pliny."

"Pliny on."

"Access planetismal catalogue."

"Accessed," the flat monotone said. Geologists never seem to get the hang of personalizing their computer programs.

"Identification by sample number." Parvati read the chalked number off the side of the core sample.

"Working," Pliny said. "That number corresponds to planetismal numbered 7877, Outpost catalogue August 1, 2011, confirmed Star Guard catalogue confirmation and update September 5, 2011."

"Location."

"Working. Out of plane, eleven percent. Out of ecliptic, nine-point-four percent. On my mark, sixteen hundred hours, twenty-three minutes Outpost standard time, January 17, 2012, location of 7877 is twenty-one degrees, twelve minutes ex Outpost heading 095, accelerating four-point-zero-two-three-two kilometers per second relative to Outpost orbit. Mark. Do you wish to compute an approach?"

"Negative. Pliny log off," Parvati said, and looked over at me.

"7877?" I said, bouncing up and down on my toes. "Which one's that?"

"7877Tomorrow," she said. "The *Conestoga* claim."

"No," Caleb said. I think it was maybe the tenth time he had addressed me directly in the four and a half months since we'd come back from vacation.

"Caleb, I—"

"You are not going back there," he stated.

It is a sad but indisputable fact that whenever someone tells me flatly that I can't do something that I immediately decide I can and will. I could feel the slow burn coming on. "I was not aware," I stated, "that the activities of the Terranova Expedition leader came beneath the authority of the Terranova Expedition's security chief."

It is also a sad but indisputable fact that the madder I am, the more pompous I get.

"Besides," I added nastily, "it was my impression that you gave not one single, solitary damn who I saw or what I did or where I went—"

"I'm sorry," he said.

"—and if you think that after almost five months of the silent treatment you can—"

"Star, I've been about ten different kinds of a jerk."

"—just waltz in and tell me—"

"Maybe more."

"—what I can do and where I can go—what did you say?"

"I am an idiot," he said.

I did not disagree.

"I stopped being mad at you a long time ago."

"You couldn't prove it by me," I said, still smarting. I was ready for a fight. I didn't want to stop yelling. I wanted him to yell back at me. I wanted to throw things. I didn't care that half my section heads and all of my family were standing around watching. I wanted to draw blood, and not mine.

"Star," he said, and his voice went all black velvet and brown sugar on me. I stiffened my spine. "I am sorry, God I'm sorry. I am one sorry son of a bitch. I've never behaved like that before in my life." He swung away, running one hand through his hair. "I've never had kids before. It changes things. It changes everything."

He glanced at me, and away. "After I was done with wanting to blow the *Conestoga* out of the Belt, I took my mad out on you, because you were entirely right. We all came here to be able to mind our own business. They have their lives to live, and we have ours." He paused, and looked at me steadily out of those clear green eyes. "I made you pull rank on me. I've never behaved like that before in my life," he repeated. "It's taken me this long to forgive myself, not you."

When Caleb apologized, he did so comprehensively and with style. "Caleb—"

"You're still not going to the *Conestoga*," he said calmly.

"What! Why, you—"

"Alone."

There was a lot of silence in our cabin.

"Or tonight," he added, and reached behind me to open the door. He stood there, holding it open, and waited.

Crip stirred. "Natasha?" he said to Mother.

"Yes, dear," she said, and they left our cabin. Simon and Charlie followed with Alexei. Leif scooped up the twins. In fifteen seconds we were completely alone.

"Thank God," I said devoutly, a while later.

"What?"

"I was afraid I'd forgotten how."

Caleb's laughter was deep and reassuring.

At about midnight, he went down to the galley and made dinner: pork roast (out of the meat vats) basted with apple liqueur (brewed in a vacuum still), served with wild rice (grown in Geodome One) and sautéd mushrooms (Geodome Three), and chocolate mousse (from some of the newly harvested cacao beans) for dessert. The fat on the pork was crisp, the vegetables were tender without being mushy, and the mousse was to die for. I love to eat, but if I had to do the cooking, my idea of a tasty, nutritious meal, elegantly prepared and simply served, was a jar of peanut butter with the lid off and a spoon stuck in it. I fell in love with my husband all over again.

The next morning we met at the hub airlock. The team was composed of Caleb and I, Ursula Lodge and Kleng Qvist, Leif, who still insisted he was the only one who could talk to the *Conestoga* crew on their level, and Mother, our only and, I may add, self-proclaimed resident anthropologist. We didn't bother with a solarsled; this time we powered up the scout, with Crip piloting. Charlie saw us off. Before sealing the hatch she gave me one sharp, all-inclusive glance, transferred her beady little eyes to Caleb and ran a second survey, and allowed herself a knowing smirk. I pulled the hatch to, just missing her nose.

Crip matched hulls with the *Conestoga* and we latched on to their main airlock. It wouldn't access.

"Do you want me to force it?" Caleb asked.

We'd been hailing the *Conestoga* all the way there, with no result. They couldn't have missed the resounding clang when we locked on. We couldn't just go down and do what we wanted on Tomorrow; we'd be jumping their claim and violating the most sacrosanct canon of the Belt code. On the other hand, if I gave Caleb the go ahead to break their lock, we'd be violating the second most sacrosanct canon of the Belt code.

But this was just too important to walk away from, and whatever else he was, Lavoliere was a scientist. Once I explained, I was sure he would understand the urgency. I gave a reluctant nod. "Do it."

It took him about two minutes. The hatch gave and we swarmed inside. They were waiting for us. It wasn't coffee and cookies this time, or lunch. It wasn't a laser pistol or a sonic rifle designed to kill without piercing the hull, either. "What is that?" I said to Caleb out of the side of my mouth.

"AK-47," he replied the same way. "The Kalashnikov. Won the War of Independence in Vietnam. Semiautomatic model. Big clip."

"What's a clip?"

"Rounds. Bullets."

"Bullets?" My voice went up high and cracked. "How many?"

He squinted. "That one holds thirty."

"Oh." I swallowed. I had to ask.

What this meant to me was that the rifle, held none too steadily by an obviously terrified but equally determined Lavoliere, fired material projectiles. After the load went through me, chances were it would go through the hull, and *that* meant that if I didn't bleed to death, I'd be finished off in the explosive decompression immediately following. I suddenly found it very hard to breathe. "You shoot that thing in here, Lavoliere," I said, "you'll compromise the integrity of your seal. Put it down."

"Why should I?" Lavoliere said, his voice shaking as much as his hands. "You're going to kill us all anyway." The muzzle of the rifle jerked up and down and swung back and forth. That section of my chest toward which the muzzle of his weapon seemed to be pointing the most often felt very cold. Behind him what looked like the entire crew complement of the *Conestoga* was jammed into the passageways leading into the room, straining to watch us without putting themselves into the line of possible fire. He waved them back and hooked his toes more securely into footslings to steady his aim.

"Lavoliere," I said, trying to make myself sound calm and rational, not an easy thing to do when staring down the maw of a twentieth-century antique, "I give you my word. I have no intention of harming anyone aboard this ship or the ship itself, I just want—"

Lavoliere actually cocked the damn thing. Somebody yelled and I was almost knocked loose from my handhold. It was Ursula, who kicked off the hatch and caromed into Lavoliere. Something cracked. Someone screamed. Something cracked again. I heard an ominous hissing noise. I'd heard it before, and it scared me as much as it always did. "Pressure leak!" I shouted. "All hands, emergency stations!"

One of the Eves kicked her way into the room. Her eyes were wide and terrified but she swam and pulled and fought her way to the opposite bulkhead and a red locker I hadn't seen before. I caught on and went after her. I got there just as she popped the locker and pulled out the sealant kit. Bodies were jamming themselves back up the passageways in a frenzied rush and zerogee didn't stop them from hurting one another as they clawed themselves as far away as possible. All the better.

Then Eve and I pushed off for the center of the lock. She pulled out the flambeau. Her eyes still wide and fearful, she looked at me. I nodded. She ignited it. There was no fire, only a cloud of smoke, thick and bright yellow. I watched the smoke. It eddied around in the center of the room for a bit. Then it began to swirl, slowly at first, and then more rapidly. I followed it down to the hole in the bulkhead. It wasn't much, maybe three centimeters across, but it was whistling like the gypsy rover. I beckoned the Eve down and we had it patched in sixty seconds.

I looked up. The bright yellow cloud was slowing now, its remnants dispersing gently into corners. "Dammit, where's the other one?" I said. "He shot twice, he hit something. Where is it?" Something brushed against my cheek and I swiped at it impatiently. I looked at my glove. It was stained red.

Startled, I looked up. There were other globules, floating around me, intermingled with wisps of yellow fog.

"Can you imagine, Caleb," Lodge was saying, "arming yourself with a weapon that fires solid projectiles, in vacuum?" She'd finally managed to wrest the rifle out of Lavoliere's hands and was emptying the chamber. "Nuts. Plain, ordinary, everyday nuts."

There was a kind of a horrible gurgle, right behind me. She looked up, and all the color left her face.

I knew at once. I knew before I turned. I knew before I looked. I knew before I touched. I knew.

Caleb was directly behind me. He had removed his helmet when we entered, so I could clearly see the gaping wound in his throat, the deep red venous blood pumping slowly out of his cruelly torn dark skin.

He was looking at me, straight at me.

He spoke.

"Star—" he said.

"Love—" he said.

Then that horrible gurgling sound again.

He tried to smile. The blood bubbled out from between his lips, broke away to join the other precious droplets, drifting, floating, wandering about the room, away from him.

He seemed to reach out to me with his enormous gloved hands, gloves, like mine, stained red, stained with the vain effort of holding himself together, of clutching to consciousness, to being, to existence. To me.

And then he stopped smiling. His hands stopped reaching. And the life drained out of his green eyes.

Someone else tore Caleb's laser pistol out of its holster. Someone else kicked Lodge in the chest when she tried to get it back. Someone else paused momentarily when a blond, blue-eyed kid latched on to her arm with arms, legs, and teeth. Someone else shrugged the kid off, backhanding him across the face in the same movement. Someone else shook Mother off their back like an annoying mosquito, someone else elbowed Crip in the groin and left him doubled up, gray-faced and gasping. Someone else sighted down that long, long barrel, to line up the terrified face of the *Conestoga*'s leader in the twin sights. Someone else waited for him to break. Someone else waited for him to beg. Someone else waited for him to cry, and sob, and plead.

And then someone else squeezed the trigger. Someone else kept on squeezing that trigger, squeezing it and squeezing it and squeezing it and *squeezing* it, until long after the batpak ran out, until long after Lavoliere was nothing but a shapeless mass of charred material and crisping flesh.

Claire and her crew were on Tomorrow like flies on a dog. They quartered and subdivided and sectioned. They mapped every crack longer than a toothpick and they measured every crevice thicker than a dime. Parvati putted up in the thump truck and set off a series of seismic booms, recording the resulting sonic resonances on squares of limnofax she laid over Tomorrow's topographical map. And then they got out the Kepler-TT optic cannons. The samples came out of the surface in perfect tubes ten centimeters in diameter and ten meters in length. Parvati and every jackleg geologist Claire could conscript or commandeer went to work dissecting them.

It took every man, woman, and child Outpost could spare, working three weeks of twenty-five-hour days. At the end of that time Claire went into a huddle with her team and didn't come up for air for three more days, at which time she sent out for a geochemist and someone trained in time-lapse geophysical analysis.

The following Monday. D day. Claire had us assemble in the galley. Everyone came who could fit. Leif, his bruised and swollen face beginning to return to normal, kept close to Mother. He wouldn't look at me.

"Before y'all like to jump down my throat, it's oil all right," Claire said, or I thought that was what she said. Her accent was so thick that morning that it was difficult to understand her words. "Crude. Black gold. Raghead blood. Dinosaur piss. Call it what y'all want, it's oil. Anybody who says different don't got the sense to pour piss out a boot without directions printed on the heel. And yes, it's indigenous to 7877Tomorrow. That rock is about as thick with oil as Atlanta was carpetbaggers after the War."

Her brown eyes held a hard glitter and she had a set grin fixed to her mouth that looked part snarl. Her team was clustered behind her, tense with suppressed excitement. "What else?" I said, because there obviously was something else.

She drew herself up to her full height. "They should have called it Yesterday." We all looked puzzled, and she said, "7877Tomorrow. They should have called it 7877Yesterday. This stuff didn't grow there. It was put."

" 'It was put'? What does that mean, 'it was put'?"

Claire leaned forward with her hands flat on the table and said deliberately, "I am saying that 7877Tomorrow was once part of a larger celestial body whose inhabitants used refined petrochemical products in large quantities and stored them against that use."

We sat there like dummies, gaping at Claire.

She nodded. She appeared to be enjoying herself hugely. "It's an artificial reservoir," she said. And she added, "Or I should say, it was."

Mother gave a soft, queer little sigh. Charlie said flatly, "This is a joke, right, Claire?"

The last thing I'd thought we'd be needing in the Belt was a paleontologist, or an archaeologist.

Or an archaeoastronomist. We needed someone up in the study of the astronomy of ancient peoples. From minute traces of an organism that looked like a bald paramecium, Charlie and Claire dated our find, or the destruction of it, as being twenty-six hundred years old. Whatever petroleum-producing, petroleum-storing intelligence was present in Belt orbit at 600 B.C. must have gone up with one hell of a bang to leave nothing but barren rocks behind; it had to have been noticed on Terra. After some wild speculation and a lot of one-shot, dingdong hypothesizing, Sam Holbrook finally said it, tentatively, maybe even a little fearfully. "There used to be a planet here." When no one contradicted him, he got braver. "Maybe more than one? There are four major clusters of planetismals in the Belt. Perhaps there were four planets orbiting in the same plane."

The room was silent while that sank in, and then Simon gave voice to the other thought preeminent in our minds. "What happened to them?"

Sam looked over at him. "Do you really want to know?"

There are almost as many theories about the formation of the minor planets as there are minor planets. The original theory was in fact that a planet broke up, with four variations on the major theme: 1) that the breakup was caused by an explosion, origin unknown; 2) that a too-rapid rotation caused a deterioration and eventual disintegration; 3) that a tidal disruption did same; 4) that a collision between two planets did same.

Later, telescopic studies advanced the notion that the planetismals developed along with the rest of the solar system from a swirling nebula of gas and dust that gradually agglomerated into larger and larger bodies, and the single-planet breakup theory went out the window. "Some astronomers," Sam said, "speculate that Chiron was once an asteroid, others consider the Trojans to be lost satellites of Jupiter and not asteroids at all."

"Phobos and Deimos look like asteroids," someone said.

"And Io, Europa, Ganymede, and the rest of Jupiter's satellites could have been asteroids transformed into moons by Jupiter's gravitational pull," Sam said, nodding.

"This is all very interesting but it doesn't get us any forrader," Simon said. "What happened to whatever was *here*?"

"And how?"

"And why?" Mother said softly.

"For now, we'd better concentrate on what. Look, that big a bang this nearby must have registered with someone on

Terra. All I can remember about celestial explosions from my astronomy course is the Crab Nebula."

"Recorded by Tycho Brahe in 1572," Parvati said, nodding her head.

"Recorded by him in 1572, yes," Sam said, "it exploded in 1054. Brahe was one of the first astronomers with the guts to put down in writing what was really happening overhead."

"The Crab Nebula was visible in broad daylight, wasn't it?"

He nodded again.

"We need something like that, only about two thousand years previous," Claire said.

Sam got up. "I'll have Maile send off a priority message to Maria Mitchell," he said. "Their library has all the old records, including the first Chinese sightings of Comet Halley, collated and filed on disk. If anyone has a record of an astronomical event the size we're looking for, Tori will."

"Good. We could use some kind of independent confirmation of what we've found here."

"How could it have been so totally lost to us?" Mother wondered aloud. "What happened to them? What happened?"

We were all frightened, and uneasy with it. Where there might have been a world, and people like us on it, now there was none. It reminded us of the near chaos on Terra. There wasn't one of us over twelve who hadn't been born on Terra. It didn't bear thinking of.

"Six hundred B.C.," Maggie Lu said thoughtfully. "Lao Tzu."

"Lao Tzu?" Charlie said. "What's that?"

"It's a he. He taught around 600 B.C. He instructed that harmony was with the unseen, and with nature. Tao, the way, and te, the power."

There was a brief silence. "Maggie, is there something you're trying to tell us?"

"And Confucius," she said, ignoring Charlie. "He was born in 551 B.C."

"And what did he preach?"

"He didn't preach, he taught. He never posed as a prophet or a messenger of God."

"Okay, what'd he teach?"

"That to love men is *jen*, the essence of humanity, the universal moral force."

"Maggie—"

"The pharaoh Necho," Akhenaton Sadat, a Star Guard, said. "It was about 600 B.C. he ordered Africa to be circumnavigated, wasn't it?"

"Zoroaster in Persia," said Sayyid Kajar, one of Claire's geologists. "He founded the first monotheistic religion on Terra, one with a dual force. Ahura Mazda, the force for good, and Ahriman, the force for evil."

"The Jewish prophets in Israel," Ari Greenbaum chimed in.

"And Siddhartha Gautama," Parvati Gandhi said. "Born on Terra about 600 B.C. or so. So it is written."

"Okay, okay," Simon said irritably. "So the destruction or the disappearance or whatever of the planet or planets, or whatever, in this orbit came at or near the same time Terra was lousy with seers. So what?"

"Do you know what Siddhartha means?" Parvati said.

Arrested, Simon said slowly, "No. What?"

"It means 'goal reached.' "

There was silence in the galley for a long time.

Simon stirred. "I see where you're heading with this, and I will acknowledge that there is room for speculation, but—"

Mother said firmly, "We must stop shipping asteroids to Terranova, dear. We must stop excavating rocks and start mapping them, inside and out, instead. We must stop as many miners as we can from exploiting their claims any further until each has been examined for artifacts."

"I knew it," Charlie said fatalistically.

"What!" Maggie said.

Charlie looked at Simon and added, "I warned you what would happen if you found out that anything higher on the food chain than a plankton made that crude."

Simon looked at Mother and said, "Natasha, you are out of your mind."

"We dare not risk the destruction of further evidence of the existence of life in the Belt," Mother reiterated.

Crip said crisply, "And what happens to the Terranovan ore shipment schedule? To the Homemade construction timetable?"

"And what if we do shut down operations?" someone else said. "I for one did not come all the way out to the Belt to sit around twiddling my thumbs."

"Nor I!"

"Me either!"

"Do you wish," Mother said calmly, "to be known as the people responsible for erasing what may be part of the prologue to human history?"

"Now wait just a goddam minute." I looked around. Maile was on her feet and without the trace of a smile on her face. "We're talking abut a history that may or may not have existed, three thousand years ago, on the strength of one small puddle of crude and the remains of what may or may not have been its container."

"Maile, dear," Mother said, "we simply cannot take the chance of destroying what little evidence may remain."

"I," Maile stated, still on her feet and still unsmiling, punctuating every phrase with a thump of her fist that shook the table, "left the Big Island because there wasn't anything left for me. Sheraton built on all the beaches, Libby's bought out all the macnut and sugar plantations, and Onizuka Spaceport appropriated everything in between. I came to the Belt to find a new life, and make a new home for myself, and I will not be dispossessed again!" By the end of her speech Maile was shouting. Until that moment I hadn't known she could shout, and judging from the expressions on the faces of those around me I wasn't the only one.

"Maile's right," Maggie, the first to recover, said. "This may concern our history, but do we preserve it at the expense of our future?"

"Are you willing to take the responsibility of destroying your children's heritage?" Mother said stubbornly. "We must preserve the integrity of the site for study."

Roger piped up from his seat next to Zoya. "If there were living, growing things out here once, I want to know about them, right down to their gene structure. We can't just go on melting down possible evidence of their existence." Next to him Zoya rose to her feet, threw out her hands, and delivered a passionate oration in Russian that lasted by my chronometer for four minutes and twenty-seven seconds. When she resumed her seat Roger said, "And Zoya feels the same way."

"And I," Ari Greenbaum said.

"I'm afraid I must disagree with my distinguished colleagues," Whitney Burkette said, very stern. "We are behind schedule as it is, don't you know. We can't slow up something as innovative and essential and, may I say, as potentially profitable, as 'A World of Your Own' production on the off chance a bald paramecium twenty-six hundred years old once occupied—what? A planet? We have no conclusive evidence of its existence." His walrus mustache was beginning to bristle. He stroked it down. "It could have been a ship. We *do* have conclusive evidence of ships built and piloted by other races than our own."

"Crude oil on an F-T-L ship?"

"It doesn't necessarily have to be a Librarian ship," Mother pointed out.

"Mother is right," Charlie said with reluctance. "We have to know one way or the other. We owe it to whoever was here before us."

"This is beginning to sound like a goddam Sierra Club meeting," Maggie said ominously.

"We owe it to our children to carry on with what we're doing," Simon said, glaring at Charlie.

"We owe it to ourselves to stay employed," Crip said, glaring at Mother.

Mother looked stubborn. Charlie looked furious, Simon enraged. Everyone started yelling at the nearest available target. I left the room.

The twins were waiting when I got back to our cabin. So was one of the p-suit techs. She had Caleb's suit in tow. She looked nervous. "Yes?" I said.

She fidgeted. "I thought—what do you want me to do with Caleb's suit?"

I looked at it. Caleb had been a large man. He and I had both needed suits tailored for us. "Ask Maile if she needs a spare," I said. "She's almost as big as he was. Or turn it over to the Guard."

I turned my back. The door closed behind me. I fed the twins peanut butter and jelly sandwiches, bathed them, and put them to bed. I read them the next chapter of *The Pearl Lagoon*. As I read, Sean crawled down out of his bunk and into my lap. Paddy slid her hand into my free one, and leaned her head against my arm.

"Where's Daddy?" Paddy asked, for the thousandth time.

"He's gone," I said.

"When's he coming back?"

"He's not coming back, Paddy."

"Why not?"

"Emaa says it's because he's with the angels now, Paddy."

"But Mommy doesn't believe in angels, Sean," Paddy replied, tears welling up in her eyes.

"I do so," I lied.

"So that's where Daddy is?" Paddy said, sniffling.

"Yes," I lied again.

"Will we ever see him again?"

"Yes," I lied for the third time.

I resumed reading. We fell asleep together, on Paddy's bunk.

—10—

Sleeping Alone

The moon has set, and the Pleiades;
it is Midnight, and time passes,
and I sleep alone.

—Sappho

The One-Day Revolution on Terranova was nothing compared
to the skirmishing that occupied every waking moment on Outpost for the next week. There wasn't a friendly conversation
that didn't end in a shouting match. There wasn't a meal
that didn't finish in a food fight. There wasn't a job that
got an inch closer to being done before one of the riggers
on it downed tools and stamped away in disgust. And then
it got personal.

Early Wednesday morning I stumbled down to the galley
for coffee and found Crip huddled on a bench with a jacket
bunched beneath his head, trying to sleep. That night Charlie
was routed out of bed to treat a beauty of a shiner Maile said
she got when she ran into a door. You can't run into a door
on a space station. On Thursday the league playoffs for tridee
basketball were scheduled. I toyed with the idea of canceling

them. Mother counseled against it. "Better they take it out on the court, dear," she said.

I don't know that "better" was the adjective I would have employed. The score was tied at the half and stayed that way until the final buzzer sounded, by which time every member of both teams, first and second string, had fouled out. "Well, dear," Mother said, preparing to rise from the bleachers next to me, "if I'd wanted to see a fistfight, I would have gone to a hockey game."

Friday evening the Globe Theater Company put on a production of *The Cherry Orchard* in Piazzi City Square. It took the Star Guard to break up the riot that greeted the curtain call. Simon and a group of like-minded Outposters and miners treated the actor who played Lopakhin to a night out in Piazzi City, finishing up at Maggie's. Saturday's performance was canceled.

On Sunday, I left the twins with Charlie and suited up to go EVA. I clicked on my helmet, checked to see that all the lights were green, and cycled the lock. Outside I attached my tether, pulled myself over to the jetpack rack, and fumbled through them until I found one whose gauges read full. I spent another ten minutes untangling and detaching my tether and pushed off. I nudged the comm switch with my chin and said, "Outpost Traffic Control, this is Star Svensdotter."

"Outpost to Star, go ahead."

"I'm stepping outside for a bit. Permission to move out five klicks on two-forty, there to maintain position until further notification."

There was a click as Traffic Control accessed my locator beacon. "Okay, Star, gotcha. What're you doing out there?"

"Rubbernecking." I pushed off and maneuvered with my thrusters until OTC, following me on their grid, told me I was where I wanted to be.

I hung there, kicking my feet over the edge of the universe.

Outpost floated five klicks in front of me, outlined against the expanse of space, white opposing its black, less than minuscule against its immensity, so brightly illuminated by Sol's rays that I had to switch on my helmet polarizer. And yet it was dull in comparison to the innumerable stars burning brightly at its back.

Space stations are never outwardly neat, and Outpost was no exception. A beehive of bombs tethered themselves to one arm by a single slender strand of steel. PVAs unfolded themselves in geometric precision inside the rim. Geodomes popped out all over like mushroom caps. Stabilizers tangled with heat radiators and heat radiators fouled antennae and mirrors rotated slowly, bringing the sun inside.

The first day we'd spent together, Caleb had wanted to know where I lived on Terranova. I'd told him, in a tiny house all by itself in the foothills of the Rocky Candy Mountains. "Sounds lonely," he had said. And I'd replied, "Sometimes. Sometimes just alone. I like it that way."

I'd been alone since we'd come back from Tomorrow, but not lonely. The twins were always there. So was Simon, trying not to sound sympathetic. Looking at me and then looking away hastily, to grab for Charlie's hand and hold it so tightly she winced. Charlie, who knew me better and so said nothing at all, was just there. Mother brought me coffee with one hand and printouts of obscure texts of Schliemann's discovery of Troy with the other, and told me how from then on *The Iliad* and *The Odyssey* were more than the sum of a blind man's telling of fanciful legends. Proof of the existence of Troy, Mother pointed out, had changed the way Terrans studied their history. And Crip and Maggie and the rest of the crew, always dropping by the cabin on little or no pretext. I'd never had so many offers to baby-sit, or to dinner, or to help with administrative duties. I realized I hadn't seen a miner in weeks. The crew had been running interference and I hadn't even noticed.

The swelling on Leif's face was down and the bruises had faded. He still avoided me. I didn't blame him. If I could have, I would have avoided myself.

If only we hadn't taken that sample. If only I hadn't recognized that damned crude for what it was. If only we'd never heard of Lavoliere, or the *Conestoga*, or 7877Tomorrow. If only—

Enough. You can't blow your nose inside a p-suit helmet. I called OTC for clearance and triggered my thrusters.

Back inside the station, I called Archy. "Archy, notify department heads that there will be a station meeting tomorrow—no, make it Wednesday—after breakfast in the galley. Attendance is mandatory. All personnel, I say again, all personnel must attend. Pull in the Star Guard, the people in the assaying office

on Ceres, and all of Claire's crew. Anyone who has to be on
duty must stand by on their communits. Get Maile to set up
a bounce to anyone who's off station and can't make it in on
time. Get it?"

"Got it. What's going on?"

"I'm calling a cease-fire."

"And about time, too."

Three days later I told my crew how it was going to be.

Outpost had the equipment and the personnel to find new
rocks, catalogue them, and analyze them before either (A)
putting them to use or (B) leaving them strictly alone. Very
well, then, we would carry on with our charting and core
sampling and specimen gathering.

At the same time, we would pay special attention to anything
that might conceivably be organic or man-made in origin.
Anything we found would be run by Outpost's newly formed
archaeology department. I took the path of least resistance and
named Mother head of the department. Archy rifled through
the personnel files and turned up an agrotech with an under-
graduate minor in anthropology and a biotech who had worked
one summer on a dig in Mazatlan. When Mother squawked
over their combined lack of qualifications, I reminded her that
we were almost two AUs from the University of Cairo, that
they were the best qualified people we could come up with,
and that they held the singular virtue of being on the scene.
Bob Shackleton volunteered his services, and Leif nominated
himself aide-de-camp, completing the employee roster.

Shackleton knew more about archaeology than the rest of
them put together, and he reminded us, "As yet, all we've got
to go on is an ecofact."

"The crude."

"Exactly."

Claire bristled. "What about the reservoir?"

"I don't know that I'd qualify something in that many
bits and pieces as an artifact." Shackleton shrugged. "I'm
no expert. I make maps. Anyway, before we start asking
questions about who and why and how and where, we need
to know when. The good news is, if there is anything left, it's
been floating around in a vacuum. No friction, no erosion. No
tourists chipping bits off to put on their mantels back home.
What we find, if anything, might be in decent enough shape
to at least date."

"What's the bad news?"

"The bad news is, whatever blew whatever this was apart did a thorough job of it, and we're talking a search that will incorporate billions of square kilometers. We'll be lucky to find anything as concrete as even the remains of an oil reservoir anytime soon."

"And if and when we do?"

"What are we looking for, anyway?" Strasser said. I'd called him in as a sort of amicus curiae. If Outpost stopped buying ore, the miners would be interested in knowing why.

"Anything that looks like—well, let me put it this way. Anything that doesn't look like a hunk of rock."

"And then? Always supposing we find something that doesn't look like a hunk of rock?"

Simon's irony was heavy-handed but Bob was unfazed. "We try to date them." He looked down at a list. "There are different techniques for different materials. If we find pottery, ceramics, that kind of thing, we can date its age up to thirty-five thousand years with TL, or thermo-luminescence. And, on Terra at least, pottery preserves a replica of the earth's magnetism at the time of firing. Archaeomagnetism, they call it. There's no reason to think this planet didn't have a magnetic field. All planets do."

"Mars doesn't," Sam said. "Or not much of one."

"Oh," Bob said blankly. This is what comes of specializing in one field. Bob's long, earnest face still looked faintly startled whenever one of us addressed him directly. For four years he had been regarded and treated as at best a nonproductive nuisance wished on us by capricious and publicity-hungry expedition planners; now we were responding to his words as supplicants before an oracle, and he didn't quite know what to do with his newfound authority.

"And that'd only help us if we had some kind of frame of reference," Simon said. "An ocean bed to take a core sample of, say, to match the sherds to, so we could place the time they were made. We don't. We won't."

"We haven't been all the way around the Belt yet, Simon," I said.

"Do you honestly think—"

"I stopped thinking when I smelled sulfur on my hands a month ago where no sulfur should have been," I said. "And knowing is always better than not knowing. What else you got, Bob?"

"If we find bones, teeth, antlers, ivory, we can use the fun techniques."

"Fun?"

"F-U-N. Fluorine, uranium, nitrogen. They're like C-14, time passes, their levels change in whatever material they exist in, we count what's left and take a guess. Fluorine and uranium's no good for anything younger than ten thousand years, nitrogen's just the opposite."

"What about C-14?"

He frowned. "Carbon dating? It works, but it's clumsy, time-consuming, and inexact. It worked easy on the petroleum because petroleum's a hydrocarbon." He thought. "If we find charcoal, it'd be worth the hassle. Otherwise, I'd hold the process in reserve for anything we find that's *really* old."

"How old?"

"Older than fifty-seven hundred thirty years. Plus or minus forty."

There was a pause. "How are we supposed to tell?" Steve the zoologist asked timidly.

Bob looked taken aback. He laughed. "Damned if I know."

There was another pause. "I'd kill for some good old-fashioned tree rings," Simon said finally.

In the meantime, I decreed, we would continue work on Homemade I, since most of its interior—and any evidence of previous life—had been smelted away by the pahoehoe. We were already at work with the MeekMakers. Claire would continue shipping rocks to Terranova, after a thorough examination had pronounced each one free of artifact or corpse. Charlie spoke for the majority of the closet Luddites when she said, "That sounds reasonable," but Mother was still displeased. "If you think by a cursory examination of the surface features—" she began.

"Not cursory, Mother," I said patiently. "We'll be careful." She looked at me from beneath a suspicious brow and I said, "Very, very careful. We'll use thump trucks and core samplers. We'll quarter and map each rock minutely. We'll run sonagrams of every meter before we okay it for use. And we won't buy ore from a miner's claim without running a survey of it first. I'd like to point out that this is adding considerably to the lead time of each delivery to Terranova and to the fish farm's timetable and delays payday for miners who sell to us, and that everyone has agreed to it is a minor miracle for which we should thank God, fasting."

"Dear, I—"

"Mother," Charlie said warningly.

Mother said gently, stubbornly, "Carlotta dear, I merely wish to ensure that Esther realizes how important it is to locate and preserve any clue to the Belt's past history."

It had been a long, hard, very loud month. I looked at Mother. I stood up.

"Star." Charlie's voice was plaintive. Her eyes pleaded with me. Charlie very seldom asked me for anything. She demanded, she ordered, she insisted, often at the top of her voice, but she very seldom asked.

I forced myself to sit down. I poured out a cup of coffee with a shaking hand. I stirred cream and sugar into it. I blew on it. I sipped it. When I could trust myself to speak and not scream, I said tightly, "Mother, I am sick and tired of fighting you on this every step of the way. You want to tell the prospectors they can't prospect and the miners they can't mine? Fine. Be my guest. Have at it." Mother looked at me, surprised, and I said, "Go ahead, go on. I won't stop you. I'll green light your p-suit for you. I'll charge up your solarsled. I'll lock the coordinates into the IMU. I'll tell you what, I'll even see to it that you get a decent burial."

"The Star Guard—" Mother said.

"The Star Guard, Natasha, is a security force, not a hit team for Outpost," Perry said, spacing her words precisely.

"I know that, dear, but—"

"They have a responsibility to protect and defend their paying customers," Perry said in a louder voice.

Mother, mercifully, fell silent. "All right," I said. "Now this is what we will do. Archy, are you on?"

"Always, Star."

"I don't know why I find that reassuring. I want you to get together with Maile and put out a special edition of the *Outposter*. Include all the information we have up-to-date on what we found on 7877Tomorrow. Include a summary of our conclusions and how we reached them. Broadcast it hourly over KBLT, run a loop over Channel 9, run off five thousand hard copies for Ceres, and of course no one gets off the station without reading it and carrying a fax or a tape of it to their claim."

"How about using the Star Guard for distribution? They get around, you know."

"They do indeed. Perry?"

"Sounds good. I'll tell Caleb—" There was a dreadful silence. "Sorry. It's hard to—" She stopped again. "I'll tell Ursula about the Guard distributing the fax."

"Thank you," I said steadily. "Archy, front page, above the fold, box a boldface appeal from me to notify Outpost of anything anyone has found that might fit in to our theory."

"How about a reward for any artifacts found?"

"Another good idea, Arch. Mother, you hear?" She nodded, and I said, "Make sure Bob dates anything brought in before you buy it."

Mother looked affronted. "Certainly, dear. I would have done that in any case."

"The only way Mother would be satisfied is if we chased every miner and prospector out of the Belt and then left it ourselves," Charlie remarked later.

"Keep it down. I just got them to sleep." I stripped off my jumpsuit. "I could sleep for a week myself. God, but I'm tired."

"Me, too," Charlie said.

"Go home and go to bed, then."

She nodded. "Only one more thing to do, Star."

"I know," I said. "I'll work up something in the morning.".

She left. I followed her down the corridor in my mind. Simon put his arms around her. She snuggled into his shoulder. She tucked a leg in between his. He wrapped his arms loosely around her waist. They slept.

Before it's sex, before it's companionship, before it's friendship even, love is lying down next to him at the end of a long, hard day, with nothing more to look forward to but the steady beat of his heart against your ear, and an uninterrupted night's sleep.

I spent four hours the next morning writing and rewriting a short description of the find on 7877Tomorrow. I speculated on what it might mean. I summarized the dissenting opinions among my own crew. I listed the options we had considered.

I explained the course of action we had decided on. I felt it was succinct, well reasoned, and sure to convince Helen that we were doing the right thing.

"Dream on, Star," Archy said.

"Thanks a lot, Archy," I said. "I appreciate your support." And with that Maile forwarded my letter to Helen.

Helen's response was an unnerving silence.

"Nothing?" Charlie said.

"Not a word."

"When did you send the message, Star?"

"A month ago."

"And nothing since?"

"Like Simon said. Not a word."

"Oh." Charlie thought. "Is the link down?" she said hopefully.

Simon shook his head. "Maile says it's traffic as usual, confirmations of composition-and-course schedules, personals for the crew, news. Nothing else."

"Hell," Charlie said.

"Yeah."

"I keep thinking about all those interviews and press conferences she gave for the Homemade."

"I know. So do I."

"She hates the press."

"That's not quite fair, Charlie," Simon said judiciously. "She doesn't just hate the press. She hates, loathes, despises, detests, abhors, and abominates the press."

Charlie swallowed. She sat up and squared her shoulders. "Well. All that public relations business was her idea."

"It certainly was."

"And construction is progressing."

"It certainly is."

"It's not as if we've trashed the entire schedule."

"Certainly not."

"She can't kill us, after all. She can't even eat us."

"No." I could tell by the look in my sister's apprehensive brown eyes that Simon didn't sound as sure of himself as she would have liked.

Five weeks, three days, and seventeen hours later, Helen Ricadonna, originator of the Big Lie, founding mother of Terranova and perpetrator of the Terranova Belt Expedition, disembarked from a Volksrocket at Ceres. She hopped a solarsled to Outpost, marched into the galley, planted herself across the table from me, and said grimly, "Now. Would you mind repeating that, please?"

Two months later Frank arrived with a deputation from the British Museum, and we gladly turned Outpost's Department of Archaeology over to them. The agrotech and the biotech returned to their respective departments. Mother, Leif, and Bob stayed with the team, and amused us at dinnertime with the latest theories propounded by the archaeology department on what had happened to the Belt civilization, if it hadn't gone up with the bang. Six hundred years before Christ in Terran history, there was plenty of fodder for speculation that any survivors might have made their way there.

Mostly I listened without comment, but one evening I said, "Have any of you ever heard of Ionia?"

"Sounds Greek to me," Simon said.

"Ha, ha. Ionia was a community of Greeks who lived in the western islands of Greece from around 600 to 300 B.C. They were the radical scientific thinkers of their time. The Ionians didn't buy the idea that the universe was a mystery to be divined only by the gods and taken on faith by humankind. They believed that there was reason in nature for those who studied it with care. For example. Did you know that Aristarchus, an Ionian, held that the sun rather than the earth was at the center of the planetary system, and that all the planets went around the sun rather than around the earth? Three hundred years before Christ? Eighteen hundred years before Copernicus?"

"Is that right?" Charlie said. "Are you sure?"

"Sam and Archy confirmed it for me independently. There was also Leucippus, who proposed the concept of the atom in the fifth century B.C. And, Charlie, there was a physician named Empedocles. He lived around 450 B.C., and believed that light travels very fast but not infinitely fast." There was a stir when I said that. "That's not all. He said that there were many more Terran species in far greater variety than had survived to his time, and that clearly, and here I'm quoting, 'either craft or courage or speed' were decisive factors in the survival of those species that had endured."

"Darwin alive and well in ancient Greece, two thousand years before he was born?" Simon murmured. "I like it."

"He killed himself jumping into Aetna," Sam added. "Empedocles. No wonder no one took him seriously."

"Perhaps he slipped, dear, taking a closer look," Mother suggested.

"Like Pliny," Claire said. "He died taking too close a look at Vesuvius."

"Maybe Empedocles did jump in," Simon said thoughtfully. He met my startled gaze and added, "If what we're thinking is true, wouldn't you have?"

And perhaps I would have. I like to think I'm strong enough to survive anything, Darwin's theory upright and ambulatory, but I didn't know. I'd had Orion on my shoulder now, and Sol at my feet. To be earthbound again, to never feel the jarring boot of an Express on kickoff, never again to be out in the Great Alone? If I had all that glory behind me, and Aetna and an end to the aching homesickness for the vast infinities of space before me? I wasn't as sure of things as I had been.

"It's odd, the coincidences we've found in looking at those years on Terra," Maggie said. "Lao Tzu, Confucius, Buddha, Zoroaster, and who was that pharaoh Ak was talking about? Necho? And now Star's Ionians. It's hard to believe all that spiritual and intellectual activity was unrelated."

"You think they went to Terra," Helen stated.

"Of course she does, dear." Mother sounded smug.

Maggie drew back. "We don't know for sure that there was any 'they,' " she said carefully. Maggie always hedged her bets. "We'll probably never know. I am merely pointing out an interesting coincidence of events."

Mother said, " 'It is a heart strangely un-Christian that cannot thrill with joy when the least of men begins to pull in the direction of the stars.' " Mother seemed to be experiencing an epiphany right in front of us. "Vernon Johns. You really should read up on your religious philosophers. They're not all so stodgy as you seem to think."

Maggie, almost but not quite, snorted.

Mother retaliated with, " 'And I saw a new heaven and a new earth: for the first heaven and the first earth were passed away.' Revelations 21:1."

Bob cleared his throat, and said apologetically, "I would like to point out something that we have yet to discuss, and that is that mankind was evolving on Terra millennia before 600 B.C. The chances of two life forms evolving practically in parallel are—are—hell, they're incalculable."

"Which makes it no chance at all," Simon pointed out.

"That divine spark from heaven," Charlie said, looking at Mother. "Maybe heaven was closer than we thought."

"Prometheus," Maggie said. "The fire from the gods."

Sam pointed at her and said, "You just named our hypothetical planet."

"Assuming our speculations are correct," Simon said, "assuming the original Belters fled a decomposing planet or planets, and found refuge on Terra. A purely intellectual, hypothetical speculation only."

"Yes?"

"Then what the hell happened?" he said. He was on his feet now, pacing between the crowded benches, his basso profundo voice frustrated, almost angry. "Not here, I mean on Terra. If, after breakup, a few of them made it to Terra somehow and started us on the road to scientific inquiry—come on, that's what we're all tiptoeing around saying, isn't it? Well? How did our ancestors come to toss it all away? If they hadn't, we could conceivably have had calculus by the time of Christ."

"Christ was what happened, Simon," I said.

"What?"

"Christ. In person. Terran scientists call it the Great Interruption. Fourteen, fifteen, sixteen centuries of deliberate sabotage of what the ancients, whoever they were and wherever they came from, laid down for us. Sabotage by religious fanatics who were more concerned about the bad public relations inherent in Galileo scoring one off the Church than they were in the fact that he was right."

"Jesus preached love, Esther," Mother said in gentle reproof. "Those who followed subverted his teachings for their own purpose."

"And they didn't do it all by themselves," Bob added. "It must have been a great comfort to the crowned heads of the times that their right to rule was anointed by God. Any doubt cast on Christianity would be doubt cast on their right to occupy their thrones. They would have defended the faith whether they believed in it or not."

But in the meantime, I thought, mankind lost eighteen hundred years. Less than a fraction of a second on the cosmic calendar, but, as Simon had pointed out, that second on Terra was the difference between having a little calculus with our Christ and the Dark Ages. Where would we be now, I wondered, if Aristarchus had prevailed over Aristotle? Would there have been Ptolemaic spheres to hold up the sun and the moon and the planets? Crystal spheres with sweet music to beguile mankind into a millennium of wrong thinking?

"We might just make up for it," Charlie said. "Here and now. The Belters."

"How so?"

Charlie leaned forward, her eyes bright with a new idea. "Think about the first Renaissance. There was a renewed interest in the classics. There was a boom in the arts, in literature, Dante, Cervantes, Shakespeare. The sciences took off, Copernicus, Kepler, Brahe, Galileo, et al. And." She held up a finger for emphasis. "At the same time there was a virtual explosion in the exploration of Terra, the circumnavigation of Africa, the discovery of the Americas."

"You're making an argument for these movements having been codependent?" Maggie asked.

Charlie nodded. "In the same way we've been saying the emergence of so many brilliant thinkers at roughly the same period in human history on Terra can't be a coincidence."

"And you're saying you think the same thing could happen here, now?" Simon said, his brow creased.

"Why not? The Belt is essentially a realm of islands, isolated from Terra and to a great extent from each other. Isolation guarantees free inquiry and breeds diversity. How many different political systems have you run across in your travels, Mother?"

Mother thought. "I see what you mean, dear. But you are talking about mere microcosms of societal organizations."

"But every language, every idea, every prejudice, every god known to man, all of them are represented here in the Belt, aren't they?"

"To some extent, dear, yes." Mother added, "And a few new ones I've never heard of before."

Charlie sat back, satisfied. "We may be in for some lively fights, but I'm betting on a boom time of exploration and inspiration in every field of human thought and endeavor."

"I Married an Optimist from Outer Space," Simon said. Charlie glowered up at him, silently promising retribution. He laughed and hugged her close.

"Terran hegemony doesn't seem quite so far distant, now, does it?" Bob said. "With such an object lesson staring them in the face?"

I laughed shortly. "I wouldn't bet the farm on it. Terrans have been drinking buddies with Armageddon for so long, it's not likely they'll be kicking him out of the bar anytime soon."

"I Married an Optimist from Outer Space and Got a Pessimist for a Sister-in-Law," Simon said.

"Where did they come from?" Charlie said suddenly, unheeding.

"Who?"

"The Ionians. If they went from here to Terra, could they have come from even farther out to begin with?" She turned to Simon. "You know, maybe it's not that genetic imperative you keep talking about that sent Columbus to America and Magellan around the world and us out here."

"What is it, then?"

"Maybe we're lonely," she said. "Maybe we're looking for friends. Maybe—ancestors? Roots? Our place in the universe?"

He smiled. "Like that poem you're always quoting."

"T. S. Eliot's 'Little Gidding.' Yes. Exactly. It's funny, Star," Charlie said to me. "On Terranova, you dragged us kicking and screaming into our future. And then you brought us out to the Belt and dragged us kicking and screaming into our past."

"It wasn't anything I planned," I said. And then I got out of there as fast as I could without running.

Whitney Burkette was waiting for me. "Ah, Star," he said as I opened the door to my cabin and motioned him inside. "I wondered, did you have a particular date set to begin breaking ground on the creeks in Homemade I?"

He was too close to me. I shrugged irritably. "I don't know, I haven't thought much about it. Why do you ask?"

And then he grabbed at me. His mustache scratched my face. He gripped me around the waist and pressed up against me.

I don't even remember moving. The next thing I knew, Whitney Burkette was lying in a crumpled heap in a corner of the room, one leg bent up behind him at an awkward angle. His face was bloody. He was missing teeth. He was unconscious and breathing stertorously.

"Auntie!"

I turned. Alexei was standing in the open doorway, his face white. "Go get your mother, Alex."

He swallowed hard and his eyes flickered between Burkette's body and myself. "Are you okay?"

"Go get your mother, Alex. Now."

"What'd he do?" Charlie wanted to know.

I took a long time to answer. "He kissed me," I said finally. "He touched me."

"Was it worth half killing him for?"

"Yes."

She looked at me, anger and exasperation and a dreadful kind of pity in her eyes. "Star," she said, placing a tentative hand on my arm. "Nothing worthwhile comes without cost."

I had to close my eyes against the wave of rage that swept over me then. When I opened them, Charlie's face changed. Her hand fell from my arm and she backed away from me. She didn't ask me any more questions or make any more comments and I was grateful in a detached sort of way. I didn't want to hurt anybody else. Not really. Not that day, anyway.

The next rock due to be launched for Terranova would be a test run for Maggie's processing plant. Although we were sacrificing the speed of an Express system for a propulsion plant that was incorporated into the refining process, adding six months to the time in-flight, when the rock arrived it would be about twenty-three percent near-pure grade silicon. Roger and Zoya were already inside Homemade I, breeding dead dust into living soil. Claire was out scouting around for the second new world. My, how life was moving right along.

"I got an idea," Lodge said one day. She wanted to start a delivery service, incorporating the Star Guard's patrol routes. Every item would be C.O.D. I told her to go ahead with it as long as she didn't need any help from me.

The twins were into everything on board the station and off it. They'd had their own p-suits since they were two; they kept the techs busy enlarging them. "I guess it's time I started thinking about some kind of training for the twins," I said to Charlie one day.

"You mean put them in school?"

"That's what I said." She chuckled, and I said, "What?"

"Nothing. They're only four years old, Star."

"We were in school at four."

"That's because we were both rabid overachievers."

"Roger tells me Sean's showing a real aptitude in the geodomes, and Sam Holbrook says Paddy can already count in parsecs."

"What would you've done if one of them had wanted to teach twentieth-century American literature?"

"Strangled them in their sleep," I said.

"This from the woman who insisted on incorporating *The Complete Works of William Shakespeare* into Archy's data base before we kicked off from Terranova."

"I guess." I yawned.

She was watching me. "Sleepy?"

"Not really. Just tired."

"Star—"

"Star," Helen said, coming in. "Just the person I wanted to see."

"What's up?"

She poured herself a cup of coffee and sat down across from me. "You know Natasha still wants to go to Mars."

"What's the problem? Put her on a ship."

"Seriously, Star, I've got an idea."

"Do you?"

She and Charlie exchanged glances. "Don't you want to know what kind of idea?"

"What kind of idea?" I said obediently.

"Transportation."

I made a noncommittal noise only because Helen clearly expected some response.

"Transportation where?" Charlie asked finally.

"Everywhere," Helen said. I was watching out the viewport. A solarsled parked and a p-suited figure wearing a Star Guard badge embarked and began the hand-over-hand journey to the lock.

"Between planets," Helen continued.

"Sounds interesting," Charlie said.

I got up and went to the lock.

"Crossing the system," Helen said, raising her voice. "On a regular schedule."

I cycled the lock and popped the hatch. It was Kleng Qvist. He looked a little surprised to see me. "How was your patrol?" I said.

"All right," he said. I helped him out of his suit.

"Just all right?" Perry said from behind me.

"Mostly," Kleng said. "Jacques Honfleur's the only holdout for the archaeological survey on my route. He threatened to shoot at me yesterday, so I didn't stick around to try to convince him otherwise."

"You tell him we won't buy his ore without the survey?"

"I told him," Kleng said. "He said fine with him; he'd just sell to T-LM or SOS."

"Jacques Honfleur?" I asked.

"6111Voyageur," Kleng said. "He's sitting on a big seam of gadolinium, after five years of chipping samples from rocks scattered over eleven degrees worth of Belt." He shrugged. "Hell, I don't blame him. You go try to tell one of those old-timers he has to tear down his sluice and pack up his shaker table and kiss his dream of living out the rest of his life in the Presidential Suite in the Luna Hilton good-bye. Tell him it's all because there's a marginal chance he's staked a claim on what could be the second rock in fifty thousand that may bear the remains of what might have been a civilization on what was possibly a planet, or planets, maybe. Try saying all that with a straight face, and make him believe it." Kleng shook his head. "I don't half believe it myself and I've seen the evidence with my own eyes."

"You tell him he'd be losing money if he sold anywhere but here?"

"That's when he started shooting."

I was remembering the surprise on Kleng's face. "I'll go talk to him," I said. Their heads whipped around. It might have been funny, once. "I'm going," I said. "It's about time I got in some travel time."

Perry started to say something. I stopped her with a single look. "Take the twins this evening? Sean's with Roger, Paddy's with Sam." Charlie nodded. Helen started to say something. Charlie touched her arm. Helen shut up, but she looked annoyed. Or worried. Or something; lately I hadn't been that good at reading people's facial expressions. Simon and Leif came into the galley as I left it. "Where's she going?" I heard, and walked faster.

An hour later I was suited up and shoving off in a solarsled. "Archy, off line," I said.

"I don't think that's such a good idea, boss," he said.

"Nobody asked you," I snapped. "Off line. Now."

Silence inside my helmet was my reply.

6111Voyageur wasn't far from our present position; I was there in two hours. It would have taken half that if I hadn't let my piloting skills deteriorate over the last months. Or maybe I was just tired.

Mars was a cold and dour red ball over my left shoulder when I arrived. I braked and hailed Honfleur on Channel 9. No answer. "Come on, Jacques," I said. "This is Star Svensdotter of Outpost. I'm not armed, I'm not selling anything, I just want to talk. Give me a signal to follow in."

I waited. Up close, 6111Voyageur looked like a diseased potato with a big chunk gnawed out of one side. Its albedo was high, and I was leaning forward to adjust the polarizer on my porthole when I heard a *ping* slightly aft of where I was sitting.

I don't like *pings* of any kind when there's only the thin, unpressurized shell of a solarsled between me and vacuum, especially when I'm coasting down the home stretch of fifty thousand rocks, all with ragged edges and half of whom I am convinced have my name written on them. My exhaustion vanished, and I came fully awake for the first time in weeks. I started slapping the rudimentary control panel in front of me. I shut down the drive, I shut down the transmitter, I shut down everything I could reach. And then I sat back and listened hard.

Time passes slowly when all you're doing is listening. It was only a few moments later when I heard a kind of *splang*, which seemed to carom off the sled's nose. I squinted out the port to see what was caroming. I flinched back out of the way of a rock about a foot across that narrowly missed the bubble of my cockpit. My elbow hit the volume control on the transmitter and suddenly the cockpit was filled with yelling.

"*Allez vous en, garce!* I tell your *chien* the same yesterday!"

"Honfleur! Listen to me!" *Chink, crack, zing!* It was the crack that really scared me, and I yelled, "Honfleur, all we want is a visual survey and one core sample, a one-time test only, we're not trying to—Christ! Stop *doing* that!"

"I listen to *merde*! I hear what happens to Lavoliere when you go to survey Tomorrow! That you don't do to Jacques

Honfleur! *Ici,* he is my rock, my *aure,* I sell him where I wish!
And no *putain*—"

There was another crack and his transmission cut off. By
then I'd managed to get the drive fired up and I was history
in that neighborhood, I was out of there, I was long gone, I
was out in back of that solarsled and I was *pushing* it down
the Belt. I didn't care what direction I was going in, I wanted
away and I wanted away *now.*

I was in such a tearing hurry that ten minutes passed before
I tried to take a bearing.

I couldn't get one.

One of Honfleur's missiles must have impacted squarely on
the IMU's antennae. My space compass was dead. And for all
practical purposes, so was my sled.

I punched in the code for Outpost. "Archy? Archy, you
there?"

The transmitter was as dead as my space compass. "Two
for two, Jacques," I said. "Not bad." My mouth was dry. I
took a nervous pull at the water nozzle inside my helmet. I
stilled, holding the water in my mouth, thinking. I swallowed
and chinned for an update on my visor.

When I'd left Outpost, I'd had enough oh-two in my suit
for twenty-four hours. I had emergency tanks in the sled for
an additional twenty-four. I swiveled around to check the
tank rack.

Correction.

I had enough oh-two in my suit for twenty-four hours.

I couldn't even begin to figure out how I'd forgotten to
check for those spare tanks before I'd left Outpost.

I'd topped off my rations; the dispensers read full, and I
had additional rations tucked away in the sled's single locker.
Didn't I? Yes, they were there, but I wasn't looking forward
to feeding them one at a time through the chin valve on my
helmet and then trying to lip them up into my mouth. It was
too much like a hen in a neck brace trying to peck up corn. I'd
had to do it once before during the 1996 solar flare, when we'd
had to stay buttoned up in our suits for thirty-five hours.

I'd topped my water tank off before I'd left, and I had
drunk very little en route. The green-lettered update on my
visor listed my tank as full. I had two whole gallons, plus
whatever my overworked suit cycler could treat and return.

I felt dizzy. Probably my imagination. I made a conscious effort not to sweat. It didn't work. I took another swallow of water—what the hell, I was going to run out of air in twenty-four hours, I wouldn't need anything to drink after that. I reached up and tripped my ELB. The trouble with the emergency locator beacons, they broadcast away from the sled, and unless you had something to bounce them off of back toward you, you couldn't be absolutely sure that they were working, no matter what the go-light said.

Of course, if I'd had something to bounce the ELB signal off of, I wouldn't have been in this fix. I flipped on the transmitter and sent a Mayday. Who knew? Maybe the transmitter wasn't dead. Maybe Archy was dead. Archy'd been dead before. In between Maydays I recited poetry. I'd always liked poetry. Gardens of bright images. Ever hear the Frost poem about the man who burned down his farm for the insurance and spent the proceeds on a telescope? Now there's a man who had his priorities straight. "The best thing that we're put here for's to see," he said, and he was right. Otherwise, why'd the bear go 'round the mountain?

I sent another Mayday. So Honfleur had heard about Lavoliere. Who hadn't? Who hadn't heard of Star Svensdotter's homicidal burst of grief, the berserker Svensdotter, the hand for hand and burning for burning Svensdotter? Three teeth, a fractured femur, and a concussion for a kiss? "He that smiteth a man, so that he die, shall be surely put to death," I said. "Hear that, Arch? All that religion Mother crammed down my throat when I was too young to resist? Some of it seems to have took after all."

"*You'd do the same for any member of your crew,*" I heard Leif say. What would I do? I'd chew their ass out is what I'd do. Two wrongs never make a right. One wrong had led to another, and another, and another. I'd forced entry into the *Conestoga*. Caleb had died for it. I'd allowed grief to cloud my judgment and blunt my initiative in deciding on a course of action after the discovery of a Belt civilization. I'd almost killed Whitney Burkette for making a mild pass, nothing I hadn't fended off more or less gracefully, and far less bloodily, a thousand times in years gone by. I'd allowed my piloting skills to deteriorate to the point where I'd neglected to checklist my emergency rations before a flight. Caleb had grounded miners at Piazzi City for far less. I'd ignored the advice of my own appointed experts in making this field trip. Instead of approaching Voyageur with standard caution, I'd barged up without so much as a hello and demanded entrance.

I'd have thrown rocks at me, too, given half a chance.

The solarsled was still moving because I had yet to figure out a way to stop it. It seemed one of Honfleur's hardballs had damaged the drive in some way. "Three for three, Jacques old buddy." I couldn't shut the damn thing down, short of getting out and yanking it off the hull. The throttle was wide open. Mars was growing redder and colder and more dour on my left. I sent another Mayday. I recited some Shakespeare. " 'How like a winter hath my absence been from thee'—no." I shook myself. "Archy, Archy, Archy." No answer. Computers are like cops and whores; they're never around when you really need them.

I played with the controls, thumbing buttons, triggering switches, hoping one would jog another loose, the way the siren had worked to kick the starter over on Dad's old crabber. Nothing worked. " 'By night on my bed I sought him whom my soul loveth: I sought him, but I found him not.' The Song of Solomon, Arch. Any serious study of Christianity begins there."

I took a star sighting, humming a little. "Star sighting. 'Star' sighting. Get it, Archy?" I giggled a little, and caught myself. Hypoxia already? Couldn't be, so soon, I wasn't anywhere near out of oh-two. I sat back and permitted myself the luxury of a deep, calming breath. I knew pretty well where I was; I just couldn't get back to where I'd started. And I was headed somewhere I'd never been. " 'I will rise now, and go about the city in the streets, and in the broad ways I will seek him whom my soul loveth: I sought him, but I found him not.' "

I sent another Mayday. And another, without waiting the prescribed fifteen minutes. "I don't feel so invincible, Charlie," I said out loud. "You happy now?" I tried the throttle again. Still no response. The reversers. Nothing. " 'I opened to my beloved; but my beloved had withdrawn himself, and was gone: my soul failed when he spake: I sought him, but I could not find him; I called him, but he gave me no answer.' The prick."

I felt wetness on my cheeks. I reached up and my gloved hand banged into my visor. Still, I knew. "Gotta stop this, Archy," I said, "I don't have the water to waste on it."

Something clanged against the hull and I was so out of it by then that I didn't even jump. Other noises followed. "Probably should see what that is, Arch," I said. "Probably Honfleur trying to finish the job. Don't blame him."

Somebody started hammering aft. "That's right," I said encouragingly. "Knock off the cell drive. Very neat. Burial at space is so messy. Remember J. Moore, Arch? Were you alive then? Or you were and weren't saying."

There was a crunch. The craft shuddered. A pause. Noises, as if someone was clambering forward. More banging, it sounded like on the hatch. "Undoubtedly Honfleur, Archy," I said. "See you in the hereafter."

The hatch opened outward. A cool red light spilled into the interior of the craft. A figure in a bulbous white pressure suit stood silhouetted against Mars's surly glower. I didn't move.

"It's me, Star," someone said over the commlink.

His voice sounded so terribly familiar. A trembling began down deep in my bones and radiated out over me in a debilitating flood. "Grays?" I said, my voice high and shaky. I peered at him. "Grays, is that you?"

The p-suited figure leaned forward and clicked visors with me, and I found myself staring into anxious blue eyes. Looking into them was like looking into a mirror. "No, it's me. It's okay, Star. I've got you."

It was Leif.

"Leif?" I said stupidly.

"Yes. Hold still, I'll have you out in a minute."

I watched his pressure suit fill up the tiny cockpit. I watched his hand moving toward my harness release. "No." I slapped his hand away.

His p-suited form stilled. "Star," his young voice came over the commlink, speaking slowly and carefully, "all that's left of this bucket is a bunch of spare parts flying in formation. It's still moving at a pretty good clip. We've got to get out and get out now before the damn thing disintegrates around our ears."

Again he reached for me, and again I slapped him away. "No."

"Dammit, Star—"

"No!" I shouted. "You go.

"You go," I repeated. "You go."

I don't know how long we stayed like that. I do know

that when he moved he moved fast, one hand smacking my harness release open and the other knotting in the collar of my p-suit. He braced himself against the frame of the hatch and yanked, hard. I flailed at him, my helmet banging against the hatchway, but he was too fast for me, and then I was out of my broken craft and dangling over the edge of a black, inimical universe. He steadied us against the safety line stretched between our ships and then reached down to feel for the safety shackle at my belt. I flailed around some more, trying to kick myself free.

"Star!" Leif shouted. "Star, what about Paddy?"

The name caught at me. "Paddy?" I said, puzzled. I stopped trying to pull away from him.

"You remember, your daughter? She's barely five? She's got a twin brother named Sean?" His voice thickened and with a faint ripple of returning awareness I realized he was crying. "They both have an older brother named Leif?"

His voice broke. "Mother, please."

The ripple grew into a deluge and all the old crippling pain was back, rolling over me like a colossal wave tossing a grain of sand farther up a beach, only to have the undertow threaten to pull it back out to sea. Oh how I wanted a place above the high water mark, safely out of reach of wind and tide, high and dry, at rest. "Leave me alone," I cried. I think I was begging. "Please, just leave me alone."

"I can't."

I fought it, but it was no use. By then the young, accusing faces of Paddy and Sean were fixed firmly before me, demanding my presence. As was the tall young man with the breaking voice dangling precariously from the safety line next to me, clutching so desperately at the scruff of my neck.

If it were just me.

If only.

"All right," I said, drearily. "All right, Leif.

"Take us home."